NOBLE INTENTIONS

LJ REYNOLDS

2026

Affinity E-Book Press NZ LTD.
Canterbury, New Zealand

Edition first (1st)

ISBN: 978-1-991357-32-8 (paperback)

Editor: A Koenig
Proof Editor: Lisa M
Cover Design: Lisa M
Production Design: Affinity Publication Services

ACKNOWLEDGMENTS

Noble Intentions would never have been possible without the help of so many wonderful people who believed this story should be told. To my mentor, Annette Mori, thank you for having the patience of a saint and believing in me. Thank you, Affinity Rainbow Publications, for allowing me to join the family. E, TW, and TF, thank you for your advice and guidance. Thanks to my beta reader, Sandy Bell, for your selfless gift of your time and input. A special thanks to my cheerleaders KC, KM, MP, SG, TP, KC, and all the wonderful family and friends in my life. To our kids, and grandkids, "I did it!" Finally, I would like to thank my parents for always believing in me. My one regret is not finishing this book before my father died. He always wanted to read it. This is for you, Dad, you are missed every day.

DEDICATION

For my wife, B. You inspire me every day.

TABLE OF CONTENTS

PROLOGUE

Her heart pounded so fast she thought it was going to jump out of her chest like a lion taking down its helpless prey. At thirteen years old, she heard the police informing her dad that her mom was dead, potentially because of a drunk driver. She didn't even know what drunk driving was. She stood next to her dad, wide-eyed and paralyzed, as he embraced her. She could smell the shoe polish and leather of his work shoes on his hands. Polishing his shoes was his nightly ritual after dinner. But tonight was different. Mom was late coming home. She was at a meeting, so he cooked dinner. The officer awkwardly handed her a teddy bear while the other updated her father on what had happened. Unforeseen tragedy had struck, defying all expectations. Particularly distressing was the fact that her dad was the police chief.

The sound of a cabinet drawer slamming brought Noble back to the present. Standing outside the door, Noble took a deep breath and another moment to gather herself. In any tragic event, she knew it was her job to make every victim know she was there for them, no matter their age. She didn't want anyone to feel like she had that night many years ago. Her job was to help them overcome their trauma and offer any help they might need. *Remember, Noble, help this young victim as that officer helped you back when you were thirteen.* At the time, Noble knew they usually gave teddy bears to small children, but that they gave her one, was something she would never forget. Or the officer who gave it to her. She still had it in a box in her garage.

Before entering the quiet room, she knocked. The room earned its name because it was where they brought and interviewed young victims. It had stuffed animals, coloring books, dolls, and puzzles. These items assisted officers and detectives in helping young victims feel comfortable enough to talk about what had happened to them. Noble used her personal experience and the training she had received from the department to build a special bond with all the young victims she'd encountered throughout her career. She had the uncanny ability to connect with them—on their level and with their permission.

Noble made eye contact with the woman she assumed was the mother who stared back at her, eyes wide open, biting her lower lip as though it was her last grip on sanity. Noble glanced at the girl who was holding a pencil hard enough to turn the edges of her fingers white. She observed the girl slowly pick at the eraser, watching intently as each pink scrap fell to the floor around her feet. Noble sat carefully beside her. Her mother finally seemed to soften, giving her a slight smile.

"Hey," she greeted. "My name is Noble Gentry." The girl lifted her head, her tired, pale blue eyes finally meeting Noble's. "Most people know me as Noble, or Gentry as my boss calls me. I'm the detective who got assigned to your case."

The girl seemed to consider that momentarily, then kicked at a piece of eraser with her foot before she answered. "What kind of name is Noble?"

Noble kept her eyes on the girl sensing her mother stiffening behind her. Her voice was tight and low as she corrected her daughter.

"Jessie Alexandria Williams."

The girl instantly lowered her eyes and nodded. "Sorry, I think it's neat, but I've never heard it used for someone's name."

Noble smiled as the first hint of connection flashed between them. "That's okay. I get that reaction a lot."

"How did your parents come up with that name?" Jessie's eyes locked onto Noble's. "Is that what your friends call you?"

"That was my mom's last name before she married my dad. He liked it because it represented someone honorable. Do you know what that means?"

"Yeah." Jessie nodded as she slid the tattered pencil into her pocket. "Everybody does."

"Well, since he was a police officer, my mom and dad thought it would fit me. And that's how I got my name." She paused, waiting until Jessie met her eyes again before Noble dropped her voice to a whisper. "My dad sometimes calls me by my entire name. But that's only when I'm in trouble."

Jessie chuckled for a moment before whispering back. "My mom still uses my entire name when I'm in trouble, too. I think it's a parent thing. And I have one friend who calls me Jess."

"So, our parents do the same thing when you and I get into trouble."

"I didn't want him to do those things to me." Tears streamed down her face like water cascading over falls. Jessie stood, walked over to the corner of the room, placed her back against the wall, and slid to the ground.

"I know you didn't. No one wants those things done to them without their permission," Noble stated as she walked over to Jessie, grabbing a box of tissues from the table, and sat next to her.

"Why did he do this to me?" Tears pooled in her eyes again, then spilled over. "He's supposed to be my music teacher." Jessie sobbed, grabbing a tissue to dab the tears streaming down her cheeks.

"I wish I had an answer for you, Jessie. Let me assure you, I won't lie. We may never truly know why your teacher did what he did. I can let you know I will be here for you each step through the investigation and court process to ensure he's accountable for what he did to you. If you ever need anything, here is my business card. If you need to talk, call me. You've nothing to be ashamed of. Remember, no person can ever take away your pain, but please don't let him or any other person take away your happiness."

"Thank you for being honest with me. Most people treat me like I'm still five when I'm almost thirteen."

"Sometimes people don't know what to say or how to act. They don't want to see you in any more pain, but they don't know how to convey their feelings for fear of hurting you further. Are you okay with going over the incident with me again? If you're not ready, we can try again tomorrow. I know this is hard, but I want to make sure your former music teacher is accountable for what he did to you."

"We can do it today. Can my mom stay here with me? And if I need a break, can I have one?"

"Absolutely! I don't want to put any undue strain on you. Why don't you tell me again what happened, exactly how you remember it—not what you think I might want to hear, but the truth. I might ask additional questions, but we will take a break whenever you need it." Noble put her hand out in front of Jessie.

"Deal." She grasped Noble's hand and completed the shake.

"You ready to get off the floor and go to work?"

"Yes. I'm ready. Thanks again for telling me how it is and not treating me like a baby," Jessie replied, propelling herself up.

"How about if an officer takes you to the vending machine for a drink and a snack before we start? And Jessie, I'll always level with you." She opened the door and motioned the officer over. "This is Officer Whitmore, and she'll be your escort. I'll see you in a few minutes."

"Thank you for how you are with my daughter, Detective Gentry. The generosity you've shown her means the world to me," Jessie's mother responded as a host of emotions crisscrossed her face. "I'm ashamed that I allowed this to happen to my daughter. I feel like a failure as a parent. But I hope you can send that bastard away for a long time."

"Mrs. Williams, most people don't know what you or Jessie are going through. I'll be here each step of the way. And that includes periodically checking in on you after Jessie's case is over." Noble placed her hand on Mrs. William's shoulder, gently squeezing. "Know how deeply sorry I am that this terrible crime happened to her."

"That means a lot, Detective Gentry. I'm at a loss on why he chose my daughter. He even professed his love for her, but never again will my naivety overshadow my gut instinct."

"Mrs. Williams, you did nothing wrong. What he did to Jessie is not your fault."

"Maybe I could have done something different, especially after calling the police. You know, he called me from jail and apologized for what he did to her. Sick bastard," she uttered as the jetted air whizzed through the crack in her tight lips.

"You're not to blame for his despicable actions. He crossed a line in what he did to Jessie and broke the law. No person deserves what he did to her. You might be unsure of the future, but please believe Jessie should be number one on your important list. He took away her worth, privacy, energy, time, intimacy, confidence, and even her own voice until today." Noble's eyes blazed with fury.

"Jessie is and will always be a priority in my life, Detective."

"I never doubted you. Jessie's found her voice, who she was, and no one can take that from her. She's a survivor, and with your help, you both will hold your heads high." Noble's clenched jaw emphasized her point.

"I'm sorry for being short, Detective. Thank you for everything."

The door suddenly opened, and in walked Jessie and Officer Whitmore—hands full of drinks and snacks.

"Officer Whitmore helped me get these for all of us."

"Are you ready to begin, Jessie?" Noble asked.

"Yes, but first, can you tell me what your friends call you? You know, your nickname?" Jessie inquired.

"Okay, but besides those friends, you and your mom will be the only people who know. I have one friend who calls me Nag since my middle name starts with an A, and the other childhood friend calls me Aaron. And before you ask, I'm named after my dad's best friend. It happens to be a man.

That's why it's Aaron and not Erin, like most girls with that name."

"That's cool. As you heard from my mom earlier, my middle name starts with A, too. Thank you for telling me, Noble."

Noble knew she sounded like a broken record telling a victim she'd always level with them, but it was true. The best way to build a bond with a kid, much less a teenager, was to tell it like it was. If Noble held back anything and they found out, any trust she had gained would be gone.

"Okay, Jessie? Can you tell me about Monday, July 15, 2018? Start at the beginning, so when you first got up…"

CHAPTER ONE

Noble leaned against the door, turning the deadbolt with a sigh. She was exhausted from a grueling twelve-hour surveillance and needed sleep. Food had slipped her mind, so Noble made her way to the refrigerator, only to discover it nearly empty, except for pickles, a few cheese slices, and a half gallon carton of expired milk. "Fuck it," she growled and grabbed a half full bottle of water.

After washing down a dose of sleep aids, Noble stripped and stumbled to her bed, foregoing sleep clothes and climbing beneath the covers. Her body relaxed into the soft mattress, but her mind remained restless, filled with images of the suspect they had been tirelessly pursuing for days. He was a repeat offender who would be facing a life sentence when convicted. Noble and her partner had built a solid case against him and all they lacked was apprehending him.

When her brain finally switched off an hour later, she drifted off to sleep. It wasn't unusual for Noble to dream, but when her energy was depleted, a persistent nightmare always haunted her.

Noble was driving recklessly on her way to assist Diana on a call the night she was murdered. Her mind replayed different versions of that night, and this one was exceptionally brutal. Noble saw the cruel grin on the suspect's face as he hotwired a vehicle. He could have easily turned left and escaped without a trace. Instead, she watched as he veered right, driving towards a figure who was searching through parked vehicles with a flashlight. She witnessed in horror as he approached, struck the woman, and fled the scene. Noble's voice in the dream was always frozen preventing her from calling out a warning. When her ability to speak returned, she screamed out "Diana," jolting herself awake, drenched in sweat and gasping for breath. No one knew the exact circumstances of Diana's death, and Noble's guilt and grief wreaked havoc in her dreams.

Noble looked at the alarm clock on the bedside table. It was five in the morning. Realizing there was no chance of falling back asleep, she got out of bed to shower, dress, and prepare for another shift.

†

Noble was the kind of detective who made it a point to keep track of previous victims, checking on their healing process, and offering her support. Jessie Williams was one of those previous cases that left an imprint on Noble. Finding time in her day for a visit, Noble knocked on the front door of the Williams' house.

"Who is it?" a female voice asked behind the door.

"Detective Noble Gentry." She lifted her badge to the peephole; she knew the routine after doing it many times over the last year.

The door slowly opened, the sun illuminating an outline of a woman's body—not Jessie and not Mrs. Williams. The woman appeared to be in her thirties, with intense blue eyes seeming to penetrate her soul, leaving Noble unable to look away. They were beautiful sapphire-colored eyes that looked as precious as the stone itself.

"I'm here to see Jessie. May I come in and talk to her?" Not sure who this woman was, Noble put her head to one side in a questioning manner.

"Yes, please do. My name is Charlie Matthews, and I'm a friend of Jessie's mom, Janet."

Noble entered the entryway and checked her watch, pausing for a sign from this woman on where she should wait. Noble heard the door close and lock, and turned her attention back to the woman—blonde hair, about 5'7" or 5'8", dressed casually in jeans and a T-shirt.

"Please, come in and have a seat. Can I get you some coffee or water?"

"No, thank you, I'm good."

"How about a beer? You look like one might help you relax a little." Charlie's eyebrows collided in the center above her nose.

"Sorry, still on the clock, so I will pass on the beer." Noble pinned her crossed arms over her chest as her eyes shot this woman a narrow look, her face rumpling with annoyance. "Although you're right, it's been a long day."

"That's good to know, that you take your job seriously. Even though it looks like you're having a rough day."

"What makes you think that?" Noble countered, her jaw slamming shut and hardening.

"Well, can I be frank?" Charlie asked.

"Doesn't seem like I can stop you, so please be frank."

"You look like you haven't slept in a week and have been put through the wringer. Your top's wrinkled, and your hair is everywhere."

"Great observation skills. I've been awake all night on surveillance, so yes, tired is correct. As for my top having wrinkles, I wore my bulletproof vest over it. So far, you're right on two of the three," Noble answered. "And for the last, my hair might be all over the place, but since you're the only one here who can see it, I'll have to take you at your word." Noble closed her eyes and quietly counted to ten.

"Good to know you're diligent in your job and wear your vest. Now for your hair. Let me help you fix it before Jessie and her mom arrive." Charlie stepped over and slowly raised her hand to fix the hair sticking out.

But before her hand connected with the stubborn hair, Noble stepped back and said, "If you'll excuse me." She marched to the restroom. "I'll see what I can do myself. Be right back."

†

Charlie laughed as she watched Noble retreat to the bathroom. *I wonder if she knows how cute she is when she's nervous. She doesn't like people in her space and is unsure how to deal with "frank" women.*

"Okay, it's fixed as well as it can be in the circumstances. Did they say about what time they'd be home?" Noble asked as she sauntered back into the room.

"Jessie and her mom should be back here in about fifteen minutes. Jessie had her therapy session today, and the doctor was running a little behind. So, is Noble your actual name? It's different. Did you get teased much about being a Noble Knight growing up?"

"Well, good to know. They'll be here shortly. Yes, Noble is my actual name. And yes, it's different. No one teased me because of my first name."

"Do you come and check on all your victims from your cases? If not, why are you checking in on Jessie?"

"Checking in on people I've had cases with helps me gauge if they're living their lives as intended before a horrific incident derailed them. What better way to make sure they haven't lost their way through no fault of their own than to check on them, whether it's a phone call or an in-person visit?"

"Above and beyond the call of duty, but I can surely respect that."

"That's me, always going the extra mile. And I have no problem with a friend of the family being protective, even if it's with a cop. It's always great when you've got people in your life that will be there for you, regardless."

†

Man, I hope Jessie gets here soon, or I will get up and leave. The sound of the deadbolt turning and the creaking of the door opening brought Noble to her feet. *Thank god they're here. Now, I know how an insect under a microscope in science class feels. Who the hell is this chick, and why all the questions? She was talking about my appearance and trying to get into my space. Pretty bold after only meeting me today. I'll give her that.*

"I'm so sorry we were late, Nag…I mean Detective Gentry," Jessie yelled from the doorway, forgetting the joke that was between just the two of them.

Before Noble could answer, Jessie appeared in the living room.

"I assume you want to check on me and my life." Jessie sat on the couch next to Noble, who was standing.

"If you'll excuse me, you two can get on with your conversation. Unless you want your mom or me in here with you, Jessie."

"No, we're fine, just the two of us. Detective Gentry and I go back since the beginning of my case."

"Have a nice evening, Detective. Take care of yourself and get some sleep."

"Thank you, Ms. Matthews. You do as well. And I will take your critique under advisement."

"Charlie, my mom is in the kitchen. She said to go in there so you two can catch up."

†

Charlie waited around the corner and listened to Jessie and Noble's conversation. That detective was a tough nut to crack, but she was good to look at. Her face was kind but had a tired look with the all too familiar bags and dark circles forming. Her eyes still reminded Charlie of green pine needles poking her for attention as they swayed in the wind. She was trying to figure out if she had made Noble angry with her frankness.

†

"Where were we? Yes, on an update, what did we agree on? You wouldn't be calling me Detective Gentry? Remember, we've worked together on your case for the last year, so please call me Noble, or Nag if no one else is around."

"Sorry, I keep forgetting. We did role-play during our therapy session today with some other survivors from the group. It felt good to scream and say that the damage he inflicted on me was done. No one could undo it. All of us in the group have a choice from now on. We can let this ruin us, or we can face it directly, in our own way, and move on. None of us will ever forget these traumatic events in our lives, but we won't let them define us," Jessie declared, her shoulders back, chest out, and chin high.

"The therapist believes we're all moving in the right direction and might not need therapy for much longer. Although, she says, we can continue the group therapy for as long as we want. She feels that we're all just about healing at the same pace and can continue to maintain our friendships outside of therapy," Jessie finished, looking Noble directly in the eyes.

"That's understandable and great news. Sometimes, people don't know the level of their actions until they're held accountable for them. Tell me what you've been doing these last couple of months. Are you returning to the same school for summer school, or will you take a summer off?"

"It might be best to take a break and start back in the fall. That way, I can have more time with my mom and work my way back to being comfortable outside my house alone without her." Jessie smiled when Noble's hands covered hers.

"Okay, that's great. I'll check back with you before school starts to make sure you're still doing okay. You remind me of myself when I was younger. Tough on the outside but sensitive on the inside. Don't be afraid to let anyone see your sensitive side. Those who matter will love you, regardless. Never forget you're strong and brave; only you can dictate your story. Some people might try to take the lead, but you control you." Noble squeezed Jessie's hands one more time before releasing them and standing.

"Noble, you've shown me that pain and strength can go hand in hand, as well as being fierce and fragile. Thank you so much for investing in me and my case. Because of you, I want to be a voice for survivors. Maybe being a counselor will help me give back as much as you helped me. And I think being like you, well, it's awesome. I only hope I can live up to it and you."

"Jessie, please remember that although we met under the most terrible circumstances, I hope you or your mom will not hesitate to contact me if you need anything. I know you can do anything you set your mind to. Can you please get your mom so I can tell her goodbye?"

"I'll be right back. And thank you for being you, Noble. You've never treated me like a child and always told me the truth, even if I didn't want to hear it." She smiled as she left the room in search of her mom.

†

"Yep, I'm going to refer to you as Noble Knight from now on," Charlie voiced as she entered the room, propping her shoulder on the doorframe.

"Okay." Noble looked at Charlie through her narrowed eyes. *And here I am, hoping to leave without having to talk with her again. No luck on my side today.*

"Listening to you and Jessie talk has made me realize that we're glad you were the detective on her case. You connected with her, and for that, you deserve a huge thank you from me," Charlie stated. "I know teenagers and those types of cases are the hardest, but it helps the victim when they have a detective who can show empathy during their case. That would be why I've given you the name Noble Knight."

"Thank you, I think. Jessie is a bright young lady with her entire future ahead of her. She has my support whether I'm on duty or off," Noble answered in a steady, confident voice.

"She's like family, and you're always welcome here, Noble," Mrs. Williams proclaimed as she walked into the room.

"Same with you and Jessie. You're a great addition to my family," Noble replied.

"Thank you so much for helping my daughter. You've helped Jessie and me in ways you don't know. Being a mom is hard, and when something like this happens to your child, you feel you've failed them," she said, her eyes filling with tears. "You've genuinely helped me as well, and for that, I'm not sure I could ever repay you except with my deepest gratitude." Mrs. Williams walked over to Noble and hugged her.

"You're welcome, Mrs. Williams. Working this case for Jessie reminds me that there's still good in this world, and you must continually fight evil to bring the good to light. Jessie knows, but if you need anything yourself, contact me. Day or night," Noble answered as she put her arms around Mrs. Williams and embraced her briefly before taking a step back.

"Well, Janet, you're so right about everything regarding Detective Gentry. Honestly, it makes me want to hug her as well." Charlie stepped in front of Noble, and as she put her arms around Noble's neck, an electrical shock caused both to jump a foot apart.

"Wow! Must be that electrifying personality of yours, Ms. Matthews," Noble said.

"Woo hoo, that was an enormous shock." Jessie laughed as she walked toward the front door. "Come on, Noble, you need to leave before Charlie sends you into cardiac arrest."

"Ladies, you have a wonderful rest of your day, and you'll hear from me." Noble walked out the front door, hearing the click of the deadbolt when she reached her car. "Today has been quite unusual. I hope Jessie doesn't have to encounter someone as intrusive as Ms. Matthews on a regular basis," she said aloud.

CHAPTER TWO

One Month Later

Patrick Smith, Troy Alan, Joe Long.

Noble stood at attention as names continued over the loudspeaker for the police officers killed in the line of duty in Onserf County.

Michael Sage, Kim Bishop, Adrian Walker.

It was a beautiful day with the sun shining and a light breeze carrying the aroma of fresh-cut roses. Noble's palms started sweating, her heart rate increased, her stomach twisted in knots, and her anxiety built as Chief Raynor read the names one after the other. *They're getting closer to your name, Diana. Please let me make it through this.* That was all she thought. She couldn't blink, or the tears would start flowing freely. *Deep breath, Noble, you can do it.*

Chief Raynor continued down the list of names of officers lost while sacrificing their lives to keep the public safe. *Diana Ortega.* Noble blinked. Her throat tightened after a quick intake of breath, and a tremor overtook her rigid body as the tears started racing down her cheeks. She felt a hand softly touch the small of her back and knew her friend, Sergeant Leah Harper, was there to help.

"Breathe in, breathe out, don't lock your knees, Noble, you've got this," Leah murmured.

The breeze lifted the damp hair at her temples below her hat, lifting a heaviness off her shoulders momentarily. Noble raised her face to the sky, inhaled the scent of roses, and mouthed, "I will always love you, Diana, no matter what!"

The rest of the ceremony was a blur until they released the white doves. As they flew their designated route, one dove went off course and landed on a tree branch that hung above Noble's head.

Leah leaned forward and touched Noble's shoulder. "See, Diana is sending you a message that she will always cherish your love and she's watching over you as you continue in life."

Noble held Leah's hand and said, "Thank you, my friend! I know it's been four years, but I still miss her, and I don't think it will ever change."

"It doesn't have to change, and Diana wouldn't want you to continue down this path of destruction. The ravaging that's eating you alive inside, Noble." After squeezing her hand once, she eased up and continued, "She'd want you to get out and live your life. No one knows better than you how short it can be. You should know that it can disappear."

"I know, but I haven't met anyone who has even remotely sparked my interest like Diana. If I can find it in my heart to love again, it will happen when I'm ready to let it happen,"

Noble replied. *The only one that piqued my interest was Mrs. Williams' friend, Charlie. But then she opened her mouth, and that cleared my mind of anything happening, ever, with her. But I like how she knew all victims need someone to lean on.*

"If you'd let your friends help in that department, it might happen sooner rather than later, if you get my drift. Come on, Noble, I don't want you to find love when you're using a walker," Leah laughingly replied.

"Yeah, yeah! We'll see about finally caving in and asking for help, but not right now."

"I know, my friend. Beth and I will always be there for you, regardless! We love and will help you through this, no matter what."

"If you can help find someone like Diana and Beth all rolled into one, it might be easier to take the chance on love again," she answered with a shrug. "You're so lucky to have Beth. I want something like what you two have, which is a tall order to fill. So, if you can clone her, that would be great."

"She's great, but it takes communication, dedication, and love to make a relationship work, and she's currently unavailable for the foreseeable future," Leah stated as she looked Noble directly in the eye. "Besides, when we first met, Beth was overbearing. She asked way too many questions, and it made me uncomfortable. She enjoyed getting into my space; she was a pain by my standards," she continued easily. "Then, when I finally agreed to go out with her, she went to hug me good night, and she shocked the heck out of the both of us. Let's see about finding you someone who wants to be a friend for now and who likes to go out for coffee and watch movies."

"I never knew how you two met, but would Beth tell it the same way? Okay, deal. How about we go grab a cup of coffee?" Noble suggested, still not in the right frame of mind to drive. "Let's walk to the Coffee Hut since it's only a block away."

"Lead the way, and if you're nice, you won't even have to buy. And yes, Beth would tell it the same way. She'd say she had to storm the castle to break down all my walls to get to my heart." Noble watched as Leah's gaze was distant as if recalling a happy memory. "Like Beth always says, you and Noble have so many walls up, but are two extraordinary women beneath, when they come down. And she says we're big softies on the inside."

It was a beautiful day for a walk, and they could get an outside table at the Coffee Hut since they'd already missed the lunch crowd.

"Thanks for picking me up and brushing me off to make me look presentable today. You and Beth have been a lifesaver, and without you, I would have already sunk into a dismal abyss, and I probably wouldn't have recovered," Noble said, bowing her head. "Your wisdom and love are the main reasons you got into my heart. You're the closest thing to a sister, and I'm so grateful you've been there with me through the worst time in my life," she resumed. "Beth is pretty accurate, and that's scary. Diana was the first person patient enough to maneuver my walls and get inside. And that scared me, but in the end, it was the best time of my life."

With tears threatening to escape her eyes, Leah grabbed Noble's hands and replied, "I'm so proud of you and what you've endured. We're both so sorry that life threw you a curve ball when you were ahead, but unfortunately, life is not fair." She swallowed her unshed tears. "It's what you do during all nine innings that will help you, and right now, you're in the middle of your game, struggling to win. We will always be there, no matter if you win or lose. We love you like family, and that bond will never break."

Leah picked up her coffee cup. "To help you get through this day and help you win the game. So, let's drink this coffee and do just that." They both clicked them together and smiled as Leah's phone dinged. Noble sipped her coffee as Leah checked her text.

"Beth's car battery is dead so I have to pick her up at her doctor's office. Are you going to be okay, or would you like to tag along?"

"No, you go ahead. I'll finish my coffee and then head home. Thank you again for today, and if I need to talk, I'll call you. Give my best to Beth."

Leah leaned down, kissed Noble on the forehead. "It will get better. You merely need to believe in yourself and remember that Diana would want you to be happy."

Noble sipped her coffee and looked across the street into the park, where children ran around, swinging and playing. *Oh, Diana, we always wanted to have a family. Now that you're gone, will there ever be a desire to have a family again?*

A little girl tugging her uniform sleeve brought Noble back to the present. "Excuse me, are you a poweece woman?"

"Yes, I am. What's your name?" Noble exclaimed, a smile crawling up her face.

"My name is Elizabeth Ann, same as my grandmother's."

"Well, Miss Elizabeth Ann, my name is Noble, and it's nice to meet you."

A teenage girl walked up and apologized. She looked at Elizabeth and said, "You know you're not supposed to talk to strangers. Your mom would be unhappy with you right now."

Noble watched the little girl with fascination as she defiantly crossed her arms on her chest and replied to the teenage girl, "My mom is a poweece woman, and I'd not get into trouble."

Noble looked at the little girl and said, "Make sure you listen and don't talk to strangers, and hug your mommy when you see her today."

"Sorry to have interrupted your break," the teenager said as she took Elizabeth's hand and continued to the sidewalk.

Noble finished her coffee and smiled both inside and out. She left the Coffee Hut and headed toward her car to begin her annual time off to honor Diana.

†

Noble finally made it home at 5:30 with the pizza in her hand and was ready to tackle Diana's last boxes in their bedroom, but dinner first. Opening the fridge, she grabbed a bottle of water and a beer. What's pizza without beer? And she deserved a beer after today. Sitting on the couch and eating a slice of pizza, she thought about which boxes in the bedroom she'd start packing. Chugging the rest of her beer, she put the last slices of pizza in the fridge and grabbed another bottle. After a big swig, she slowly walked into their bedroom.

"You got this," Noble sputtered, briefly covering her face with her hands before pulling them away. "Diana always said, if anything happened to either of us, we needed to move on after a respectable time of mourning. And I've honored those wishes. Four years is certainly an honorable amount of time."

Remember, these are merely possessions, and you'll always have memories.

Noble opened the first box, closed her eyes, and drew in the scent that exploded into an image of Diana; it looked like love, unwavering loyalty, and forever. Her scent had been spectacularly unique: a warm mixture of aged leather, amber-glazed wood, cinnamon, and baked brown sugar. To Noble, it would always be the smell of home.

Diana's old high school yearbooks, her neatly folded letterman's jacket, a handful of creased, brightly colored ribbons, and medals from all the sports she had played and conquered were inside the box. Noble closed the box swiftly and made a mental note to see if Diana's mom would like to have the pieces of Diana's past that were now too painful to look at.

She closed her eyes, took a single ragged breath, and forced herself to seal up the box and move on to the next. However, she sliced into the seal with her pocketknife before a sideways glance reminded her that her beer bottle was empty. Noble tossed the knife onto the box and grabbed another from the fridge, leaning against the cool edge of the marble countertop for a few minutes before she could walk back into the room.

The next box contained Diana's sweatshirts. Noble picked out a few and hung them in her closet, then sealed the box and set it aside for donations. She dropped to her knees again and downed her beer, draining half the bottle before she stopped for a breath. *Only eight more boxes to go and the last of her will be gone.* Even the thought felt wrong. She'd planned on forever with Diana, and now she had to let go of the last of her, sealed up in cold cardboard boxes. Everything inside her wanted the opposite. All her insides wanted Noble to scream.

By the time Noble got to the last box, she'd cried every tear she had, even laughed at a few of Diana's old notes that she had a habit of leaving around the house for her, and set a few things aside in her memory. But when she opened the final box with a jumble of cards she'd given to Diana over the years, she couldn't hold her heartbreak any longer. Diana had kept every fucking thing Noble had ever given her. She'd kept every bit of Noble, and now Noble had no choice but to let Diana go.

She slid to the floor in a heap as the hot, stupid tears burned the back of her eyes, tears that dropped from her cheeks to scatter across the floor like memories she couldn't bear to look at again.

†

At 4 a.m. the alarm clock began beeping, blaring a high-pitched and unpleasant noise—the kind that caused a person to want to take a hammer to and destroy. Noble crawled over to the nightstand and smacked the snooze button on the clock repeatedly until it fell to the ground beside her. The empty beer bottle wobbled on the nightstand until it tipped over, crashing to the floor. "Shit, thank god there's carpet in here," Noble said, as she put her hand through her hair—a chaotic mess.

Realizing that she was wearing the same clothes as the night before, Noble got up and sat on the bed with her feet firmly planted on the floor, still a little dizzy from the drunk fest the night before. Four years, and she was still having nightmares about Diana's death, and drinking all those beers didn't help.

"What the hell was I thinking? I haven't had any alcohol since Diana's death. Not that I drank a lot to begin with, but damn, this can't happen again."

Knowing she had to get up, Noble walked to the bathroom and turned on the shower. Her headache was like jagged slivers of pain trying to push their way out through her eyes. Popping some Advil, Noble hoped it would help ease the memories from the previous night. Stepping into the shower, she felt the scorching water surround her body.

Yesterday was the anniversary of Diana's death four years earlier. Noble would never forget the night she lost Diana, but she realized she needed to face reality. She had known four years ago that someone had ripped everything of importance from her life. All she wanted and hoped for was gone in the blink of an eye. As they lowered Diana's casket into the deep, cold ground, Noble felt helpless and alone, even though there were at least a thousand people who attended the funeral to show their support. She secretly wished this was all a terrible dream. She'd wake up any moment, and Diana would comfort her and ease her fears. Unfortunately, this was reality, and Diana was gone. She was not coming back this time, and the realization stung.

"You got to get your shit together, Gentry. New day and new beginnings. That would be what Diana wanted."

†

Realizing the scorching water had turned cold, Noble blinked. She wiped the excess water from her eyes and turned off the shower. Grabbing a towel, she dried off and dressed in jeans and her favorite shirt. The shirt read: *Real women are cops. The rest must be up to some form of shenanigans.* Noble quietly laughed as she remembered that this shirt always embarrassed Diana when she wore it. Today would be her first day back at the Northwest District station after her yearly time off to remember Diana, and finally taking care of Diana's belongings once and for all.

CHAPTER THREE

A sudden succession of shrill rings cut through the silence. Startled, Charlie jumped up from the kitchen table, where she was enjoying her coffee and the peaceful morning. She walked over to the phone, her brow furrowed, and picked up the receiver.

"Hello."

"Hi, sweetie. I'm sorry to bother you so early, but Elizabeth is here, and I just tucked her in," Beth stated, a sigh escaping her lips.

"What do you mean she's there, Mom? I'm supposed to pick her up this morning," Charlie answered, her reply tinged with annoyance.

"Well, your ex couldn't handle Elizabeth and, with her busy social life, called me last night. I'm so glad you left her and got full custody of Elizabeth."

"Thanks, Mom. I'm sorry you got the call, but not sorry that Elizabeth is with someone who loves her and wants to spend time with her."

"How about I bring her over in two hours? That way, you can do some unpacking."

"Have I told you how lucky I am that you're my mom, and I love you?" Charlie stated as tears trickled down her face.

"Yes, but I never tire of hearing it. I'll see you in two hours," Beth replied as she ended the phone call.

Charlie's anger boiled over when she slammed her phone on the counter. "That bitch!" she yelled into her hands, cupping her face. She got up and went to log this into her notebook. The latest incident would be the last. Charlie also emailed her attorney, advising her of what had happened. From here on out, Charlie would ensure that her ex strictly adhered to the new child custody agreement. Her ex would only get supervised visits because of the damage and lack of involvement in Elizabeth's life.

Charlie had just finished unpacking Elizabeth's room when the doorbell rang. She walked to the door, looked through the peephole, and slid the deadbolt. She pulled the door open and smiled at her mom and Elizabeth.

"Come on in. It's two of my favorite people." Charlie smiled, blinking sweat from her eyes.

"What about Mimi?" Elizabeth asked, flipping her palms up.

"Well, she's my third favorite person," Charlie replied as she picked up Elizabeth, hugging and kissing her.

"Mom, let me down. I'm too old for you to be picking me up."

"You'll never be too old for me, munchkin. And four is not too old."

"Can I go see my room?"

"Yes, go ahead."

"She has the same energy you had at that age." Beth hugged and kissed Charlie on the cheek.

"Thank you so much for taking her last night. I emailed my attorney after I got off the phone with you. Thank god the new child custody order goes into effect today."

"Elizabeth mentioned last night that she doesn't want to see her anymore and is glad she's coming here today. Have you called your ex?" Beth asked.

"No. Nothing good will come out of that phone call. My attorney will handle it from now on. I will schedule all the supervised visits through her. What a shame. I can't imagine not wanting to spend time with your child," Charlie ranted, the vein on her neck pulsing, twitching, and becoming engorged.

"Some people should never be parents, Charlie. You, however, were born to be that child's mother. And she's an exceptional grandchild, but I might be slightly biased," Beth stated.

"Yes, she's exceptional. I can't wait to start this new job. I'm glad to be back home and excited to show Elizabeth the town."

"Good thing school is out for the summer, not that it matters, as she'll be starting kindergarten in September. She can spend all her time with me now that I'm retired. And she'll see Leah when she's on days off."

"I appreciate your support and all the help you and Leah will give us. It means the world to me. I'm also happy that Jessie's mom has a daughter who'll help." She grinned, exposing her perfect row of teeth. "Who knows, someday I might find the right woman to spend the rest of my life with, but for now, I need to focus on Elizabeth and work before that happens."

"Don't worry. Everything will fall into place when you least expect it. Now, let's go check on Elizabeth," Beth said as they walked down the hall.

"Mom. I love my room. Grandma, look at all my dinosaurs."

"Your mom did a marvelous job, Elizabeth. Grandma must go, but I'll see you in the morning. I love you."

"I love you too, Grandma."

Charlie walked her mom to the door and handed her a set of keys. "Here is an extra set to the house in case you or Leah need them."

"Perfect. There's a chance I'll have an extra set made for Leah. I will see you here in the morning. I love you." Beth walked out the door and down the steps.

"Mom, I love you too. Hug Mom L and kiss her for me. We all need to get together for dinner soon."

"Absolutely! Soon. We've been busy with the police officer's memorial and supporting our friend Nob during this difficult time, but I believe we're finally getting back on track," she remarked as she settled into the car.

"Bye, Mom." Charlie waved one last time as she walked inside, shut the door, turned the deadbolt, and engaged the lock. *I will have to ask Mom more about the memorial and this officer Nob when we get together for dinner. If Nob is an officer at Onserf PD, presumably she is a friend of Leah's. Or surely Leah has heard of her. Who the hell names their daughter Nob? I hope that's a nickname.*

"Hey, munchkin, are you getting hungry? I'm making a snack soon, so play in your room, and I'll come get you when it's ready."

"Yes. Can we have pizza? Yesterday, I saw a poweece woman. I told her my name was Elizabeth Ann and that you named me after my grandma. Her name started with an N, but I can't remember what it was. I got in trouble with the babysitter for talking to her."

"Remember, you shouldn't talk to strangers, even if they're in uniform, unless Mommy says it's okay. And yes, I'll put a pizza in the oven for dinner, but I will make you some apples and peanut butter for your snack."

"Thank you. I'll try to remember not to talk to strangers, but it's hard, Mom." Elizabeth turned back to her dinosaurs and started playing.

Charlie shook her head as she left the bedroom and headed toward the kitchen.

Chapter Four

At 6:30 a.m., Noble arrived at her assigned district and sat in the car for over half an hour, mustering the courage to see her coworkers. Noble would never forget that even after four years, strangers, friends, and family still asked her how she coped with her job, and Noble always replied that she didn't know. All she could do was hope her reply gave someone peace of mind, but that person was only her.

Once she cleared her head, Noble exited the vehicle and entered the district station. She hurried to her desk, staring curiously at a case file lying on top. She sank into her chair. Her old beat-up green desk looked like someone had cleaned off the top except for a file that appeared to be new and had a sticky note attached. The message instructed her to report to the sergeant as soon as she got there. She'd always loved figuring out puzzles, which intrigued her about law enforcement. Well, that, and that people loved women in uniforms.

She opened the file and stared at a mugshot of a man stapled on the side and a synopsis on the right. His icy gaze felt like it was staring right through her. The synopsis stated the suspect was an absconding parolee, originally imprisoned for a series of brutal rapes. His last victim had escaped and later identified him in a photo lineup. He'd been in prison for many years and had recently been paroled. Noble closed her eyes and took a deep breath. She got her mind into the game and read the file's contents. She always gave herself a brief pep talk before starting a fresh case.

†

It was years ago now, in February, that Noble remembered getting a case with a suspect who looked like the photo she was staring at now. At first glance, it appeared this could be Billy Russell's father, but upon closer inspection and seeing the parolee's name, the image was Billy Russell himself. How the hell could he be out on parole so fast? His eyes skewered her with an icy gaze as his mugshot stared back at her.

Noble shut the file, rose from her seat, and had taken two steps when her partner, Tony Vistole, walked into the office toward her. He had a leather jacket dangling over his shoulder, a navy-blue dress shirt, jeans, sneakers, and a friendly smile. He was her work partner and a fantastic one at that. Tony looked out for her, and she did the same for him. He was like the brother she never had.

He grabbed her arm but kept moving, turning her around and pulling her toward Sergeant Harper's office door. Noble had regained her balance as he pushed her into the office. Her eyes searched his, scanning for any sign of what was happening. Noble felt like she was watching a movie and waiting for the surprise to reveal itself, possibly in the sergeant's office. She couldn't tell if something was wrong and wondered if it had to do with the file on her desk.

"Did you read it?" he asked, his voice sounding like a kid in a candy store. As he waited for her to answer, Noble eyed him. He stared at her with a questioning look, and her curiosity kicked in. *What the hell is going on?*

"I skimmed it if you're talking about the file on my desk. I was getting ready to see Sergeant Harper, and then you ushered me right into her office." Noble's response didn't affect him; his eyes twinkled like a star in the dark night sky.

"It's great to have you back, Noble." Tony swept his brown hair out of his face. He attempted to contain his smile, but it didn't work. He'd never hidden his emotions from her. The room suddenly became a silent chamber until Sergeant Harper's phone rang.

"If you ever need to talk or need a shoulder to lean on, you know I'll always be there for you, Noble."

"I know. And believe me, I will always welcome that." She slowly put her hand on top of his.

"Can I come in?" Sergeant Harper asked.

"It's your office, Sarge." Noble claimed a chair across from the sergeant's.

Leah Harper entered her office and sat in the chair behind her desk. She had an unobstructed view of both detectives.

"I'm glad you're back at work, Noble. If you need anything, let me know," she commented, her chair creaking as she shifted her weight on the seat.

"Thank you. If I need anything, you and Tony will be the first two people I contact."

"Both of you need to look at the crime scene. I need your input on this. That's all we need—for Billy Russell to upgrade his crimes to murder instead of just sexual assault. We need to either cross him off the list of suspects or keep him as a possible. Check to see if the deceased knew any of Russell's sexual assault victims," Sergeant Harper directed. "With Russell absconding parole, it could be that he might target his prior victim's family and friends, escalating to the actual prior victims later. It's my understanding that the only victim who remains in Onserf is Tracy Snow. This would have been your case, Noble. I think it was four years ago."

"We'll head out there now," Tony and Noble announced together as they stood.

"Could we have a quick chat, Noble?" Sergeant Harper inquired.

"I'll go grab the file and meet you out at the car in five, Noble." Tony nodded to the sarge and shut the door.

"You ready for this, Noble? If you need more time to finish packing up Diana's things at home, no one will fault you, given the circumstances," she whispered.

"No, I got it all done yesterday. I need to drop off some boxes for donations. I realize that time doesn't stop when horrific things happen, and the best therapy for me is to be back at work. Working will keep my mind focused on cases and not thinking about Diana and the thousands of what-if scenarios that continuously run through my brain if it's not working on a task."

"I truly meant it when I said that if you ever feel the need to chat, don't hesitate to reach out to me, whether it's a late-night call or a coffee break in the afternoon. I want you to understand that I'm there for you and ready to help you," Leah stated. "Beth says the same and wants me to tell you not to be a stranger. It's been too long since you've been over. She's loving retired life and will spend much more time with our granddaughter now that our daughter has moved back here. And remember, I'm a friend you can lean on whenever you need it."

"Thank you, Leah. Your words mean more than I can ever express, and believe me, if I need someone to lean on, you, Tony, and Beth are on that list. And I'll finally get to meet your daughter and granddaughter as you're always talking about them." Noble smiled.

"Okay, how about you get out there and get this Russell guy into custody before he goes a step above rape and starts a killing spree for paybacks?"

†

Parking near the crime scene, Tony turned off the car and got out. He walked around and stood beside Noble, who put a strand of hair behind her ear.

"I'm sorry about rushing you into the sergeant's office. It was inappropriate. Did I hurt you, Noble? Because that's the last thing I want to do. I'm glad you're back, partner."

"No, not at all. I mean, come on, Tony, you know it takes much more manhandling to hurt me, right? I know you're glad to see me, and I'm happy to be back at work and working with you again." Noble walked past Tony to the edge of the tape. She smiled at the officer standing beside the alley and greeted him politely.

Noble's gaze canvassed the crime scene, trying to take it in. The dispersed contents and deceased body were like many other scenes she'd worked in patrol—bloody items and a stillness in the air. Noble needed a moment to glance away, close her eyes, and take a deep breath, silently questioning the limits of humanity.

The scene comprised an unusually narrow alley in the old downtown business district. The blood had splattered the rear businesses' walls, almost like a twisted painting. Displayed in the middle of the alley was a butchered body covered in a mixture of dried and drying blood. Someone had dumped out the victim's purse and scattered all its contents on the ground nearby.

"Robbery went wrong?" Tony asked from behind Noble.

"No way in hell this was a robbery. Look at the injuries she has. You can tell there's a much deeper motive than that. Almost personal. You can nearly feel the attacker's anger directed toward her." She looked upwards, and other than the sun beating down on the crime scene, drying all the blood, it appeared there would be little contamination.

Tony, standing behind her, stated, "Let's get started. I'm going to grab my gear from the car."

"Hey, can you bring me my slippers and cameras?" she yelled over her shoulder but noticed Tony walking back with only his gear. "Never mind, I'll go get them myself," Noble grumbled while heading toward the car.

Noble opened the trunk and gathered her booties, or slippers as she referred to them, and her camera, and then rejoined Tony. Both put a little Vicks under their noses, hoping it would mask the various odors of the corpse that had been baking like a burned pizza out in the heat for the last couple of hours. The metallic and urine smell alone would make anyone nauseated.

Gear in hand, Noble smiled again at the officer holding the perimeter as Sergeant Harper's patrol vehicle pulled up. Noble always felt a little sorry for the officers at the scene; they had to deal with the weather, civilians, brass, and plain rubberneckers. Noble lifted the crime scene tape slightly, crouched under, stood straight up, and engaged her camera lens before gathering intel/evidence that might help link the case to Billy Russell.

†

Noble started her disturbing assignment by taking pictures of the overall crime scene before stepping closer to the murder victim. She always took additional photos, hoping between her and the Crime Scene Unit, someone would uncover crucial evidence. The victim appeared to be a relatively young woman, about mid-twenties, her light hazel eyes staring vacantly into nothing, her blonde hair saturated with an ill-fated red, her clothes torn and soaked. Noble examined every blood spatter, every shoe print impression near and around the body, and anything that looked like evidence that could point toward who the murderer was. After completing pictures of the overall scene, she moved on to fresh sets of marked-out evidence. During their initial observation and walk-through of the scene, Noble and Tony used the yellow-plastic numeric-evidence-identification markers provided by the department, adding to the ones left earlier by the Crime Scene Unit. Every so often, Tony would glance in her direction and point at the victim, where he spotted signs of a struggle and other injuries, such as bruises on her wrists and neck, which showed themselves the longer the body was out in the elements. There was a minor comfort in knowing that the victim didn't go down without a fight, hopefully even injuring her attacker and leaving his DNA at the scene.

The worst of her injuries was the wound on her head, which was most likely the one that killed her, but the other injuries might have also been a contributing factor. The coroner would make the final determination after the body arrived at the Medical Examiner's office for the official autopsy. Lividity gave evidence that she'd bled continuously before her death and in that position.

The victim had been there a while, at least two hours. Again, Noble canvassed the crime scene, looking for anything she might have missed. She and Tony realized hours had passed, and it was lunchtime, but lunch would have to wait until they finished. Noble skimmed through all the photographs to check them against her surroundings. Satisfied that everything matched up, she stepped under the tape and joined Tony. He was waiting and observing the crime scene investigators as they canvassed and collected the evidence. Maybe they'd identify something that she and Tony missed.

"I saw nothing in or near the immediate vicinity of the crime scene that could inflict that kind of damage on someone, let alone kill them," Noble stated. "It's possible, with the right strength, any object could kill someone, but these injuries, in my best guess, would be that the weapon had to be something like a tire iron or a crowbar."

"How sure are you, Noble?" Tony asked, observing her. Tony always valued her opinions, especially when they regarded crime scenes, but sometimes reserved judgment until her theory was correct. She looked at him with eyebrows raised and arms folded across her chest. He smirked as if this would be a small token of apology for questioning her competency. "So, if we can't find the weapon, what do you think happened?" he pressed.

Noble gave him an exasperated look, which he returned with a massive grin. "Okay, let's suppose it started as a verbal argument," she began, motioning toward the scene before them.

"Good bet. That's how it started." Tony shrugged.

"You know I don't like to make assumptions, but for the sake of speculative reasoning," she spoke while making movements with her hands, "let's consider there was an argument between an unknown suspect and our victim. Now, at this phase of the investigation, we aren't sure what happened between these two individuals or even why they were arguing. But for appearance's sake, the argument turned violent."

"My gut tells me they knew each other." Tony hitched his thumb toward the crime scene.

"The unknown suspect naturally became overly aggressive and took hold of the victim's wrists, gripping them tightly, creating a bruising line, possibly leaving some of their skin cells behind, but we won't know that until the body arrives at the coroner's office and the evidence collection is complete. Hopefully, we will lose nothing crucial with the body transfer." Noble crossed her arms in front of herself.

"Go on." He nodded avidly.

"So, let's consider that the victim reacted to this act of aggressive behavior with some resistance, most likely resulting in her attempting to pull away and forcing the unknown suspect or suspects to tighten their grip on her wrists as she struggled. The suspect couldn't deal with the victim fighting back and resisting his assault, which the suspect didn't like. So maybe the suspect might be a person who likes to have control and show their power, so the suspect grabbed something in proximity that was easily accessible, possibly either a crowbar or tire iron, and swung it at the victim."

"I like where this is going." He nodded in agreement.

"She was most likely being held only by one hand, so she now could strike back, but the violent blows kept hitting her, each one causing more atrocious injuries than the last, resulting in massive bleeding, bruising, and broken bones on her body. She's weak, possibly leaning limply against her attacker, motionless in their grasp, as one of her wrists is still being controlled by her attacker. But now her attacker continues to beat her, inflamed by a hatred until finally, the suspect delivers the final blow to her head, killing her and ending the vicious attack. Realization creeps in that they murdered the victim as she hangs lifeless in the suspect's hand, with her eyes staring blankly at him."

"I was under the impression you only glanced at the file on your desk?"

"I did. Why?" Noble replied with a laugh.

"Because that's as good as word for word the account that happened in Billy Russell's last case, except the victim survived," Tony answered.

"And since it was my case, I should know it word for word because that case was difficult to forget." Noble, lost in thought, looked down at her notebook.

Twirling the pen above the paper, she looked at her notes. It was uncanny. She'd remembered so much. It horrified her as the scene unfolded slowly. The gruesome images stuck in her mind. She forced herself to clear her thoughts and refocus. Most images would fade with time, but the vision of every victim would never entirely leave her thoughts. Noble blinked twice and shook her head. She lifted her gaze and inhaled deeply. She turned toward Tony, staring instinctively at the same blood-spattered crime scene. His mind was most likely racing just as quick, if not quicker than hers, filled with the same horrific images, missing only one thing: the killer.

"Tony. Are you okay?" she asked, placing her hand on his arm. He jumped slightly at her touch and looked at her, eyes as blank as the victim's. Suddenly, it seemed like a realization sparked in his eyes.

"Oh yes, I'm fine," he replied, clearing his throat. "Ahem, yeah, so excellent theory."

"It would have been better if you had paid attention and listened." Chuckling, she smiled at him. This caused him to shrug his shoulders and raise his arms as if giving up.

"Hah, I was fortunate," Tony remarked. A hush fell over them as they sensed another person stepping into their work bubble.

"It was a satisfactory theory, but I'd rather have cold, hard facts to present to Chief Raynor instead of just some theories," Jacoby, the patrol sergeant remarked. "Can you explain why sex crime detectives are present at a homicide scene? Your delay prevents officers and detectives from completing their work in a timely manner. Their jobs are far from finished." Sergeant Jacoby glared at Noble and Tony for a few more seconds before turning and walking toward the crime scene.

"Sergeant Harper, advised by Chief Raynor, directed us to come and canvass the crime scene because this case might have a connection to some sexual assaults, ma'am." Noble spoke loud enough that Sergeant Jacoby could hear her as she was walking away.

"I can't stand her," Tony murmured, expressing his strong dislike for the sergeant, which Noble shared.

They both continued to wait next to their vehicle to observe the evidence collection and be of some help if needed. The coroner's van was on its way to remove and transport the body. The best part of the day was watching Sergeant Harper talk to Patrol Sergeant Jacoby after her unprofessional rant. With schooling over, Sergeant Harper left.

After several hours of processing the scene, with evidence bagged, tagged, and loaded into the crime scene van, the coroner's vehicle pulled up. Doc, the driver, stepped out along with an intern, a college kid named Brian. Noble waved to Doc and watched him do his job, not wanting to get in their way. Doc usually preferred to do the task and talk later. The victim always came first. Soon, they would load the body and take it to the coroner's office, where hopefully, they would determine the cause of death.

†

Noble and Tony returned to the office to update Sergeant Harper. It would be nice to return to the station, change into clean clothes, and get something to eat. They'd spent several hours at the scene, and their workday was over.

Tony turned to Noble. "You want to go out for drinks and dinner tonight? I know you've had a lot going on, which might overwhelm you on your first day back, but I found this little bar out on Ventura. Are you in?" he asked.

"Not tonight. I need a good night's sleep before we get going on this case. I'll need to be fresh so I can focus, and we can get an arrest." Noble backpedaled to the door.

"Now that you mention it, it's probably not a good idea. I'll stay home and read or catch something on the television."

"Alright, I'll see you tomorrow at zero-dark-thirty."

"Good night, Noble," Tony replied as he shut down his computer and headed home.

Noble walked out to her car, thinking that there was nothing he could have done to cheer her up, but at least she was smiling, showing signs of bouncing back quicker than before. The only thing Noble wished Tony would do was get some sleep and be ready to tackle this new case head-on in the morning. He always had a tough time sleeping when they got a fresh case. Usually, it was a live victim, but regardless, they knew someone was out there with that person's blood on their hands. Probably her least favorite thing about the job was finishing her shift before solving the case.

†

Once home, Noble sank onto the couch. She closed her eyes, took a deep breath, and leaned back on the cushion. If this was her reaction to her first memories of the scene, she wondered how she'd be able to handle the others. Noble pushed herself out of the couch and went to the kitchen for a glass of water. She couldn't find the sleep that had been eluding her for weeks, if not years, but would once again have to put the television on, hoping any sleep would come quickly and uninterrupted.

†

"Mom. I'm ready for my bedtime story," Elizabeth yelled as she flipped open her dinosaur book.

"Did you brush your teeth? Say your prayers? Say goodnight to all your animals?" Charlie asked.

"Yes, Mom. How do you know I talk to my animals?"

"A mom knows these things, sweetie."

"Why doesn't Mama Naomi? She always tells me not to do that, and that the animals don't have feelings and can't talk back."

"Well, she's wrong. All your toys and stuffed animals have feelings. It's in the parent handbook that they do. Maybe Mama Naomi missed that day in training."

"She's missed a lot, but I'm glad you didn't. I love you, Mom."

"Oh, sweetie, I love you, too. Now, can you tell me which dinosaur this is?"

"It's a big one, Mommy."

"It's called a Tyrannosaurus rex. Or you can call him T-rex for short. They can be as tall as forty feet and are meat eaters. They have powerful legs and short arms." Charlie looked down at Elizabeth, and she'd already fallen asleep.

Charlie closed the book, kissed her forehead, and turned off the light before going to the living room. Grabbing her glass of wine off the coffee table, she sipped her favorite Zinfandel and relaxed into the cushions. *Tomorrow is going to be here soon enough.* With a groan, she got up, took her last sip, walked to the kitchen, and put her glass in the dishwasher. After one last trip around to ensure she had locked all doors, she went to her room and climbed into bed. *Someday, there will be that person who thinks Elizabeth and I are important enough to spend time with and love.*

Elizabeth ran into her mom's room, panting. "Mommy, can I sleep with you tonight? Only until I get used to the new house."

"Come here, sweetie. Are you scared?" She reached over and lifted Elizabeth into bed.

"Yes, just a little. I love you, Mom," Elizabeth declared as she snuggled in next to her and closed her eyes.

"I love you too, sweetie. Get some sleep."

CHAPTER FIVE

Billy Russell sat in the run-down motel room, drinking a beer he had stolen from a homeless man, trying to figure out how he would get Tracy Snow. "I need a plan. That bitch will pay dearly for what she's done. This time, I'll see to it. There's no chance I'm going back to prison," Billy muttered to himself.

He still had some abrasions from where his ankle monitor had been before he cut it off. Small scabs with dried blood, along with the beer, fueled his anger. Billy turned on the sound of the TV and saw his face appear on the screen. The local news was running a news report, and the newscaster was talking as the camera panned over to an officer giving a statement.

"An Onserf-area parolee who was wanted for failing to check in with his parole officer is now being tracked for removing his ankle monitor. If anyone has seen him, please contact 494-STOP. He's considered dangerous. Russell's lengthy criminal history dates to at least 1999, when authorities charged him with multiple offenses, including indecent exposure, burglary, and kidnapping. He's currently out on parole for sexual assault and attempted murder. He's spent several stints in and out of prison, spanning most of his life. Russell will face charges of failing to register as a sex offender and absconding parole. Again, if seen, please call 494-STOP and don't confront."

"Who the fuck does she think she is? Fucking Chief Raynor, I just might take care of you like I intend to take care of that bitch, Tracy," Billy yelled at the TV, spitting saliva and beer on the screen as he paced in front of it. "No bitch is going to tell me what to do or say no to me ever again…she's lucky she lived last time, but I won't make the same mistake." He continued talking to the TV as the newscast ended.

Billy set his alarm for 2 a.m. and lay on the bed, remembering the women he'd had to teach that he was in control until they took their last breath. There were only two that he wished he'd had more time with, that female cop he'd had to run over because she was close to catching him with that bitch Tracy. She was hot and would have been fun to control. It was a damn shame that he'd had to run her over like a dog. If he hadn't heard her sirens, he'd have been able to have fun with her and Tracy. Make no mistake, whoever got in his way would wish they hadn't. Because, once he killed Tracy, after having a little fun with her, he'd leave this town and start over.

†

Billy Russell sat outside Blades Brewery watching for that bitch, Tracy Snow, who needed to be put into place. She made him go to prison, and she was going to pay with her life. His lawyer had discovered a loophole that reduced his sentence, making him eligible for parole. He couldn't wait to get his hands on her again and see the fear in her eyes when he finished what he started the last time. And then he'd watch her eyes dim as he killed her for putting him in that hell hole called prison. She'd not be as lucky this time with just a beating. He'd never forgotten her face and would patiently wait for his chance to finish her. His daddy taught him early in life that men rule and any woman he wanted had to succumb to his needs.

†

It was after two in the morning when Tracy and Vera wrapped up their final table cleanup. "Oh my goodness, my feet are absolutely throbbing," Tracy exclaimed.

"Are you going to be okay, knowing that Russell guy is on the run?" Vera asked.

"I am frightened. I realize he's determined to finish what he couldn't four years ago. I handed over the letters he sent me to the police, and they assured me they would increase their patrols in this area, in case he discovers my current address," Tracy mentioned.

"I'm staying with you tonight, and that's that!" Vera declared. Tracy switched off all the lights, and they made their way to the apartment above the bar.

†

Billy saw the lights go off inside and waited for someone to exit. After about ten minutes and no movement, he took one last puff of his cigarette and flicked it into the street. "Either the bitch went out the back, or she's staying at the bar. Believe me, you're going to pay and pay dearly," Billy mumbled as he slipped into the shadows and walked down the street to his car.

†

Tracy was cautious as she moved the drapes aside, giving her a view from the window and onto the street. She saw a slight orange glow fly out from behind a tree across the street and the outline of a person walking away in the shadows. Tomorrow wouldn't come fast enough. She could relax with undercover police inside the business while she worked until they caught Russell.

Tracy walked back to the door and made sure all the locks were secure before joining Vera on the couch and putting her feet on the coffee table. Vera had poured them a glass of wine and turned on the television. The glow of the TV illuminated the otherwise dark room. Tracy feared turning on the lights. Billy Russell or any other crackpot might notice someone living above the business, and it was a known fact that she owned it.

A repeat of the news came on, and as Vera was turning the volume up, the screen showed officers out on the scene of what the police were saying was a homicide. The homicide had occurred in the 1100 block of West Moss Avenue, and the victim appeared to be a female. They released no further information pending identification of the victim and contacting her immediate family. The police were asking for the public's help, and if anyone had any information, they should call 494-STOP, the CrimeStoppers number. It was okay if they wished to remain anonymous.

"Dear god, that poor woman! Could this be Russell?" Tracy gasped as she tried not to vomit.

"What're you saying, Tracy?" Vera asked her with concern in her voice.

"You know that Billy Russell is out. I wouldn't put murder past him at this point. This can't be happening."

"Let's get some sleep, alright?"

"Thank you for staying with me, Vera. It means a lot."

CHAPTER SIX

The next day, when Noble got into the office, she saw Tony sitting at his desk, head down, staring at the many reports they'd have to fill out. She didn't see any evidence packets, so she assumed they were already downstairs, or Symonds, the crime scene tech, had come up to collect them himself. Mackie Symonds hardly ever left his office. Noble made her way over to Tony's desk. Noble mimicked Sergeant Harper's deep, authoritative voice, saying, "Vistole." His head snapped up from the reports.

"Absolutely, ma'am," he started, but shot a glare at Noble, who was laughing at his response.

Noble handed him his coffee, still chuckling. She made her way to her desk across the room. Once seated, she leaned back, closed her eyes, and inhaled deeply.

Tony's muttering reached her ears. "Ha-ha, real funny, smart ass!" There was a hint of minor irritation in his tone, but the grin on his face told a different story when she glanced over at him. Taking a sip of his steaming coffee, Tony beamed. "Thanks for this. It really hits the spot."

Noble smiled at him in return. She then looked back at the many open-case file folders and the newly assigned cases in the computer and sighed. Damn, she needed to get caught up. Noble grabbed a pen, turning it in her fingers as she skimmed through the many reports related to the murder.

"These reports will keep us busy all day, unless there are any urgent issues we need to tackle." Tony's cheerful smile was evident above his coffee cup.

"Other plans? Since when do I make other plans when we're working on a big case? So, there's nothing important on today's agenda, right?" Noble asked, hoping to get away from her desk.

"Well, Dr. Redmond should conduct the autopsy on our Jane Doe sometime today, if you could check up on that…"

"Hey, wait up a minute! Why do I have to go to the autopsy?" Noble asked, glaring at him.

"Well, for one, I'm going down to talk to Mack and see if he got a hit on Jane Doe's DNA. And two, you can hold your stomach much better than I can. It would be better if you went instead of me. He'll let us know when he's about to begin or finish, depending on if he wants any company." A slight smirk crawled onto Tony's handsome face.

"Gentry!" Sergeant Harper yelled from her office. "Vistole," she continued.

Tony glared at Noble with an accusing look.

"What?" Noble replied. "Don't look at me like that. I wouldn't call my name?"

"Gentry! Vistole!" Her yell got louder and sounded more irritated as she called for the two detectives. "Where are you two at?"

Noble glanced at Tony as they both jumped and hoofed it across the office and down the hall where Sergeant Harper stood waiting for them.

"Yes, ma'am, my apologies, ma'am," Tony and Noble's voices echoed. The initial bewilderment of being summoned to the sergeant's office so early in the morning faded as Sergeant Harper regarded them with a curious gaze.

"Noble, is the evidence downstairs with Mack Symonds?" Sergeant Harper asked as Noble discreetly rolled her eyes.

Noble often thought Leah, or rather Sarge, liked to pull their chain and mess with them. Not bothering to speak, Noble and Tony nodded as Sergeant Harper continued, "And who'll observe the autopsy, collecting or logging any additional evidence and making notes?"

"That's me, ma'am," Noble replied, noticing Sarge's gaze shift in her direction. "Dr. Redmond mentioned he would give me a call when he was set to begin."

"So, I take it you two will be tackling those reports?" Sergeant Harper glanced around the corner at the towering stacks of files on their desks. Noble, catching her drift, nodded to her own mountain of paperwork.

"Yes, ma'am, we were just getting started." Tony gestured to where Noble had been standing, but when he turned to look at her, Noble was sitting at her desk, head down in a report. Sergeant Harper stood staring at him. "Oh, sorry, ma'am, I'll just head back to my desk and get back to work," he finished, about to turn away.

"I'll believe that when I see it, Vistole," Sergeant Harper remarked as Tony turned to his desk. "Oh yeah, and by the way, Tony, when your partner heads out for coffee, it would be fantastic if you could ask her to grab one for me as well!" she added, a smile spreading across her face as she winked.

Tony sat as Noble chuckled a little. Tony hadn't been in the unit as long as Noble, so he had little practice with Sergeant Harper and her remarks.

"Don't take it too seriously, Tony," Noble called out from the other side of the room, shuffling through a stack of reports. "She recognized that you work hard, so don't let her bring you down." She shot a quick look at Tony and noticed a smile beginning to form on his lips. Leaning in, he resumed his tasks.

"I don't put in the same effort as you do, so I suppose that's why she seems to prefer you," Tony commented, focused on his files.

"Yeah, but that's because she's our sergeant first and my friend second. Forget about it and keep doing what you're doing, and if she jokes about coffee with you, then she likes you," Noble replied.

They let the silence engulf them as they read page after page of reports. The only sound was the clicking of the computer mouse when they looked through additional images of evidence on their computers. After a few hours of understanding the gruesome scene, they needed to canvas and analyze. They closed the files on their desks and cleared the pictures from their computer screens, and attempted to relax just a little. It only seemed a moment before Noble's phone rang, ending the silence. Her hand shot out and picked it up. "Detective Gentry, Sexual Assault Unit, how can I help?" A familiar voice met her ears, and a smile radiated from her face.

"Hello, stranger," Dr. Redmond from the autopsy department greeted. Noble knew why he was calling, but it was nice to hear his voice. "Are you the one who wants to view the autopsy on Jane Doe?"

"Yes, I am. Are you about to start?" Noble asked as she was collecting her notebook and pen.

"I am. How long till you can be here?" he asked.

"I'm walking toward the stairs now. Give me about ten to fifteen minutes. I will walk over to your office. See you in a few, Doctor." Noble hung up the phone. She looked at Tony and smiled at him as she stood. "I'll see you later today. You know, you truly ought to give autopsy another chance. Getting reacquainted with all aspects of the job might do you some good. And besides, you know you'll have to attend another one, eventually." With that parting comment, she politely waved goodbye to Tony and approached the stairs next to their office. Once outside, she began the short trek over to the morgue.

"Well, be still my shocked heart. If it isn't Noble Knight."

Noble stopped in her tracks and turned around to the familiar, annoying voice. "Hi, Ms. Matthews. Fancy seeing you down here."

"I'm just getting some information in the hall of records. You probably thought you'd never see me again."

"Well, it had crossed my mind. Although I figured it would be at Jessie's house if I did. I'm sorry, I need to go. I've got an appointment at the medical examiner's office."

"Most people at the morgue have time on their side. So being a few minutes late won't make them any more alive. Take a deep breath and slow down. All this constant running will wear you down. You need to take better care of yourself. And if not for you, think about all the victims you won't be able to help if you're bedridden and exhausted."

"True, but the doctor conducting the autopsy is punctual and doesn't like to be kept waiting. Have a great day, Ms. Matthews."

"You keep saving the day, Detective Noble Knight. I'll see you around, hopefully. Maybe someday it might be under better circumstances." Charlie smiled as she began walking toward the hall of records.

"I will, and you never know what might happen. Thank you for your concern about my wellbeing," Noble stated as she made her way to Doctor Redmond's appointment. *Would I like to see her around someday? Maybe, but I need to get my head back on the case. There's time to think about that after I save the day.*

As Noble entered the coroner's office, it seemed like minutes slowly passed while the elevator music played through the ceiling speakers, causing Noble to chuckle slightly. No one who worked in this building ever showed symptoms of being calm; she never could understand or get why they'd even attempt it.

When the automatic door opened, Noble exited, walked over to the employees entrance, stepped inside, and found a gown, gloves, booties, and hat. Pulling the clothing over her own, Noble then continued walking through the double doors into a sterile autopsy room. Dr. Redmond turned around to look at his visitor. Even though the mask covered most of his face, his eyes showed the smile hiding underneath. In their type of job, it was good to know she put a smile on people's faces.

†

"And how has your day been so far, Noble?" Dr. Redmond asked, his voice muffled by the mask covering his mouth.

He knew how affected Noble might be, specifically in cases where the victim was young and violently murdered. But his question needed answering.

"Fair-to-middling. I had a meeting already with Sergeant Harper this morning. Sarge was messing with Tony, and I think he needs to learn to take it with a grain of salt. I know that if he doesn't, he will make his job even tougher for himself while he's in this unit. Wow, it's been over a year and a half since Tony joined me in the unit. How is your day going, Doctor?" Noble asked, redirecting the questions away from herself with ease.

"Let me think for a minute. You've been up there for what? Six years. It was during your third case together you sent him over to me for the first time, wasn't it?" he remarked, making Noble laugh out loud at the memory of Tony's pale-white face after his first viewing of an autopsy. "If I recall, that was just over a year ago. Remember, you were cranky since you didn't have a partner to help you with the caseload. You should be happier now that you've got Tony around!"

"Yes, I've finally got used to having him around. He's an excellent partner, a great guy, and like family. And just between you and me, Sergeant Harper likes Tony. She knows how to make him uncomfortable and unsure of himself. She did that with me until I called her on it. We've been friends ever since."

Dr. Redmond chuckled at her comment. He was aware of her views on Sergeant Harper, the respect that accompanied them, and the bond they had forged over the past six years. "Let's skip the small talk and focus on the case that brought you here," he indicated, gesturing toward Jane Doe on the metal table.

†

He'd already cut her open before Noble's arrival. It didn't appear that Noble had missed much, as the incisions looked fresh. The victim's organs looked like a mess from internal bleeding and bruising. "Sorry, I was a couple of minutes late. Got stopped by a civilian."

"No harm, no foul. Your victim suffered extensive injuries, but she put up a fight, as you can visually see from the defensive wounds along both her fists."

"Tony and I thought so, but with all the blood, it was difficult to tell," Noble muttered, not expecting the doctor to hear.

"Yes, I fully expected you to think of that once I realized it was you out at the crime scene. That's why I mentioned it to you. There's more evidence I found on the body that's already downstairs with Mack," Dr. Redmond answered.

Noble nodded in response as she wrote notes on what he was telling her.

"As you can see, even without the injury on her head, she'd have eventually bled out and died. There was no way she'd even have made it to the end of the alley, regardless of how hard she tried. And I doubt she could have even crawled, let alone make any attempt to walk because of all these wounds." Dr. Redmond pointed to the additional injuries on the rest of her body. "We've already sent her clothing downstairs. However, as I know how your mind works in cases like these, it gives you a reason to come and visit my lab, so I saved this information for you." He picked up a smaller version of a fingerprint card from the tray.

Noble smiled slightly and thought she liked visiting Mack, but she enjoyed going to the lab so much more.

"Hopefully, you're telling me you got some good impressions that could help identify the weapon used, possibly a crowbar or tire iron?"

"I can always count on you to get it right, Noble. A crowbar was the weapon of choice used on this poor girl. Look here." He pointed to a distinct bruise on her side. "The weapon's impact was minimal, which caused only a bruise, thus creating and leaving a shape indicative enough to show that it's a crowbar. I sent Mack a picture earlier, and he agreed with my findings." He smiled as Noble, deep in thought, wrote notes on her notepad.

"Does that mean the cause of death was the injury that she sustained to the head?" Noble asked as she could see the puzzle pieces moving into their correct places.

"Yes, that was the decisive strike. Within seconds, death occurred. Even if the assailant hadn't inflicted such severe injuries as those visible on her body, this one would have been lethal regardless." He gestured as he revealed her skin and muscle to show the numerous contusions and trauma affecting the inner layers of her torso, legs, and arms. "If you look closely, you'll notice a clear bruise line around her neck. It seems the suspect gripped her firmly, but not enough to cause asphyxiation, merely to restrain her, if only temporarily," he indicated, pointing to the subtle bruises.

"Were you able to determine the time of death?" she asked, knowing that this was one of the most crucial puzzle pieces and one that Doctor Redmond prided himself on determining.

"Yes," he replied while sifting through his documents. "Alright, I've managed to pinpoint her time of death to somewhere between midnight and one that morning."

"Wow? That's interesting. What was she doing late or early that morning in that part of town?" Noble asked as she made a note of the time.

"That's for you and Tony to figure out."

"Oh, sorry, Doctor Redmond." Noble chuckled a little as she nodded to him.

"I'll make sure to send my report out promptly after I double-check everything. Now," Doctor Redmond stated, capturing Noble's attention, as she lifted her gaze from her notepad and met the doctor's eyes, "I trust you've all the pertinent information you need for the investigation. You'll come back and visit soon, right? It can get quite lonely down here, and I genuinely enjoy your company."

Noble smiled again at the doc. "Why don't you try to come by my office sometime? The atmosphere is unique. You might even say pleasant." Noble laughed.

Dr. Redmond was older than her and a lovely man, but he sometimes came across as trying a bit too hard. Today, though, he was doing fine. He knew she was a lesbian, but that didn't deter his flirting with her any time the chance arose.

"Now, I suppose you ought to get this recent information to Mack, or we might never find out who your victim is."

"I will see you around, Doc. I might even take you out for drinks once this case is over. It appears Tony wants to collect on his outstanding rain check, so you can join us if you'd like." Noble smiled and headed toward the door, and just before it closed, she heard him call out to her.

"I will hold you to that, Detective!" he said as the doors shut again.

†

Noble returned to her office, quickly entered the building. As she approached her workspace, she noticed Tony sitting at his. She bypassed her desk and placed the envelope in front of him. Noble kept the same gloves she wore while handling the print card to prevent any contamination. Tony would be the one to bring the gloves to Mack, so Noble placed them on top of the envelope. Noble looked up and glanced around the corner toward Sergeant Harper's office, but she saw no sign of her.

"She's meeting with the primary officer first on the scene, you know, the uniform who called it in," Tony replied to her non-verbal question. "Mack went with Sarge to get a verbal overview of what first happened and to make sure no additional evidence was located. Otherwise, I'd have already been downstairs with Mack getting information on our case," Tony explained as Noble sat down at her desk and reviewed her notes from earlier today.

"Thanks, Tony. When you go down to get additional information, do you mind taking the envelope?" Noble asked. "I want to keep the chain of custody."

"Sure, no problem. I'm sure he'll be happy to get them. Hopefully, we will make an identification with these prints."

"I hope so, too." Noble slowly laid her head on her desk and took a deep breath, causing herself to cough and grimace in pain.

Tony chuckled and handed her a bottle of water. "Sorry, Noble. I should have seen that you were coming down off your high and got you some water, coffee, or food to help you out.

It seems we're creatures of habit and forget the effects we might have when working on a case like this."

Noble smiled, thanking him for the water, although she probably would have preferred to throw up and get it out of the way. Opening the bottle, she took two swigs, hoping it would help clear her mind of the crime scene and the gruesome images she had seen. She coughed a few more times and forced herself to drain the contents of the bottle and not throw up. Refocusing her brain, she started writing her follow-up report from her earlier meeting with the doctor.

Sergeant Harper and Mack returned from the field. Sergeant Harper continued walking past them, but Mack stopped, sitting beside Noble's desk. He quietly rapped his fist near the edge like knocking on a door.

"Yes?" Noble asked while laughing in response to his knock. "How may I be of service to you, Mack?" Noble continued, swiveling in her chair to face him. His long hair partially covered his eyes, bangs if you will, and blocked his big expressive brown eyes that were full of energy and a bit of mischief as a smile lit up his face, displaying straight, perfectly white teeth.

"Doctor Redmond advised me you might have some prints for me." He nodded once toward the reports on her desk and pointed at the one on the top of her stack.

"I just gave them to Tony, so technically, he has them," Noble replied, pointing in Tony's direction. "He was going to bring them down to you once you and Sergeant Harper finished in the field. Doc gave them to me so I could hand deliver them to you. Also, our Jane Doe's primary cause of death is a head injury, as Tony and I suspected, but even without that major injury, she'd have died with all the internal and external injuries from the assault inflicted on her."

"Thanks for the update. So, what are you doing later after your shift?" he asked. Noble heard Tony's faint sigh of exasperation, and she chuckled a little.

"Sorry, Mack, I'm not interested. You know I don't date men," Noble replied. Whenever he saw her, he couldn't pass up the chance to ask her out. He always knew her answer would be no, but he enjoyed trying because it lightened the mood while working tough cases. "And you should know by now that I don't go out during a case. Once it gets solved, you can come out with Doc, Tony, and me, and we'll get drinks. You might even catch a ride with Tony." Noble swiveled her chair toward Tony and gave him a questioning look.

"Hey, Mack." Tony turned around in his chair in response to his name. "Hell yeah, I'll give him a ride," he replied, smiling. "Noble got those prints. How're the other things with DNA coming along?"

Noble understood that he always preferred to talk about the case and was trying to divert the subject away from the night out with drinks. It was great to hang out with some of the gang because one of them always went off-topic, and then the others would eventually follow, never wavering. It was entertaining to watch things unfold among great friends.

"Alright then," Mack replied. "Come on down. I need to update and review some evidence with you." Mack gestured toward the stairs leading down to his office's floor. Noble knew he preferred to use the stairs because he didn't like to be in small spaces, but occasionally, it was a requirement, especially when going out in the field with Sergeant Harper. She always expected him to meet in her office before they left.

†

Noble didn't see Tony for most of the afternoon, and when he returned, he was reserved, other than being adamant about Noble checking out one of the lab reports. The end of their shift came, and Noble felt like there was something that Tony wanted to tell her, or maybe he was keeping something from her he didn't want her to know. She watched Tony, and he looked as if he was ready to explode out of his seat. All the while, Sergeant Harper kept walking in and out and inquiring about what they were still doing there.

"Damn, we got no hits on who our victim might be," Tony expressed frustration, noting the lack of leads on the identity of the victim. "Without identifying our victim, we've no solid leads. We searched the National Missing Person database, but there weren't any hits or anything remotely close that matched our victim's physical description. We're clueless about where this case is going to take us."

"It's okay, Tony. We'll catch a break eventually, then we can determine if this is Billy Russell's doing or someone else's, and then put whoever is responsible behind bars for the rest of their lives." Noble squeezed Tony's shoulder. "I'll see you tomorrow."

"Have a good night, Noble."

She headed home after a long day at the office, feeling like they'd gotten nothing of importance accomplished. She always took her work home with her; it helped her pass the time and gave her something to think about when she went to sleep. She was tired of all the nightmares, the havoc they were wreaking on her, and the lack of sleep she'd been experiencing. She read her notes and wrote additional questions regarding their case. The feeling of the pen moving gently on the paper would hopefully trigger a memory or make something stand out in the reports and help spark something that could bring closure to this case. The only bright spot today was running into Charlie Matthews; she wasn't sure how to take that. *Oh boy. I need to get a grip.* Noble laughed at this surprising thought.

CHAPTER SEVEN

"Hey Charlie, don't forget the boss wants to see us before we leave for the day," Mike bellowed, running his fingers through his hair.

"Okay. Thanks for showing me around today. You truly were a lifesaver. Things have changed a little since I last lived here. I can't believe how much the downtown area has grown."

"Yeah, it's great for the city, even though it gives us more work," he muttered.

"I ran into a cop that works for the Onserf Police Department while I was heading to the hall of records. Her name is Noble Gentry. Do you know her?" Charlie asked.

"She's a rather good cop, from what I've seen and heard. I've met her several times when we've worked joint operations with her department." Mike fidgeted with his watch band. "Having her on your side is a godsend because she handles all the details. She's not one for mistakes and wants everything delivered to the district attorney's office, complete with a bow."

"This was my second time running into her. The other was at my friend's house, whose daughter was the victim of that music teacher last year. The case that just ended recently. I grilled her that time." Charlie laughed. "She doesn't know I'm in law enforcement."

"Well, I'm sure you'll eventually get around to more formal introductions. She's become a recluse since her wife died four years ago," Mike revealed. "But once you get to know her, you'll see that she's a humble woman who likes to do her job and do it right the first time."

"Oh wow, I didn't know she'd been married. Do you know what happened to her wife?" Charlie whispered, her voice gentling. "Maybe I won't give her too much grief the next time I run into her."

"Her wife, Diana, worked for the Onserf police as well. She was responding to a call of a woman screaming and being assaulted in her apartment. When Diana arrived, she got out of her vehicle and radioed in that she was in foot pursuit of a white male who was fleeing the scene." A sigh escaped his lips. "Noble was trying to reach her on the radio, and the last transmission from Diana was that the suspect was in a white Ford LTD, going southbound on McKenzie Street approaching Baymont Avenue, and that he was heading straight toward her. Within a couple of minutes, Noble and the assisting units arrived at Diana's location and found her unresponsive in the middle of the street." Mike rubbed the back of his neck. "The suspect had run her over and left the area. She died on the way to the hospital, and the suspect is still outstanding four years later."

"Gosh almighty, how horrible. I remember my parents talking about it." A pained look marred her face. "Four years, and the suspect's DNA is still not showing up in the system? I hope they get him. I'm sure she'll want some closure."

"Believe me, there are a lot of cops that want to make that arrest," he spat. "Diana was highly respected and loved by her department and the community. Her family has a long history with this city, so everyone is still hoping."

"You can add me to the list. I hope they get him soon. Four years is a long time to wait for closure. I don't know how I could ever lose the woman I love like that. It would tear my heart out."

The sound of a phone shrilling brought her attention to the present. She looked at Mike, who reached for the phone on his desk.

"Agent Taylor, how may I help you? Yes, ma'am, I'll let Charlie know. And yes, we're all caught up on the cases from this morning, except for two follow-up reports we're typing now. Understood, no overtime is in the budget. We'll head out shortly for the day. Thank you. Have a nice evening yourself."

"Well, it sounds like our meeting with the boss got canceled?" Charlie inquired.

"Yep, and there's no overtime, so we must finish these reports in the morning," Mike grumbled as he turned off his computer.

"Great, I'll be getting off early. And it's a night that the grandmas are keeping Elizabeth overnight." The words were a jagged whisper on her tongue. "I've no social life. I need to work on that."

"Come on, Matthews. One night of peace won't hurt your social life. It's good to spend some time alone and relax. I'll try to set up a group outing with some people soon, and you can meet them all." He ripped out a laugh. "It's a mix of people from our office and Onserf police. It's a well-rounded group; you can start networking and building friendships there. That's if you want to."

"Sounds great. Just let me know when. I need to secure my mom for babysitting duties. Have a great evening, Mike."

"You too, Charlie. I'll see you tomorrow," he remarked while exiting the office.

Charlie grabbed her bag and headed out of the office to her car. On the drive home, she stopped and got some Chinese food. As she walked through the door, she grabbed a glass and poured herself some wine. Sitting on the couch, she pulled out her laptop and searched for Noble Gentry. While waiting for her search to appear, she devoured her dinner and took a big sip of wine.

"I can't do this. This doesn't feel right. Maybe, maybe not, but when I run into her again, I will let her tell me about her life. It will be more truthful than some newspaper articles. Noble Knight is proving to be more intriguing by the day." Charlie finished the last sip of wine in her glass and headed to her bedroom for a good night's sleep.

Chapter Eight

The next few days involved trips to forensics, DNA, and sometimes autopsy, but what caught Noble's eye most was Sergeant Harper. She spent most of her time next to her murder board or pacing back and forth across her office. Noble had her ideas on the case, but Harper always questioned them and made her go back and use various inventive ways to move the case along with the endgame of solving it. They sometimes butted heads, not because they disagreed but because they went about different ways of finishing the puzzle so both could see the complete picture and make an arrest. They had distinct styles of doing things, and sometimes Harper forgot she was the sergeant and not the detective anymore. Noble loved this about her, but sometimes she'd drive Noble insane.

Tony and Noble voiced their theories to Sergeant Harper and Tony passed her messages regarding the labs. Sometimes, Sarge's restlessness, which followed her actions, made work around the office much more exciting and livelier for the unit.

Noble's thoughts strayed back to the case, and she found it odd that no missing person's report regarding the victim had been filed yet. Wasn't her family worried? Didn't she have any friends or an intimate partner who might notice her absence in their lives? Noble gripped the pen in her hand, thinking over everything about this case to help give her an account of what had happened to Jane Doe.

Noble arrived at the station early, finding Harper and not Tony at her desk. She was sitting in Noble's chair. Noble quietly entered their office and let the door swing shut behind her. She didn't know what to do. Did Harper want to talk to her or maybe even yell at her? Was she in trouble, and Harper was there to tell her firsthand? She continued advancing in Harper's direction without knowing what the issue could be. She might as well get it finished instead of prolonging her anxiety.

She paused at her desk and, with a composed tone, asked, "Harper, what are you really…?"

"Ah, Noble," she cut her off midsentence. "Noble, I need to talk to you about something."

"Well, um, Harper, unless you're also waiting for Tony," Noble responded, pointing toward Tony's empty desk.

"Who?" Harper asked, following Noble's hand pointed at the desk. "Oh, Noble, no, I don't need him for this conversation."

"Anyway, what did you need to talk to me about?" she prompted, hoping to get back to her current case and finish it as soon as possible.

"Yes, right? What were you saying?" Harper murmured.

"Harper, you wanted to talk to me," Noble reminded her.

Feeling uncomfortable, Noble looked at Tony's desk, silently wishing he'd glide through the door. As if her wish came true, Tony entered the room and took two steps before his eyes questioned the scene in front of him. The smile on his face changed to one of confusion as he put his keys back into his pocket. He held his old, weathered-leather jacket while a neatly ironed, crisp green shirt was tucked into his jeans. The finishing touch were his tennis shoes, which barely looked like someone had tied them and completed the casual look.

Noble frequently made remarks about his clothing choices because of the casual T-shirt she wore under her blazer jacket, jeans, and comfortable dress shoes. Lucky for her, it suited her.

Noble smiled at Tony's arrival. "Hey!" Noble called, trying to distract him from Harper, his confused expression causing her to laugh.

Tony's eyes looked toward Sergeant Harper as he saw Noble shrug her shoulders discreetly. He appeared to be in the dark as much as she was. Noble was stepping in Tony's direction, but Harper reached across Noble's desk and grasped her forearm. It surprised Noble. Even though they were friends, Harper always kept it business in the presence of others, not wanting anyone to think she was giving preferential treatment to her friend.

"Can we please continue this conversation in my office, Detective Gentry?" she asked, making it more like a question than an order.

Noble knew something must be going on if she wanted a meeting with merely the two of them. Noble nodded quietly in response and followed Harper into her office. As they both passed Tony, he appeared confused, almost as if he wanted to say something, but kept silent. Noble gave him a reassuring smile as she entered Sergeant Harper's office and closed the door. Noble worried that something was wrong with the case. Or that something might be wrong with her friend.

Sitting, Noble's eyes focused on the white walls of Harper's office. They were hard not to notice, as they were radiant. It was almost as if Harper had barely moved in, and everything was in mint condition. The entire station was the same color but felt less intense than the white here. Harper closed her office blinds so no one could see their conversation or body language. The last time she did this with Noble in the office, she'd been the one to tell her about how the department had mandated that Noble see a therapist after Diana died.

Noble shifted in her seat, feeling uneasy as she came to the realization that when the blinds were shut, she hated being in Harper's office. The desk was a black cherry, and there seemed to be a massive canyon between them. She smiled when she realized Harper didn't lock her office door, which was good. She could leave voluntarily if she needed to flee, and that immediately calmed her.

"Noble, I'd like to talk to you about your job." Harper took a seat, leaned forward, her hands clasped on the desk.

"What about my job?" Noble demanded, feeling like she had to force the conversation out of Harper.

Harper was a rare breed who was usually straightforward and to the point. Noble expected her to be more direct, since she and Harper were friends. *I wonder what the hell Tony is doing right now.*

"What if you had a tailor-made job to fit your abilities?" Harper asked, probably hoping to gauge her reaction.

"Leah, I mean Sergeant Harper, my current job exactly fits what I enjoy doing right now. Sergeant…" Noble saw the beginning of a smile on Harper's face. She could tell Harper was trying to hint at something, but she wasn't sure she wanted to know what that was.

"Noble, I'm considering your qualifications and Vistole's."

"What kind of job?" Noble questioned as she played along.

Even though her frustration level was rising, she did not want to test Harper. She sensed Harper was getting irritated as Noble tried to take charge of the conversation. Most people would show interest in getting a better job, but Noble liked her current assignment, was good at it, and wanted to stay put.

"Dammit, Noble, sometimes you make me want to pull my hair out. My granddaughter doesn't even do that." A groan accompanied the roll of her eyes. "I'm asking you to be my acting sergeant when I'm gone, like on vacation or out sick. I want you to be my right-hand woman."

Noble had expected her to say many things, but that was not on her list. Noble stared at Harper with what she suspected was a dumbfounded look. *What?* Losing Tony as her partner played repeatedly as her mind went into overdrive.

"You're my best detective, and I wanted to extend a formal offer to you once I got the green light from the higher-ups. It can only be one person, and you're overqualified," she articulated with deliberate clarity. "The unit dynamics will stay the same, you and Tony will still be partners. However, he needs to understand that there will be times when you'll be in charge, and I expect him and the rest of the team to respect that. I trained you when you were a rookie, so I know firsthand that you can handle this extra responsibility with your eyes closed."

"I'm not sure what to say, Harper." Noble was at a loss. She'd get a promotion, but Tony and she would still be partners. She knew Tony would be happy for her but happier that their team wouldn't get broken up. Her dream had always been to become a detective. This additional responsibility would prepare her for the future if she wanted to be promoted.

"Hey, Noble, I'm not sure I've ever seen you at a loss for words." An amused expression appeared as Harper studied her. "You don't have to answer me today, but I'd like it soon."

"I'm sorry, Harper, I mean Sergeant Harper, but I will accept your job offer. If it's any consolation, only a few people have rendered me speechless." She smiled so hard that the corners of her mouth were introduced to her ears. "Thank you for the opportunity to grow and learn from your continued leadership. You had me worried there for a moment that I might be going to a new assignment." Noble felt a colossal weight lift off her shoulders.

"Excellent, I will inform the staff that you have accepted the acting sergeant position so they can update their paperwork and your file." She drummed her fingers on the desk. "You know, Noble, it's great to see you back at work with a smile. I was concerned we might need to intervene." Her expression softened as she looked at Noble.

"Thanks, Harper. It's great to be back at work, and I'm trying to get my personal life together. Diana would kick my ass if she saw me sitting at home sulking. She'd expect me to move on like I'd expect her to do the same." She shifted back in her seat as if it made shifting her thoughts easier. "I decided this was the last time I would take a vacation unless it was to make new memories. I've realized that Diana will always be a huge part of my life and my past, and I will honor her by becoming a better person, willing to change in this cruel world." Noble's mouth quirked upward. It was not a forced smile from the past, but a genuine half smile, ready to forge ahead on an unknown journey.

"Noble, you'll be fine, and Diana will always be proud of you, no matter what. She'd be ecstatic that you took this offer without blinking. It would show you're thinking long term, not simply for now but for your future. Diana would want you to celebrate that future with someone eventually, and she'll know that you always hold a special place in your heart for her. Vistole will be there right next to you, like a sponge taking it all in so he can continue to learn and be like you, which is a damn excellent cop and detective." Harper raised her left eyebrow as if waiting for Noble to disagree with her.

"I won't disagree with you." She'd learned that she'd take her life in her own hands if she did. "But I will make you proud of me, on the job and off, for the rest of my life," Noble replied as tears filled her eyes, her lips quivering as she smiled. "Thank you for taking a chance on me and believing I'm ready for my next career phase. Maybe you can continue to be a wonderful friend and help me wade through life and entry to the dating world someday." Noble ended with a full-blown, deep, belly laugh.

"It would delight Beth and me to watch and help you in both phases of your life. I can say that the work portion should be a breeze, but the relationship part could be dangerous." A grin sprang across her face. "Sometimes, you might get a rotten apple before you find that pristine Golden Delicious you want to make your own and take a bite out of. Or something to that effect." She snorted through her laughter. "You can tell Tony now as you're getting fidgety. I'll talk to you later. Try to come by after work tonight to grab a bite of food with everyone. Char and Elizabeth will be there, and it's about time you meet them."

"Depending on how much I can get done today, I'll try. You always talk about them and I'm excited to meet both.

Besides, I need to get all the dirt on you and Beth." Noble raised a challenging eyebrow.

"Out. Get out now and get back to work. You're lagging today," Harper scoffed with a laugh.

Noble stood, hurried around Harper's desk, and hugged her. "I won't disappoint you." She moved toward the door, opened it, and returned to her desk.

She'd already answered all her emails and phone calls before her conversation with Harper. While she waited for updates on the murder victim, she would go through the case file again. She had to be missing something that was in plain sight. Tony was sitting at his desk, and Noble smiled at him as she neared, but instead of smiling back, he glared.

"How come you had to go behind closed doors with Sergeant Harper? What was it about? The case? Why wasn't I invited if it was about the case?" he rattled off in quick succession, impatient for the answers to his questions.

"What do you mean? What was what about?" Noble queried in return, prolonging his torture.

"You know what! Why was Harper so persistent in talking to you behind closed doors that she about dragged you into her office?" he grilled, showing that his patience was thinning regarding being left out of the meeting. "Oh shit, I guess I should make sure you're not being disciplined or fired before I rattle off. Well, were you disciplined or fired?"

"What the hell gave you that idea, Tony? Are you flipping kidding me? No, to both the discipline and being fired!" She skewered him with an unflinching look. "Sergeant Harper wanted to know if I'd become the acting sergeant of the unit. We talked about her expectations of me and what the job entails. The meeting had nothing to do with the case." Noble continued walking to her desk and sat. She switched the screen on, and there it was. Well, at least she wished that one of the recent emails would optimistically give her case hope.

"Wow, you're going to be the acting sergeant! Congratulations, Noble. You deserve it." A wide grin crinkled the corner of his eyes. "Ah, man, will they get me a new partner? I'm not ready to partner up with anyone else. Did she tell you anything about that?" Tony rambled on as he placed his hands over his eyes and took a deep breath.

"Per the sarge, we will remain partners, but she wanted it stressed that when I'm the acting sergeant, you're to listen to me as if she were here." Her tone brooked no argument. "She doesn't want anyone to think I'm taking it easy on you because we're partners. Are you clear about that, Tony?" Noble challenged. She needed him to understand that business is business, and there would be times she was in charge. He would have to respect that.

"I understand there will be instances when you're in charge, and you'll have no problems with me. I'm glad we still get to be partners." A relieved look washed over his face.

"Let's finish up so we can head home and relax for the day," Noble insisted.

†

"I need to come up with a plan so I can find that bitch. Damn, TV stations running my photo are pissing me off," Russell yelled.

Russell paced around the motel room and noticed no proper ventilation except a barely working air conditioning wall unit dripping water onto the carpet. There was an unpleasant, musty odor. The stale air in the motel room smelled like a breeding ground for mold and mildew, as if a pipe had broken and flooded onto the carpet that nobody had ever replaced.

"I need to leave here for a few hours so this smell doesn't kill me. I know what I can do," he said as he went to the bathroom and took the razor out of the bag he'd stolen from the barbershop last night. He meticulously shaved his head, beard, and mustache, giving him a new look. "All those bitches think I'm a dumb shit, but I'll prove them all wrong. Right, Daddy? They won't know what hit them. Thank you for being the best teacher I ever had. I'm going to shower and see if I can slither around town without being recognized like some damn rock star. This might be fun, and I can experiment with some women until I can find the right time to kill that fucking whore."

Chapter Nine

Charlie looked at the front door. "Knock, knock, anyone home?" she called as she entered through the open doorway.

"Well, if it isn't my favorite daughter. Come on in, sweetie. How was your first day at the new office?" Beth inquired, smiling lopsidedly.

"Mom, I'm your only daughter and your only kid," Charlie replied as she wrapped her arms around mom.

"So, how was it? I see you still have all your hair." Beth laughed as she marched with Charlie to the kitchen.

"A new boss, a new partner, and a lot of other new stuff are happening in my life right now. It could be worse. I have to learn how they operate and be ready to go if anything arises. Although I think my partner and I will work out well," Charlie answered as she poured herself a glass of water.

"I'm glad to hear that. You've wanted to transfer here for a while, and I, for one, am so happy it's now as opposed to later," Beth replied.

"It sure is great being home again and closer to you and Leah. I've missed spending time with you both. And I know Elizabeth will love it here," Charlie stated. "What're you cooking? It smells delicious?"

"I'm cooking a tri-tip in the slow cooker, potatoes, and a salad. You're welcome to stay. That way, you can see Leah when she gets home from work. She'll be happy to see you," Beth commented as she lifted the lid to check on the meat.

"It's not like Elizabeth and I have anything to do or anyone waiting for us at home. So, we will stay for dinner. I will be with the two most important people in my life—other than Elizabeth. It can't get better than that!" Charlie declared. "Where's the munchkin?"

"In the living room watching her favorite dinosaur movie." Leah smiled from ear to ear. "Oh, sweetie, someday we'll just be distant thoughts for you when you finally find the right person to share your life with. I bet you get invited out on a date within the month. You can't rush love, but sometimes it can bite you in the ass if you're too slow to recognize it."

"We'll see…" The words trailed into the kitchen as Charlie turned around to find her daughter.

"Honey, I'm home." Leah entered the kitchen. "Oh gosh, well, what do we have here? Get over here and give me a hug, princess."

"Oh, how I've missed the attitude, Mom L." Charlie squeezed her in a bear hug.

Beth joined in on the hug and started singing "We Are Family." Charlie couldn't remember a time when being happy didn't include being home. Mom and Mom L were the foundation of who Charlie had become. She had been excited when she could transfer back to the local Department of Justice office. Maybe she could look to add someone special to the mix and complete her dreams of sharing her life and growing old with her forever girl.

"Mommy, Mimi, and Grandma, I want to dance, too." Elizabeth intertwined her arms with her mom and Mimi.

"Let's boogie, Elizabeth." Leah twirled around in a circle.

"Charlie, why don't you set the table? Leah, you can pour our drinks once you're done dancing. I'll bring out dinner." Beth shooed them away to complete their tasks.

"Yes, dear. Yes, Mom," Charlie and Leah replied as they spun around and headed to do their assigned tasks.

"So, tell me about your first day at the new office," Leah asked Charlie once they had sat down for dinner.

"It was okay; I need to get into the swing of things. Also, I like my partner; that's a plus." Charlie took a massive bite of her tri-tip.

"Wow!" Leah stared at Charlie, trying not to laugh as she struggled to chew.

After the last bite of tri-tip traveled down her throat, Charlie looked at Leah and stated, "What? I've missed Mom's cooking."

"Our daughter was telling me earlier that she's single but looking. And after seeing her shovel all that meat into her mouth, I might know why." Beth laughed as she held her stomach.

"Mommy, what does it mean when you're single?" Elizabeth asked as she chewed her lip.

"Well, munchkin, you know how Grandma and Mimi have each other? I don't have that other person to share my life with. It's you and me, kiddo. And if that's how it's supposed to be, then so be it," Charlie replied. Her words came out delicately, wrapped in a whisper.

"I hope I get another mommy. You can hold my hand as we walk and swing me. And even better, you can read me a bedtime story and watch my favorite movies with me," Elizabeth announced as she chewed her tri-tip.

"I'm so lucky to have you for a daughter, Elizabeth."

"You're the best granddaughter," Leah and Beth expressed, their voices sweet and smooth like syrup.

Laughter filled the table as Elizabeth expressed her fondness for Mimi.

"Back on my status, Mom L. Do you have any single and willing-to-mingle women who work in your district? I need to broaden my horizons, so maybe I'll swing by your station and have a look," Charlie pressed.

"Oh, no, you won't, young lady! I can still put you over my knee and spank you. I don't need any trouble; my officers need to focus, and by being focused, I mean on work." Leah jabbed a finger toward Charlie.

"Oh, come on honey, isn't Lieutenant—" Beth blurted as the question popped from her tongue.

"Hell no, don't even go there, Beth!" Leah grunted, pinching the bridge of her nose.

The trio erupted into a laughter fit, including a snort or two. Leah gulped her beer, closed her eyes, and declared, "I've missed you, princess."

"My love for the two of you has no boundaries. I promise not to stalk any women in your district unless we meet somewhere else and they work there," Charlie replied as she dodged a napkin thrown by Leah.

"I guess the positive side is that you kept your mom's maiden name, so I can claim not to know you. I haven't even told my good friend Nob that you transferred back." Leah laughed as she took her last sip of beer.

"Wow, I think I will hyphenate my name, so it says Matthews-Harper, but on second thought, I enjoy having my identity and making a name for myself." She grabbed her napkin off the table. "No offense to you, Mom L, but I don't want to be that person people talk about for riding on the coattails of their parents." Charlie hoped she hadn't hurt Leah's feelings.

"No offense taken, princess! I have faith in you and respect your decision. I'm so proud of you, and it's nothing to do with your last name but with the woman you've become," Leah replied as she collected the dishes from the table and headed toward the kitchen.

"You know, Leah is right. We're so proud of you, and that's all there is to it." Beth grabbed Charlie's hand on the table. "I'll leave you two to talk about work while I clean the kitchen. Elizabeth, come help Grandma."

Leah came back into the dining room with two fresh beers and took her seat. "We have a case right now that I might call your boss to ask for a team to assist us on." Leah took a swig of beer from the bottle.

"Oh, by all means, can you tell me about it?" Charlie probed as she shook salt on the top of her beer bottle.

"We have a sex offender on parole who cut his ankle monitor and is on the run. It's possible he's tied to a recent murder. Regardless, we need to get him back into custody as soon as possible," Leah continued as she gave Charlie a synopsis of the case.

"Sounds like a great case to assist you on, get the lay of the land, and meet some officers I'll be working with to build relationships outside of the DOJ," Charlie said. She couldn't wait to read more on this case.

“I’ve got my best detectives, Nob and Vistole, assigned to the case. They’ve made headway, but with your unit’s help, I think we can get this guy off the street faster and hopefully limit his rampage through the city,” Leah replied as her phone buzzed with an incoming call.

“If you need to answer that, I’ll go help Mom and Elizabeth.” Charlie stood and meandered toward the kitchen.

†

“What’s up, Noble? Do you or Tony have a lead you need to check out, and you’re letting me know you can’t come over tonight.” Leah wanted to know after she answered her phone.

“Yes. Sorry,” Noble replied.

“Okay. Keep me updated on whether something pans out or not. Send me a text unless it’s an emergency. I will let Beth know you can’t make it. She made you a to-go bag a few minutes ago; maybe I will bring it to work tomorrow. Stay safe.” Leah wrote notes in her small notepad that she always carried.

“I will do that, boss. Give Beth a big hug and kiss for me—and not one of your hugs and kisses, either. That would be wrong on so many levels, and I don’t need Beth thinking I’m crushing on her.” Noble laughed.

“Holy crap, Gentry, you talk like I’m some deviant. I’ll relay the message and await your response about your lead later,” Leah replied as she ended the call.

Leah stood and walked into the kitchen, where Beth was finishing the last cleanup.

“I’m to give you a chaste hug and kiss from Nob.” Leah gave Beth a hug and a soft sweet kiss.

"Let me guess, she had to chase some lead, so she won't stop by tonight to get her to-go bag?" Beth replied as she hugged Leah back.

"You know her so well. What a shame she's not coming by, or I'd have introduced her to Charlie. Anyway, where is she?" Leah answered as she kissed Beth's neck.

"She checked on Elizabeth and then went to the restroom."

†

"Everything okay with your phone call?" Charlie questioned as she moved into the kitchen.

"Yes. It was my lead detective on the case we were talking to you about earlier. She was giving me an update," Leah replied as she lifted the trash bag out of the container, tied it up, and headed outside to the trash.

"Sounds like you'll meet her soon, anyway. She's become a wonderful friend, and she's been working for Leah for the last six years in sex crimes," Beth mentioned, knowing Charlie might have some more questions.

"Alright then. Elizabeth and I will say our goodbyes as soon as Leah returns and head home to get a good night's rest before work tomorrow. I hope Leah calls my boss soon so I can start strong and help her with the case," Charlie replied as Leah returned in the middle of her response to Beth.

"I'll be calling your boss tomorrow. Come here and hug us so you can leave for home. I know you and the princess need your beauty rest. Well, that and coffee." Leah laughed as she and Beth waited with open arms.

"Don't forget about me down here," Elizabeth said as she glanced at all three.

"That will never happen," all three stated simultaneously.

"Aren't you the funny one? I think we got you out of a box of Cracker Jacks. Is there any way we can pack you back in the box to quiet you down?" Charlie proposed as she hugged Beth and Leah together.

"No can do, princess. I'm out for the duration. And I'm not a contortionist. Ask your mom," Leah replied as she moved quickly to avoid the pinch from Beth.

"We love you both, and I'll talk to you tomorrow," Charlie said as they approached the entryway.

"We love you too, sweetie," Beth and Leah replied before they shut the door.

"Our girl is all grown and ready to tackle the world." Beth squeezed Leah's hand.

"Yes, she is. And if Elizabeth had her way, she'd be well on her way to adulthood, like yesterday. Are you ready for bed?" Leah asked, grabbing Beth's hand and leading her toward the bedroom.

"Only if we can practice your contortionist skills. I've got the exercises, and it doesn't require sleep," Beth replied as she released Leah's hand, sauntered past, and, as they ran the rest of the way, removed her top and let it fall to the ground.

"Oh yes, practice, practice, practice. I love how you think." Leah caught up to Beth, kissing her as her foot kicked the door shut.

†

"I need to get some timers so I can have lights on when I get home." Charlie pulled into the garage and punched the opener to close the door.

As soon as the door was down, she exited her car and opened the back passenger door to find Elizabeth fast asleep.

As she picked her up and closed the door, Elizabeth mumbled, "Noole. You can help me save the dinosaurs."

"Sleep talking again, I see. Let's get you inside and into bed." She locked the back door and dropped her bag on the chair in the kitchen. She laid Elizabeth on her bed and gently pulled down her sheet and blanket, careful not to wake her.

"Noole, I want to be brave like you, Mom, and Mimi," Elizabeth mumbled again.

"I need to ask her who this Noole person is tomorrow. Although, it's common for kids her age to have an imaginary friend." Charlie headed toward her bedroom and face-planted on the bed, with one final thought before sleep finally consumed her. *I hope Mom L calls my boss tomorrow so I can start working on this case.*

Chapter Ten

Noble clicked on the email icon on her desktop computer and noticed ten recent emails she needed to open and view. Her face lit up when she clicked on the fourth one and realized the message might give their case a leg in the game. Her heart frantically beat like drums at a rock concert, marking her memory of this crucial emotional moment. There mightn't be any hits related to the collected DNA in the database, but finally, they'd have a place to start. *It's a solid lead!*

Noble quickly stood and headed toward Harper's office. She knocked on the door but was too excited to wait for a response.

Noble opened it and called to Harper, who was sitting at her desk looking over paperwork. "Sergeant Harper, meet me in the interview room."

After practically barking her order, she shut the door. She knew it was frankly rude, she should have mentioned something a little more besides ordering Harper, but Noble was too excited to care. Running the scant distance down the hall and skidding to a stop at her desk, she collected her notepad. As Noble arrived at the interview room, she saw Tony inside, waiting with a man named Samuel Adams.

Noble explained to Mr. Adams what they needed to do and then excused herself to get a pen since the one she usually kept in her notepad must have been left on her desk. As Noble was going through a commonly used desk outside the interview room looking for a damn pen that worked, Harper entered from the common hallway.

"Hey, Noble, next time, a little synopsis would be much better than ordering me to the interview room. Hell, for a minute, I thought I was at home, and you were Beth!" she blurted as she approached Noble. "Next time, take a minute and fill me in on what you have so I don't have everyone in our unit looking at me like a deer in the headlights when I came strolling out of my office to meet you here. I think they thought I might make you disappear, and they wanted no part in saving you or selling their souls to the devil," she concluded, but Noble hadn't even looked at her at this point.

"I'm sorry, Harper. I read one of my emails, and my brain went into overdrive. Next time, I will be more thorough in my information sharing and try not to make you feel like Beth is in the substation ordering you about," Noble replied, her eyes rolling skyward.

"I appreciate it. Now, what've you got?" Harper urged.

"Again, I'm sorry for being rude, but someone came into the substation and made a report of a missing person. It's a female. I'm hoping it's our Jane Doe. Tony is with him in the interview room now. Tony wanted to advise you, but he was already with Mr. Adams, so I came to do it, and here we are," Noble explained.

"They're both in there right now? Were you planning on being in there also?" Harper suggested.

"Yes, and I'll be heading in there shortly if I can find a damn pen with some ink," Noble growled in frustration as she continued to look through the desk drawers, but her perseverance paid off when she discovered a box of pens. She pulled out one and scribbled on her notepad until black ink appeared.

"Now that you've got your pen, get in there and find out the identity of our Jane Doe," Harper announced, lightly grasping her upper arm and leading her to the interview room door. "I'll observe from out here, and if I have questions, I will knock on the window so you'll know and can come out here." She shot a glance from the corner of her eye. "Also, I'm going to tape the interview. That way, it will already be recorded if it starts heading toward him being a suspect. So, don't worry about stopping the interview and coming out to do it," Harper added as she sat in a chair behind the glass with her pen and notepad.

As Noble entered the interview room, she saw Tony had the kit to take DNA samples from Mr. Adams. Tony had been in the room with Mr. Adams, and Noble suspected he'd built a rapport with him.

"Mr. Adams, I'm going to sit here and take notes while Detective Vistole asks you some questions."

"Oh, okay. And what is your name again, Detective?"

"Sir, it's Noble Gentry."

†

Harper decided that while she was on the other side of the glass, she'd also write Mr. Adams' overall appearance, his responses to the questions they inquired about, his answers to those questions, and the entire process of how he'd handle this interview. Even though Harper and Tony both were taking notes, it was standard procedure to video and audiotape anyone they thought could be a potential suspect. Harper set up the equipment and started recording the video and audio tapes. One thing that was sure: it was better to be over-prepared than not prepared. It would help Tony and Noble avoid slowing down any momentum they might get during the interview.

†

Noble positioned herself to Tony's right and directed her gaze toward Mr. Adams, who was seated across from Tony. She noticed a sealed evidence packet sticking out from Tony's portfolio binder and wrote a note to remind her to ask Tony about it. Noble wrote Mr. Adams' physical description and continued to listen to their conversation.

Short, brown, spiked hair, expressive green eyes, a casual, loose-fitting, maroon hooded zip-down sweatshirt, and a pair of faded blue jeans. She noted his forehead appeared to be glistening with a light coating of sweat, possibly from the bright light in the interview room. A bead of sweat gradually made its way down the side of his face and fell onto the interview table. Every so often, he'd raise his arm and wipe off the sweat covering his face, falling into his eyes, and dropping onto the table. He was blinking his eyes often, and it was unknown if it was from sweat or if he was nervous about being in the interview room.

As she observed Mr. Adams, her attention was drawn to his complexion and posture. There was a sense of unease emanating from him. His left arm was tightly crossed over his chest, creating a barrier between him and Tony, who sat across from him. A secure watch adorned his left wrist, adding a touch of elegance to his overall appearance. Resting on the metal table in front of him, his right hand rhythmically tapped the surface with his fingertips. With a slight lean forward, his attention fixated on the mirror behind Tony. He focused on the glass like he was staring at Leah, who sat on the other side, observing the interview. Mr. Adam's eyes were fixed on the glass, but there was no way he could see Leah. How did he know Jane Doe? Friend? Lover? Brother? She watched as his eyes glanced at his watch and he shifted in his seat.

"Detective Vistole, is someone standing on the other side of the glass?" Mr. Adams asked. His tone carried an unexpected warmth, considering the uncertain circumstances they found themselves in. He gestured toward the glass in Harper's direction. Tony and Noble swiveled their heads in the direction Mr. Adams pointed. Feeling annoyed, Tony swiftly turned back and locked eyes with him.

"Yes," Tony replied.

"Who is it, if you don't mind me asking?" Mr. Adams moistened dry teeth with a swipe of his tongue.

"It's my supervisor, Sergeant Harper. Don't worry about her," Tony informed him. Mr. Adams appeared to be relaxing a little but still had a look of concern on his face, his shoulders slightly hunched forward.

"Do I need a lawyer?" he questioned, keeping the question as light and straightforward as possible. He was not doing anything that anyone else might do if they were being questioned in an interview room.

"I don't know," Noble replied before Tony had a chance to, her voice appearing colder than needed. "Do you?"

Mr. Andrews looked around in confusion before his eyes landed on the glass again, making a silent plea. Maybe to Sergeant Harper, but Sergeant Harper could do nothing for him.

"Look, I'm unsure why I'm getting beseeched with all these questions. I wanted to see if someone here could help me. I mean, Bridget sent a text message to me, and it mentioned she was going to drop in and visit her parents, you know, an unannounced visit, as she called it. But then I hadn't heard from her." His mouth pressed into a bloodless white line. "I became worried, so I called her parents, who hadn't heard from her. Her mom, Susie, is worried. She misses her daughter and wants to know where she is." His nostrils flared with anger. "Her going this long without talking to her parents or me is out of character. I'm scared that something has happened, and I want to know if she's okay!" he uttered suddenly, in a slightly panicked tone. Noble jotted the mother's name and Mr. Adams' relationship with Jane Doe.

"We're sorry," Noble replied, her voice soft and calm. She knew this was the best form of dialogue when someone was distraught and did not know where their loved one was or if something tragic had happened to them. "But please give us her parents' full names, telephone numbers, and address so we can contact them." Her tone had an immediate impact on Mr. Adams.

"Oh, sure. Is there anything I can do to help? Mick and Susie Shelton are her parents. They said one of them would always be home until they heard from Bridget." He gave them the address and telephone numbers. His voice was still on edge but much calmer. Noble jotted down the names, numbers, and addresses for later reference as the questioning continued.

"Sorry again, but Susie is her mother's first name?" Noble asked, trying to confirm the information she wrote on her notepad.

"Yes, Susie is her mother, and Mick is her dad. I'm not Bridget's father but a close family friend. Sometimes, she looks at me as a father figure. If everything had gone my way, I'd have been her dad." He lowered his head. "It might as well be me because her dad is not father-of-the-year material. She loves and visits her parents weekly to see her mom." A sigh escaped his lips. "Bridget wouldn't have ever been disrespectful to her dad when she was there. Her mom tried to make the best of the situation. Despite their strained relationship," Mr. Adams stated as if he had forgotten why he was at the police station.

"So, can you confirm if Bridget has been seeing anyone or ever mentioned being bothered or harassed by anyone within the last month?" Tony continued. Noble sat back in her chair and watched him write Mr. Adams' responses. They made an excellent team.

"Last week, she mentioned having problems with her new boyfriend, Rusty. And he was asking a lot of questions about a friend. I can't remember her name." He shifted in his seat. "Bridget mentioned that he scared her. She told him to leave and then went into the bathroom and called me. I guess she waited in there for about an hour before she had me pick her up in the alley. She didn't want him to follow her." A painful look marred his face. "All she told me was that he had become aggressive over the last week and that she had never seen that side of him before. She felt shaken for two days, and now she's missing." He placed both hands over his face and took a deep breath. When he removed them, she could see the despair that eked from his eyes.

"Are you suggesting that her boyfriend might have harmed her? Did Bridget tell you his last name?" Noble asked as she stood from her chair.

"Yes, that's what I'm trying to say. No, she only said his first name, and I didn't ask because she was upset. I'm not sure what happened, but it must have been sometime after Bridget called to ask me to pick her up at her parents' home. She never made it. So, do you know where Bridget might be? I hope you can find her with the information I gave you," he asserted, his forehead creased with concern.

"That's why we're thankful you came in and made a missing person report. As soon as her parents get here, we will talk with all of you and give you an update," Noble stated, her voice matter of fact and emotionless. All hope left Mr. Adams' face as he looked like a dose of reality had smacked him in the head. The news wouldn't be the kind he wanted to hear.

"Bridget…Bridget has to be all right!" His voice was flat and disheartened as tears fell.

"Mr. Adams, can you sit here with Detective Vistole while I call the Sheltons and see if they can come to the station? Is there anyone you'd like us to call for you?" Noble offered as she placed her hand on Mr. Adam's forearm. The silence spoke volumes; his nonresponse was as good as a no. The poor man looked dazed, confused, and numb, almost as if he couldn't speak.

"Noble, you go check on the status of Mr. and Mrs. Shelton's arrival, and I'll stay here with Mr. Adams." Tony stood and paced around the interview room.

Noble stepped toward the door and proceeded through to exit. Once outside the interview room, she turned to Harper. Noble knew this case would blow up in the press if it linked to Billy Russell. Noble leaned against the wall, needing something to brace her, tears pooling in her eyes as she remembered Mr. Adams' reactions. She knew she needed to be strong, but sometimes, cases like these were the hardest to work.

Harper put her hand on Noble's shoulder and gently squeezed. She placed her hand on Harper's and nodded, knowing her job was to bring closure to families. Noble would do everything she could to get that for the people who loved Bridget. A flash of memories flooded Noble's mind as she stood there with Harper.

Noble felt a hand on her back and knew her friend Harper was there to help her. "Breathe in, breathe out, don't lock your knees, Noble. It'll be fine," Harper uttered.

The gentle breeze caressed her face, allowing Noble to experience a fleeting moment of relief as she felt the weight of her pain lifting briefly. Looking up at the sky, she declared with unwavering devotion, "No matter what happens, Diana, my love for you will endure!" The remainder of the ceremony became a hazy blur until the release of the pure white doves. While gracefully following their intended path, one dove veered off course and perched on a nearby tree branch beside Noble. Harper gently touched Noble's shoulder and whispered, "Diana is sending you a message."

"Are you okay, Noble?" Harper gently tugged on her shirt sleeve, bringing Noble back to the present.

"Yes, merely remembering!"

†

Noble stood there, clenching a pen in her trembling hand. Noble took a deep breath and brushed away a tear from her eye. She needed to be steadfast in front of the family and let them know their daughter mattered.

The sound of a ding showed the elevator had arrived on the second floor. Slowly, the doors opened and revealed a man and woman. Noble edged toward them, acknowledging their presence. Any slight bit would help overall when they knew the entire circumstances of why they were there.

"Mr. and Mrs. Shelton?" Noble inquired, her voice calm and unwavering.

"Yes, we're the Sheltons, but please call me Mick, and this is Susie." He pointed toward his wife next to him.

"Please follow me this way, and we'll use one of the interview rooms, where it will be a lot quieter." Noble guided them down the same way she had accompanied Mr. Adams hours earlier. Mr. Adams was, however, in interview room number one. Noble approached and opened interview room number two, waiting for Mr. and Mrs. Shelton to enter. "Please take a seat, and I'll explain why we called for you to come here today." Noble looked at the glass, aware that Harper would be outside observing.

"When was the last time you saw your daughter?" Noble wanted to know as she prepared to write their answer in her notebook.

"It's been over a week, and we expected her to be here a few days ago, but she never showed up or called. This is out of character for her," Mr. Shelton answered as he slowly grasped his wife's hand.

"When you last saw her, did she mention having problems with anyone? Does she have a current significant other in her life right now? Was she having problems at work or with a coworker?" Noble pressed as she continued writing notes from Mr. Shelton's earlier comments.

“She mentioned nothing to me,” Mr. Shelton replied as he turned to look at his wife.

“Bridget called me three days ago saying that she wanted to talk to me about something but suggested it could wait until she saw us in person,” Mrs. Shelton stated.

“Please tell us what’s going on. You wouldn’t have contacted us to come here if something hadn’t happened to Bridget.” Mr. Shelton’s brow furrowed.

“I regret to inform you we found the body of a young woman who we believe to be your daughter, Bridget,” Noble stated as honestly as she could. It was a calm response that held sympathy as she reached across the table and laid her hand on Mr. and Mrs. Shelton’s hands, both which visually shook.

It was a heart-wrenching sight to see Mrs. Shelton as her husband embraced her tightly, comforting her with whispered words. Witnessing this tender moment, Noble couldn’t help but yearn for a similar connection in her life again. Diana would have been that person if she had not been taken away. But now, as Mrs. Shelton’s tears reminded her of her own pain, Noble hoped to find something even remotely close to what she had with Diana and perhaps even more. The overwhelming emotions made her realize that no one should ever endure such profound sorrow.

“We’d like to see for ourselves, Detective. If this is my daughter, we’ll have many more questions that we hope you can answer.” Mr. Shelton attempted to gain his composure.

“Please excuse me for a moment, and I’ll see how long till I can accompany you to the viewing room with Dr. Redmond,” Noble said. She exited the interview room to let Tony know that she’d need an officer to escort Mr. and Mrs. Shelton to autopsy to view the body.

As she exited the room, Tony emerged from interview room one. He approached her and Sergeant Harper before speaking. "I'll stay with Mr. Adams. Sergeant Harper, would you mind escorting the Sheltons to the autopsy waiting room if that's okay? He's still pretty shaken up about the possibility that Bridget is dead," Tony stated.

"That sounds good to me. I need to grab my case file and can meet you there, Sergeant Harper. I have a feeling I will need some help when they're facing the fact that this is their daughter who is dead, murdered." Noble looked at her phone and realized that she had a text message from Dr. Redmond that stated he was ready for her and the Sheltons.

"I don't mind at all," Sergeant Harper replied. A gentleness touched her lips.

Noble returned to interview room two, opened the door, and stated, "Dr. Redmond is ready for us to come over and do the viewing. If you'd please go with Sergeant Harper, I'll be there shortly."

Noble placed her hand on the small of Mr. Shelton's back and guided him toward the elevator. Noble stood behind the three of them, holding her notepad, not envying this trip because she already knew the outcome of this viewing. When the elevator door opened, she saw Sergeant Harper apply gentle pressure to Mr. Shelton's lower back and guide him into the elevator behind his wife.

Noble shuffled over to her desk, grabbed the case file, and entered the women's restroom next to their office. Splashing water on her face and patting it dry, she turned and left for the short trek to Dr. Redmond's office. Looking down at her case file, she suddenly felt like she'd careened into a brick wall that about knocked her on her ass.

"Are you stalking me or something?" Noble heard as she picked up notes that had fallen to the ground after the collision.

"Shit, I'm sorry," Noble declared as she stared at a familiar set of sapphire blue eyes. "No stalking, Ms. Matthews; I was simply heading over to Doctor Redmond's office, where my sergeant and the parents of my victim are waiting.

"I'm sorry, tough case?"

"Yes, these always are. But this is even tougher because it involves the loss of a life." She anchored her gaze to Charlie's.

"Are you holding up okay? If you ever need an ear to bend, I can be available. Give me a call, day or night. I saw how you were with Jessie, and I only wanted to extend the same courtesy if you need it."

"Thank you. I need to go, but I will keep you in mind."

"Great. Here is my number. Don't hesitate to call."

"Yes, ma'am." Noble took the piece of paper and put it in her pocket.

"Goodbye, Detective Gentry."

"Goodbye, Ms. Matthews." Noble continued toward Dr. Redmond's office.

As Noble opened the door, she took hesitant steps toward the waiting room adjacent to the double doors leading to the autopsy viewing room. In that moment, Mr. Shelton glanced over and met Noble's gaze.

With a shaky voice full of emotion, he asked, "Do we want to go in there?" His eyes were filled with tears as he waited for her to answer. Upon hearing the question, she saw Mrs. Shelton and Harper take a few steps back toward them and wait for her to respond.

"Sir, only you can answer this question. But I will tell you, you'll not have complete closure until you know for a fact, other than our word or a photograph, that this is indeed

Bridget, your daughter," Noble replied. It was as straightforward as she could be, with the utmost respect to the Shelton family, but these interactions with families deeply impacted her.

Raising his trembling hand, he turned toward his wife, grabbed her hand, and declared, "We're ready. We need to bring our baby home if it's her."

Sergeant Harper trekked through the automatic doors, and everyone followed. Noble kept her distance, knowing this time Mr. Shelton didn't need a hand on his back guiding him because he had his wife by his side, but she stayed close by. Once inside the viewing room, Dr. Redmond excused himself and went into the autopsy room, where a body lay under a crisp, clean, white sheet. He shuffled and stopped at the head of the gurney and spoke into the microphone hanging down from the ceiling.

"Let me know when you're ready, and I will turn down the sheet," he stated, his voice a monotone as he looked out toward the Shelton's.

"Whenever you're ready, Mr. Shelton." Noble squeezed his shoulder, showing her compassion, comfort, and a slight urge to move him to the next step.

"We're ready, Detective," Mr. Shelton said, his expression drawn in agony.

Dr. Redmond folded the sheet down, exposing the top of the victim's head. He stopped and laid the sheet down when it reached the victim's shoulders. He then turned on a brighter light so the Sheltons could view the victim's face. Noble turned toward Mr. Shelton, and she saw hope disappear from his face in a fraction of a second. His eyes erupted with tears like a volcano spewing lava for the first time. His knees buckled slightly under him as reality revealed this was their loving daughter. He crumpled to the floor, sobbing, as his wife got down on her knees to console them both. Noble kneeled next to him.

"Yes, it's our daughter," Mrs. Shelton said as she hugged her husband on the ground.

"I'm truly sorry for your loss, Mr. and Mrs. Shelton," Noble sympathized. Words were not enough, but Noble hoped they would comfort the man, father and husband, sitting next to her. After a short while, the Sheltons stood, wiped away their tears, and tried to regain their composure as best as possible.

"May I tell her goodbye one last time?" Mr. Shelton pleaded, turning to Noble as he removed what appeared to be a picture from the inside of his jacket.

Noble turned her head and stared directly at Doctor Redmond, looking at him for guidance and an answer.

"Yes. Noble, please bring them both back," Doctor Redmond said as he watched all four slowly enter the room.

Mr. and Mrs. Shelton said their goodbyes to Bridget, told her they loved her, and were sorry they weren't there when she had needed them most. Mr. Shelton leaned down and softly kissed his daughter's cold, pale cheek as his lips trembled again.

"Oh god, Bridget, why?" Mr. Shelton clenched his teeth as more tears fell.

"I'm sorry—" Noble's heart hammered in her chest.

"What couldn't she tell us? What was she afraid would happen? Who'd do this to her?" Mr. Shelton continued as he locked eyes with Noble. "That's our baby girl in here, and I want to know why!" he spat the words out through gritted teeth as despair eked from his eyes.

"I understand all too well what you're going through, Mr. Shelton, and believe me when I say this, sir, I will do everything possible to bring the individual responsible for murdering your daughter to justice," Noble answered as her pulse pounded in her throat.

"Thank you, Detective. That's all I ask of you," Mr. Shelton replied as he hugged Noble in gratitude. "I'm ready to leave." He grabbed his wife's hand and took one last look at his daughter lying on the cold metal gurney.

Harper nodded to Doctor Redmond as he recovered Bridget with the sheet. "Thank you, Doctor Redmond." Sergeant Harper followed Noble and Mr. and Mrs. Shelton into the viewing room.

Noble felt a bit of numbness and loss for the Sheltons as she knew what they were dealing with after viewing their daughter. Noble waited until they were in the initial viewing room and pointed toward a small sofa, gesturing for them to sit. Noble knew they needed some time for their daughter's death to sink in.

"Take all the time you need. Detective Vistole and I will assist homicide with working on your daughter's case, and I will keep you updated every step of the way, either via phone or in person." She knelt to look at them directly. "Here are my desk and cell phone numbers. Please call if you remember something, find something you think might be useful, or if you need to talk. I'm a phone call away." Noble softly laid her hand on top of the Shelton's hands.

"Thank you, Detective. I want justice for my daughter. We will head home now to plan for our daughter's burial and continue our grieving in private." Both he and his wife stood.

The four of them exited the room. Once they arrived at the lobby, Noble walked them to the door.

“Do you need me to have an officer drive you home?” She raised the subject, wanting to ensure they’d be okay.

“That won’t be necessary, Detective, as our friend is waiting outside to do that. He was at our house earlier when we received the call and offered to bring us,” Mr. Shelton answered as he shook her hand.

Noble stared out the door, watching Bridget’s parents leave, thinking about Bridget’s last hour before she took her last breath.

“Come on, let’s go.” Noble felt a hand press her shoulder slightly and felt Harper lead her back toward the room they’d left mere minutes before. “Will you please have a chaplain sent to Mr. and Mrs. Shelton’s house to help them through this process?” Noble suggested to Harper.

“I’ve already contacted them, and they’ll be there later today,” Harper replied.

Noble and Harper returned to the department in silence, allowing each other the space to get back on target once they went inside headquarters. They entered the side entrance and climbed up the flight of stairs. Noble knew it was going to be even more discouraging since they’d have another person to tell regarding Bridget’s death. Sergeant Harper waited outside interview room one.

Upon returning to the room to talk with Mr. Adams, Noble saw him seated in the chair, completely consumed by sorrow. His body trembled with the weight of his grief, and tears streamed down his face. Tony sat quietly beside him, waiting for some sign of whether Jane Doe now had a name. She nodded yes, stepped over to the corner, and waited for Tony to update Mr. Adams and ask additional questions.

“Mr. Adams…” Tony started, apparently unsure of how to lead off. “The Sheltons have identified their daughter, Bridget, and permitted us to tell you." He watched from under his brow. "I want to say I'm sorry for your loss."

Mr. Adams sat silently, his eyes vacant as he brushed away stray tears.

"Is there anything else you think we should know that will assist us in our investigation?" Tony asked. Mr. Adams shook his head. "Okay, I'll call and have an officer respond here so they can take you home."

"No," Mr. Adams interrupted. "I'll speak to both when I get home, to help them with anything. Hopefully, I can ease the burden with everything they must do to prepare for burial."

"Here is my business card in case you need to contact me regarding any additional questions you might have." Noble nodded in response to his sudden outburst as he got to his feet, gripping the card.

"Wait, there's one thing, not sure if it could be relevant," he started. "The other day, while Bridget was visiting, she'd gotten off the phone, and I could have sworn she was yelling before I entered the room and interrupted their conversation. It appeared Bridget had been crying about something, and when I questioned her about it, she said it was nothing. She implied I shouldn't worry as it was not important. I believe she mumbled something about an empty threat, but I can't be sure. I hope this helps shed more light on the investigation," he finished as he crossed his arms over his chest.

Tony nodded and stood. "Thank you, Samuel. We'll contact you if we have any further questions, okay?" After Samuel exited the interview room, another officer escorted him out of the building.

"I'll get Detective Clark to write up and execute a search warrant on Bridget's phone, including calls and text messages and everything else you can do on your phone nowadays. I'm curious if it was her father she was arguing with or possibly this guy, Rusty."

"Me, too," Noble replied as she closed her notebook and stood up from the chair.

"Me three," Harper's voice came from the doorway. "I'm not sure we should have let him leave yet."

"Sarge, I'm sorry, but I think he needs some time to grieve," Tony hinted, gesturing toward the door, but stopped when Sergeant Harper raised her hand.

"I understand completely," Harper responded, her voice sounding unusually gentle.

"I'll get an update from Detective Clark." Tony nodded as Harper held the door for him.

"Vistole," Harper voiced, rounding on him, her tone not as soft as before but more authoritative. "I want Tracy Snow contacted first. We need to see if she knew Bridget Shelton and, if so, in what capacity." There was a deep-set frown on her face. "You or Gentry can call her on the phone or go to her club, but I want answers today if there's any relationship between the two that would link Bridget's murder to Billy Russell." She rubbed her temples.

"Okay, Sergeant. Let's ask Tracy Snow to come to the station so we can fill two needs with one meeting. We can question her about Bridget and find out if she ever met Bridget's boyfriend," Noble proposed as she picked a piece of lint from her sleeve.

"Let's get on it. Do what you must to make it happen today," Harper barked.

"Okay, Sarge, I'll get on it right now." Noble returned to the office and sat at her desk, opening her notebook and dialing the business number for Blades. Entering the numbers on her desktop phone, she waited for the ringing. After three rings, someone answered.

"Hello, Blade's Brewery. Tracy speaking. How may I help you?" Her voice was so quiet it could probably be drowned out by whistling.

"Hi, am I speaking with Tracy Snow?" Noble queried as she raked her fingers through her hair.

"Yes," she replied, "and may I ask who's inquiring?"

"My name is Noble Gentry. I'm a detective in the Onserf Police Department." Noble wondered if she would remember her.

"Yes, Detective Gentry. I remember you from my trial involving Billy Russell. I hope this is about him absconding parole?"

"Yes, it is. Could you meet me at the downtown police headquarters later today, about three o'clock?" Noble stated.

"I'll be there!"

CHAPTER ELEVEN

"Hey Mike, have we gotten any updated information on Billy Russell?" Charlie asked, the chair creaking as she shifted her weight on her seat.

"Nothing concrete. I know the state parole analysts are running the data from his ankle monitor to see if we can locate where he cut it off. Somehow, it's taking a little longer than normal. I checked in with the Onserf Crimestoppers office, and calls were slowly coming in."

"If he's got half a brain, he should have already altered his appearance. I will print out his various mugshots to see how he looks in all of them. It'll give me a better idea of what he might look like now." She tilted her head to the side, a curious expression on her face.

"His funds were minimal. So, he's sleeping on the street, or someone is hiding him. He'll slip up somewhere because, reading his file, he always screwed up enough to get caught," Mike replied after a long moment.

"Let's hope so. If Russell is involved in this case, it's not over yet because if he's linked, he would have nothing to lose as he has already escalated from rape to murder. I doubt he's thinking about going back to prison. So, I guess he will go after Tracy Snow and get out of town."

"If it wasn't for her ripping off his hooded mask while he was raping her and fighting him, then I think he'd have never seen the inside of a prison cell. Detectives at Onserf PD believed he committed more sexual assaults, but he always wore a condom and made the women shower before he left." Mike flexed his hand. "And he shaved his body, so there was never any trace of evidence at the scene. I mean, who the hell shaves their entire body other than a professional swimmer?" He raised his eyebrow at her in disbelief.

"Wow, how did they know he shaved his body? This guy needs to be off the street yesterday. He's a threat to the community."

"When they arrested him, stubble covered his entire body. Do you know that prickly hair that grows back after you shave? I guess he was the talk over in sex crimes at Onserf PD." Mike screwed up his face.

"Man, I can't stand stubble on my legs. I don't know how anyone could stand it on their entire body. It must have itched like a motherfu—" Charlie replied, the thought setting off an avalanche of uncontrollable shivers.

"Whoa, hold up. Shouldn't you be watching your cussing since you've got a young child?"

"Why do you think I'm saying it here and not at home?" She threw her arms open.

"Listen to what I'm saying, Matthews. It will carry over at home, and you'll be in big trouble." He laughed.

"Thanks for the pep talk, Taylor. And now I'm knocking on wood because you jinxed me." Charlie's knuckles wrapped on the desk.

"I hope it works for you. On that note, I'm heading to the records department to get some of Russell's prior case reports." Mike clambered to his feet. "When I get back, let's go through them all to see if we can find the needle in the haystack where he might hide out."

"I'll finish up a couple of follow-up reports and be done by the time you get back," Charlie said, pointing to her watch to indicate the time.

"While I'm over there, would you like me to say hi to your Detective Gentry? It must be fate you two keep crossing paths." Mike grinned. "I can make a special trip to her office to let her know you're thinking about her. I'm good friends with her partner, Tony Vistole." Mike laughed as he dodged the pen flying in his direction, which bounced off the wall toward Charlie.

"Be on your way, Taylor, and bring some lunch back for us while you're at it. Hit the roach coach by the department and grab my usual, please," Charlie said as she looked at her computer screen and laughed.

"Will do. I should be back within the hour," he said.

†

"Great, you're back. My stomach has been growling for the last half hour," Charlie said as she grabbed the bag Mike extended to her.

"I got a lot of reports for us to go through. This guy has been a shitbird his entire life. I could get older reports when he was a kid and needed to be placed by CPS."

"Child Protective Services cases will shed some light, and we need any help we can get," Charlie said as she took a big bite of her chicken sandwich.

"Yep, the guy probably didn't get enough hugs from his mom or something. Who knows what triggers these assholes!"

"Now, Mike, since he's such a shithead now doesn't mean he deserved what happened to him when he was a kid. But let's find out because we're looking for the missing puzzle piece in all these reports."

"Oh, Detective Gentry and my friend Tony were meeting with Tracy Snow, so I couldn't tell her hi for you."

"Be quiet, knucklehead, and start reading one of those reports. Thanks for lunch. I'll get it tomorrow."

They each began reading different reports to see if they could uncover anything new to help them find his hiding place.

"Man, I see what you mean. Russell's dad was a sick fuck. He made his kid watch as he raped his mom and kept telling him that all women should obey men." His brow furrowed as his mouth turned grim. "And when he didn't watch like his father told him to, he'd beat the shit out of the kid. This first report introduces Billy Russell to law enforcement and other agencies. You were right. No kid deserves that."

"See, never assume till you gather a little intel to confirm it or not. Something must have led him to turn into his father and despise women. Hate is not a built-in trait, rather it is learned." Her expression slid into a frown.

"Based on the report I'm reading, I'm unsure what the trigger could be," Mike said.

"It must involve a woman. I bet one rebuked him, which sent him into a tailspin," Charlie replied.

"Well, Tony said they thought he'd done a bunch of other rapes before Tracy Snow and maybe a couple after. Remember, they had a tough time linking him." He absentmindedly cracked his knuckles.

"We'll get him. He'll make a mistake. I hope no one else gets hurt before we catch him. I can't wait until the Onserf's sex crimes sergeant contacts us to assist on the case," Charlie said as she opened another case file.

CHAPTER TWELVE

A few minutes before three, the secretary's phone rang, and she gave instructions to the person on the other end. Hanging up the phone, she looked directly at Noble. "Your three o'clock appointment is here and on her way up via the elevator," she said as she looked at Noble.

"Thank you, Linda." Noble stood and strolled toward the door. She stepped into the hallway and heard the elevator's screech as it stopped abruptly on their floor.

"Thank you for coming to see me today, Tracy," Noble said as she greeted Tracy once the elevator doors opened.

"You're welcome, Detective. Hope this monster gets caught before he hurts anyone else," Tracy stated, smoothing down the seam of her skirt.

They strolled into the open bay where Noble's workstation was, and she directed Tracy to sit in a chair next her desk.

"I need to start by asking if you know anyone named Bridget Shelton," Noble inquired.

"Yes, I do, why?" Tracy's face scrunched up in worry.

"Tracy, I'm sorry to inform you, but Bridget Shelton is dead, murdered, and we're trying to see if it's related to Billy Russell and your case…" Noble's words trailed off.

At this moment, Noble heard a sob, followed by uncontrollable tears falling from Tracy's eyes. Noble leaned over and gently took Tracy's hands, attempting to console her. She knew what she was going through and would do everything she could to get the monster Billy Russell back behind bars and make it for good this time.

After a good half-hour, Tracy looked at Noble and asked, "How?"

"We received an anonymous call regarding a woman lying in an alley. When units arrived on the scene, they located the deceased body of a woman, her identity unknown." Beyond that, nothing would sound appropriate, so Noble offered nothing further regarding the scene. "While we were investigating the case, Mr. Adams came in to file a missing person's report on Bridget. From there, we could contact Bridget's parents, who came for an interview. Once we believed our Jane Doe was most likely Bridget, we had her parents make a formal identification of the body."

As Tracy appeared to process the loss of her murdered friend, possibly at the hands of the man who had attacked her years earlier, Noble observed various emotions playing out on her face. The whole world seemed to be moving in slow motion as the quietness enveloped the room. Noble found it necessary to break the silence and ask Tracy a few more questions.

"Do you know if Bridget was seeing anyone or had a steady boyfriend?" Noble asked.

"Yes, she'd been seeing this guy named Rusty for the last couple of weeks. Our schedules had been so busy lately that we hadn't had time to get together, and I hadn't had the chance to meet him."

Noble heard another sob and Tracy's shaky voice.

"Why are you asking if Bridget had a boyfriend? Do you think her boyfriend was involved?" Tracy's hand covered her mouth.

"We're trying to establish a timeline and see who Bridget had contact with in the days prior to her murder. We can't rule out anyone until we confirm their alibi, and we can check them off our list." Noble's eyes connected with Tracy's.

"I understand, Detective. If there is anything I can do to help you with your investigation, all you need to do is ask," Tracy said.

"Do you know Rusty's last name, by chance?" Noble asked. "Any additional information about him would help. It will help rule him out, or we may need to look more closely at him."

"I believe she said his last name was Williams, and she'd met him at the coffee shop by her house. He supposedly runs his own business. I will need to look through my text messages and get you the name of his company because I believe she mentioned it at one point." Tracy shifted in her seat. "I don't know what he looks like, and I can tell you she never sent me a picture of them together, but she mentioned he was camera shy." Her words fell out in confusion.

Tracy looked at her phone as if waiting for all the answers to jump right out at them. Noble admired Tracy's strength, especially after realizing her friend's murder might have a link to her own case.

"Have you gotten any strange calls, anything suspicious left at the bar, or any men visiting the bar, that's left you feeling uneasy?" Noble asked, gazing at Tracy with renewed focus.

"I was looking out my window above the bar the night the police released information on an unidentified woman murdered in an alley, when I saw a figure behind a tree flicking a cigarette into the street," Tracy replied confidently.

"How do you know it was a cigarette? Was there a streetlight? Did you see anyone? Did you call it in when it happened? The next morning?" Noble cocked an eyebrow in surprise.

"There was no streetlight on that part of the street, but I saw the ember, and I assumed it was a cigarette and not a cigar. I glimpsed a shadow, and then it disappeared." Tracey paused before continuing, "But I had my friend Vera proceed to that area the next morning, and she found a cigarette butt in the vicinity. She picked it up with a napkin and put it in a sandwich baggie. I brought it today hoping you could do something with it," Tracy said, handing the baggie to Noble.

"Thank you. It could be a great help." Noble put on a pair of latex gloves and placed the baggie in an evidence bag. She labeled and sealed it with packing tape from her desk drawer. She then put a vertical line down on both sides of the envelope over the tape along with her initials. "Again, why did you wait until now to bring it in?"

"The next morning, I called the police department. I left my name and number but assumed they would call me when someone was available, as this wasn't an emergency. I placed it in a locked drawer in my office and kept it safe." She absentmindedly cracked her knuckles. "So, when you called and asked me to come in, I brought it because no one had come to collect it or returned my call." She scrunched her shoulders against her neck. "I haven't had anyone suspicious in the bar, and the only calls I've gotten are occasional hang-ups," Tracy said, grabbing an antibacterial towelette from her purse and cleaning her hands.

"We have no more questions for now, but if anything arises during the investigation, you'll be my first point of contact. I want to keep you informed because you could be the key or partial key to the investigation." Her smile flattened. "However, if you have questions, reach out and contact me. Regardless of whether you think it might make a difference or not. It's better to have asked than possibly let something important go unaddressed because you were unsure or thought it might be silly to ask." Noble's gaze clamped onto Tracy. "Here is my business card with my cell phone number on the back. You can contact me, day or night. Please call, even if you just need someone to talk to," Noble said, knowing it was the right thing to do, and they'd make it through this case as they'd done in the prior case.

"Thank you, Detective Gentry. It means a lot to have you working on the case," replied Tracy. "I still can't believe his sentence got reduced, and he was allowed parole," she added.

"Oh, and Tracy, I've heard and said these words many times, but I'm sorry for your loss," Noble said, pausing momentarily. "And the next time I see you, I hope to have made significant progress in this case, and we can get him back into custody and throw away the key," Noble finished.

Tracy stood from her seat, put her hand out, and shook Noble's hand, saying, "Thank you." She walked toward the elevator to exit the building.

†

Noble sat in her chair and took a deep breath to control the tears attempting to escape from her eyes. Realizing Tracy had given her the full name of Bridget's boyfriend, she jumped up with the evidence envelope, ran down the stairs, and headed toward Detective Clark's office to update Tony.

Startled, Chris and Tony looked up when Noble skidded to a halt in Detective Clark's doorway. Panting like she'd run a marathon, Noble entered the office and said, "Hey guys, I got the name of Bridget's boyfriend." She bent over, clutching her side, trying to catch her breath. *Damn, I need to get back into shape.*

"Are you messing with us?" Tony and Chris responded, sitting straighter in their chairs and looking at her, waiting for the name.

"No, I wanted to run down here to exercise. Yes, really!" Noble had by now caught her breath. "Chris, run the name Rusty Williams in all the databases to see if we get any hits. I want this guy found so we can eliminate him or place him on the person-of-interest list. And Chris, I don't care if there are fifty matches. We need to go one by one to eliminate them from the investigation. Start with the ones with local addresses and check if they might be on probation or parole," Noble said.

"I'll also see if any of the numbers in Bridget's phone have Rusty Williams listed as the primary account holder," Chris answered.

"Thanks, Chris, because I believe I remember seeing a number on her phone multiple times and calls made at various times during the last couple of months," Tony said.

"Possibly like a boyfriend calling to talk with his girlfriend or maybe checking up on her, like there could have been some trust issues?" Noble inquired.

Chris was looking through some paperwork when he said, "We've already tried to search the number through our systems, and it has come up empty. The next step is a search warrant to find the account holder's name."

"We're heading back to our office. Please get in touch with us as soon as you get the search warrant signed and the account holders' names from their respective companies," Tony said.

Noble and Tony were silently heading back up the stairs toward their office when she suddenly spoke. "He probably has his phone off, so we can't track him, especially if it implicates him in Bridget's murder. He could know it would take time to get a search warrant, and he needed time to get rid of more evidence or completely vanish from town," Noble said in frustration.

"We'll get him, Noble. Criminals always make mistakes."

Noble rarely wore her emotions on her sleeve and out for her coworkers to see, but this was personal. "Quit looking at me like I have one eye, Tony. We all have a case occasionally that gets under our skin. Alright, this is one of them!" Noble said as she stopped halfway up the stairs to look at Tony directly.

"Okay, Noble, calm down and take a deep breath. Let's sit at our desks and brainstorm this case from the beginning. Work it out on the dry-erase board, put all the reports on the briefing desk, and see what we have and need. Maybe it'll click on what we might have missed to help us get one step closer to solving this case," Tony answered.

"You're right, let's go," Noble replied. "And can you believe Tracy brought in a cigarette butt wrapped in a napkin, thinking maybe it was Russell watching her business the other night?"

"No shit. I can take it by the Department of Justice Lab on my way home. And for the record, Noble, your work gets under your skin in every case. But don't worry, that's why it makes you the best detective for the case because you care and want justice for the victims," Tony said, taking her arm to guide her the rest of the way up the stairs toward their office.

"Thanks, Tony."

†

It was after four o'clock and getting close to quitting time. Noble tossed her pen and notepad onto her desk, pushed her chair back, and stood. She knew there wasn't much more they could do today. Despite that, she continued to pace back and forth behind her desk.

"How about we get the reports in order and call it a day, Noble?" Tony asked. "We can get some sleep and start fresh tomorrow with everything else."

"I agree with Detective Vistole. Both of you've accomplished a lot today, and in the morning, you can work on finding the connection to firm up the case. Hopefully, the search warrant is ready, and we will have additional information regarding Bridget's phone," Sergeant Harper stated as she strode toward them from her office.

"Okay. Tony and Harper, I'll see you bright and early," Noble acknowledged as she shut down her computer.

"See you tomorrow," Tony answered, also shutting down his computer.

"Good night. I'll be in early tomorrow, and we can all sit and brainstorm together," Harper said as she returned to her office, shut off her light, and headed toward the stairs.

Tony and Noble followed a brief time later.

CHAPTER THIRTEEN

"Hey, Mom, it's me," Charlie yelled as she went in the back door.

"We're in the living room watching dinosaurs, sweetie," Beth said.

Charlie put her briefcase on the countertop, grabbed a bottle of water from the fridge, and headed to the living room.

"How are two of my favorite people doing?" Charlie cracked a smile.

"Mom, guess what? Grandma got me a new book to read. It's about a boy and his dinosaur."

"Great, did you thank her?"

"Yes, silly. You taught me to thank anyone who gave me a gift. Can we read it at bedtime tonight?" Elizabeth whisper-shouted.

"Yes, we can. How was your day, Mom?"

"We had a fun time. We built a fort under the kitchen table, played with dinosaurs, had a tea party, and cleaned the house. Everyone had fun."

"Thank you so much for doing this. I deeply appreciate it. You're the best."

"I'd do anything for you or Elizabeth," Beth vowed. "You should know that by now. I love you both so much. And she's had her dinner and a bath, so she'll be ready for a bedtime story shortly."

"Again, thank you. I was surprised to get home this late, but we're making some headway on the Billy Russell case that Mom L and her team have. We're waiting until we get her formal invite, but we're working on our intel, so we've something to bring to the table when we get there."

"I hope you catch him soon. Leah calls me every other hour to make sure we're okay. And as much as I love to hear from her, I don't enjoy living on pins and needles with this guy out there. Sometimes, I think she forgets I was a cop, too. It's cute and annoying." Beth laughed.

"We all need to stay alert and watch our surroundings until he is caught. Would you like a glass of wine?" Charlie asked.

"Mom, Noole will also keep us safe. She's like you and Grandma." Elizabeth gave a half shrug.

"Who's Noole, honey?" Charlie and Beth both asked.

"She's a poweece lady I saw when I was with the babysitter. She told me not to talk to strangers, to hug you, and to say thank you."

"Oh, you finally remember her name," Charlie said.

"Yep. Maybe I can see her again someday. Bye, Grandma, love you," Elizabeth said as she got up with her book and tried to skip toward the bathroom.

"Brush your teeth while I say goodbye to your mom. Then, you'll be ready for your storytime. I love you, too, and I'll see you tomorrow." Beth snorted through her laughter.

"Do you or Mom L know an officer Noole?"

“Name doesn’t sound familiar, but when I get home, I’ll ask Leah,” Beth said as she hugged Charlie and strolled out the front door.

“Love you, Mom, and I’ll see you tomorrow,” Charlie said as she watched her mom enter her car and drive away.

Charlie tiptoed into Elizabeth’s room and saw her fast asleep with the book on her chest. She pulled the covers up, kissed her daughter on the forehead, turned off the light, and left the bedroom. She entered the kitchen, put some leftover pizza on a plate, and decompressed in the living room.

CHAPTER FOURTEEN

Noble went to work the next day, wide awake and ready to tackle the case. She wouldn't let anyone or anything get in her way until they solved it and someone was in custody. In her mind, Noble believed the last puzzle piece was the name of the individual who committed this murder, and Billy Russell's name kept creeping into her thoughts as the individual responsible. Noble sat at her desk, picked up her phone and dialed Chris's office number.

"Hello?"

"Hi Chris, it's Noble," she said.

"Oh. Hey Noble. How can I help you this fine morning?" he asked.

"I didn't get to ask you yesterday, but I wanted to know if you got any hits on the name Rusty Williams."

"Yes, there was a hit." He hesitated midsentence, and Noble heard his fingers tapping on the keyboard. "Rusty Williams' name is on a report about six years ago in which he physically assaulted his girlfriend," he concluded. "I've requested the case file and hope to have it by the end of the week. They're overhauling the system, and cases from five years ago are being processed by hand until they can be scanned. We won't know the girlfriend's name until we get the case report."

"Thank you, Chris; you're the best!"

"Well, I try." He laughed.

"So, does it show an address, or will it wait until we get the case?" Noble solicited.

"Yes, I have it right here. It won't be of any help, though," Chris advised.

"Because?" Noble urged, wanting answers, but knowing the sound of his voice meant unwelcome news.

"Noble, I'm sorry, it shows the address as on Frank Road, and we know it isn't current since it's the house where we board all high-risk sex offenders when they get released on parole." He gave a long, low sigh. "We know he's not there since we can't find a record of him showing a conviction for a sex crime."

"No." Noble sat back in her seat. Those words deflated any realm of hope and knocked her back into reality.

"Sorry, Noble. I've searched all the databases, but there's no updated address. I will put out feelers to all adjoining agencies, probation, and parole to see what we can find out about Rusty Williams," he replied.

"No," she said again in disbelief.

"Noble, this guy, Rusty Williams, obviously appears not to want to be found," Chris said.

"Dammit!" Noble shouted at the phone, standing quickly with her right thumb and index finger pinching the bridge of her nose. "You keep searching, Chris; don't give up, there has to be an explanation. No one will throw in their towel that easily." She took in a shuddering breath. "We need to check his phone to see if he's turned it on. There must be something we're missing about this boyfriend, and we need to do everything we can to find out what he's hiding." Noble slammed her hand on her desk.

"Again, I'm sorry, Noble. We've got a crew dedicated to finding him, so we'll keep plugging away till we do," Chris said in a croaky voice.

"Please call me the second you get any alert about his cell phone and someone turning it on. We want to know why this bastard is avoiding us." She exhaled a groan rivaling a squeaky hinge. "Either he's involved, doing something else that's illegal, or he's got some dumb luck following him," Noble sputtered. "And Chris, thank you for going above and beyond on this case. I appreciate it," she said, softening her voice.

"I will, don't worry, Noble; I will," he stated before hanging up the phone.

Noble sat slumped in her chair, head back and eyes closed. Feeling someone was watching her, Noble opened her eyes and looked directly at Tony. He looked ready to make some smart-ass comment but then thought better. At that moment, she cursed herself for how personal she'd allowed this case to become. Then again, she had a personal stake in every case they assigned her.

"Don't even think about starting," Noble said, looking Tony directly in the eyes, daring him to question further. Everything was put on hold.

†

"Another homicide," Leah called out. "Grab your gear," she barked the order firmly.

"Sarge, are you putting us on another case besides Bridget Shelton? We're making some headway, and another case might interfere with that," Noble asked hesitantly, almost pleading with Harper.

"Have a little faith in me, you two. I don't think this is an original case," she said over her shoulder as she stepped toward the elevator. Noble and Tony grabbed their gear and followed.

When they got outside, Harper legged it to her car and signaled for Noble to get into their vehicle next to hers.

"Follow me," Harper said.

Noble was annoyed at not being advised of what was going on. Climbing into the car, not wanting to disobey Harper's order, she looked at Tony.

"What the hell is going on? Noble, I don't want another case, but we can't choose who we help or don't help." He grunted. "I understand you want closure of this case because it might involve one of your prior victims, but we need to see what's happening. I can't believe I'm saying this, but Leah would never screw with us this way," Tony said, raising a challenging eyebrow.

"Ha!" Noble replied.

"Noble, do any of those 'grab your gear' words ring a bell with you?" Tony shook with laughter.

"Hmm, 'grab your gear' does. Haven't you heard them before, Tony? If I remember correctly, you didn't know what was happening," she teased.

"I can never forget that day. It was on our third case, and I'd only been here about four months." His muscles twitched under his eye. "You were charming, but some people would say you were arrogant and only wanted to focus on one case. I had no clue what to do when Sergeant Harper yelled those words at us." Tony laughed full and long.

"Yep." Noble's face lit up with a gigantic smile at the memory from long ago as she muttered her response.

"You adapted nicely to that incident, more than I did. Even Sergeant Harper agreed," he finished with a smirk.

Noble started laughing out loud as she knew he was trying to keep her mind off things and cheer her up simultaneously. That was another bizarre case that had Noble at her wit's end.

Noble and Tony turned down another street when they saw Harper's car come to a stop. Noble looked at the building as her brain registered the location. Her stomach in knots, she quietly muttered, "No."

"Noble, what's wrong?" She could hear the concern in his voice.

"No," Noble said louder and more pronounced.

"What is it? What's going on, Noble?" Tony asked again.

"This is the old Vagabond Motel. What the hell is going on?" Noble said as she exited the vehicle and strode toward Leah.

"You would know better than me as I've never worked in this district," Tony replied, following Noble toward Harper.

"Sergeant Harper?" Noble called as she approached. Harper turned to face Noble at the sound of her name. "What exactly is going on here? You know what building this is, right?" she growled. "Bridget's murder occurred in the alley behind this building. And Neil lives here." There were only two conclusions that Noble could come up with as to why Leah wanted them there. Either something had happened to Neil, or the victim was somehow involved with or related to Bridget's murder. "I believe the anonymous caller specifically said you needed to be the responding detective, Noble," Harper said.

"Anonymous caller? Why would they ask specifically for me?" Noble pressed Harper for an answer. She realized that this was the building where Diana had died.

"Patrol officers found the body of Neil Bishop in his apartment. There was a note left on top of the body addressed to you. No one has touched it yet other than to collect it, but it's in an evidence envelope, and you can view it properly downtown," Harper answered, looking directly at Noble with soft eyes.

"Neil Bishop. I saw him last week, and he mentioned nothing about any problems," Noble responded.

"Who's Neil Bishop?" Tony directed the question at both Noble and Harper.

"Neil was the civilian who tried to save Diana after she sustained her fatal injuries. I've kept in contact with him, and we've become friends," Noble struggled to speak.

"Get your gear, Vistole; you wanted justice, so let's do it. Noble, if you need a minute, I'll understand," Harper said as she turned and marched toward the building's entrance.

Noble returned to the car behind Tony. She saw Tony lean against the passenger side door, looking at her for any sign of how to proceed.

"Well, how are you doing, Noble?" Tony asked.

Noble leaned against the car next to Tony and rested her head lightly on his shoulder. "I'd rather be anywhere else in the world but here." She didn't like feeling helpless, so she always put on a friendly face to her closest and dearest friends. Tony put his arm around her and gently squeezed her shoulder.

"Come on, let's see what we have so we can get some closure for Bridget and Neil's families," Tony said, his voice reassuring.

After the much-needed pep talk, Noble pushed herself away from the car and moved around toward the trunk. Tony handed Noble her gear. With their bags on their backs, they approached the entrance where Harper was waiting.

"I've locked down the elevators for the time being, so it might be best to take the stairs to the fourth floor," Sergeant Harper advised.

"Do you want us to clear the elevator first?" Tony asked.

"No, another team is doing that now, and a third team is working on the stairs. Keep to the right as you go up," Harper replied as she hustled up the stairs ahead of them.

"Shit, I need to exercise more," Tony complained, gasping for air after the first flight.

"I've invited you to work out with me at the department gym, but you're always too busy," Noble said.

"Jeez, Noble. Look at you; it would intimidate anyone who worked out with you. I don't know if my ego could take it," Tony joked.

"Maybe you shouldn't care so much about your ego and concentrate on your cardio. That way, the chicks will fall all over you and your 'fit self.'" Noble chuckled.

"I'll make you a deal, Noble. If I work out with you, will you promise me that within the next two months, you'll at least try going out for coffee with a woman, like on a lunch date?" Tony challenged.

The silence was unmistakable, as if the very air had bolted from the area, and time had frozen as Noble came to a dead stop.

"Deal." Noble took a deep breath and extended her hand, sealing the deal.

Looking stunned, Tony accepted Noble's hand and gripped it, saying, "You won't be sorry, Noble."

"I better not be, seeing as I'm trying to save your life, jackass," Noble replied.

"Children, now that you've made nice, we've work to do," Harper said as she looked down toward them at the top of the fourth-floor staircase with a smirk on her face.

"How much of that did you hear, Sarge?" Noble asked.

"Enough to know that you'll save Tony's life and his ego, and something about you, coffee, and a lunch date. Does that about sum it up?" Harper replied.

"Yes, ma'am," Noble growled as she reached Harper's location with Tony behind her.

"We've cleared this spot for you two to set your gear down while you enter the apartment," Harper said in her sergeant's voice.

Noble and Tony put on booties over their shoes, gloved up, and grabbed a mini pack to enter the apartment. The bag contained gloves and evidence baggies in case they found anything they deemed questionable.

They stopped at the door, looking at the familiar yellow crime scene tape. When Noble lifted the tape, Tony ducked under and entered the apartment. Noble followed, and her hand let go of the tape, allowing it to return to its original place as a barricade.

Noble looked around the apartment, slowly taking in the scene before her, and made mental observations. She had to fight back a natural gag reflex and tears that quickly blinded her vision to the horrible scene in front of her. The walls near where the violent act took place, the furniture, and the victim, Neil Bishop, were all saturated with blood.

Noble inhaled deeply, composed herself, and allowed her eyes to dry as her anger slowly showed itself and her hands clenched into fists. *Ah, Neil, you didn't deserve this! I'm sorry I wasn't there for you. You were a wonderful man, and I will do everything in my power to see that this son of a bitch is in custody so that justice can be swift!*

A slight touch on her shoulder brought Noble back to the present. As she looked, wondering why someone would touch her, her eyes met Tony's.

"Come on, Noble, let's do this," he said.

Noble removed the camera from the bag and followed. As she methodically worked through the process, she took pictures of the walls and the blood splatter on them. After what seemed like an hour, Noble could focus on the body. As she aimed the camera for the next set of photographs, she saw blank, empty eyes staring at her. She remembered those eyes being full of life, smiling at her less than a week ago. Noble shook her head to clear her mind and continued to do her job.

She noticed that Neil had suffered multiple injuries to his torso area, while Bridget had injuries around her head and body. Someone had ripped his chest open with an unknown weapon, which caused him to bleed to death. The open wound allowed some of his organs to hang out against his torn and shredded skin. There were no noticeable signs of injuries to his face, even though his blonde hair was unrecognizable as his blood was all over it. His torn shirt and jeans were now a deep red, and his brown eyes were empty of any signs of life.

Noble turned her head, and her eyes quickly scanned the room before settling on Tony and Harper, who appeared to be involved in a heated discussion. Tony's expression was one of irritation and annoyance.

"Let it go, will you?" Tony shouted. "We'll discuss it later, okay? I want to make sure my partner is okay."

Noble turned back and continued working when she heard footsteps creeping toward her.

"What was that about, Tony?" she asked, not making eye contact.

"There is nothing important we can't sort out at another time," Tony muttered.

Noble took Tony to heart regarding his choice of words, not wanting to press him. She figured he'd talk when he was ready. They finished with their photographs and notes, wanting to wrap some of this up before they took a break. She couldn't believe there could be that much blood in the human body and how quickly he'd bled out. She could still feel the loss of life, seeing his motionless body on the apartment floor.

†

It was near lunchtime when Noble and Tony stepped outside the apartment.

"Did you bring your lunch?" Her stomach gurgled in protest.

"Yes. It's out in the car. Did you bring yours?"

"Yep. Let's head on down. I'm starving." Noble's smile warmed her lips.

They handed off all their evidence collection to an assisting technician before heading down the stairs.

They stood, eating their lunch; Harper allowed that. She sometimes irritated Noble, but most of the time, she was an excellent boss—edgy at work and home. After eating, they headed back to the apartment to wrap things up.

At the same time, the boss herself was standing by the apartment doorway talking to Mr. Blasingame, the next-door neighbor, who'd called it in. Tony crept closer and stood unusually close to the interaction, as if he was trying to listen in on the conversation. Noble eyed him. It was out of character since Tony had never cared about the first on-scene or first suspect interviews before. So why the sudden spark of interest? Noble made her way over, tapping him on the arm as she passed. He jumped before getting to the point. Noble lifted the tape for them as they entered the crime scene. Dr. Redmond had called ahead and would arrive soon, giving them time to collect evidence and argue ideas. Noble started with the collection of blood for sampling. There was one splatter that seemed out of context with the rest. It was more like gravitational drops, possibly from Neil's defensive wounds. He could have fought back. From blood, Noble moved on to collecting the many prints on the scattered beer bottles left from Neil's night-time activities. One was set down carefully on the opposite side of the room. With a naked eye, Noble examined the print. It was distinctly different from the others. Someone else had been there in a calm frame of mind. Noble turned to see Tony crouched and collecting evidence from the body, but he seemed stumped by something.

"Food for thought?" Noble called, catching his attention. He looked up and rose to his feet.

"Yeah," Tony replied, going toward Noble and holding his arm out to show her a couple pieces of evidence he'd collected. "Look at these," he said, pointing to both items in his hand.

"We're surrounded by blood," Noble remarked, turning away after her comment. "It is the substance encompassing us. What about it?"

"Yeah, Noble, I know that, but look closer," Tony said, keeping her attention. "One of them is dried, Noble. Look around," he instructed. "Do you see any other dry areas with blood?" Tony asked, looking at Noble expectantly. It finally fit together in her mind. Was that what he was thinking?

"It's the suspect's. Or maybe another victim. Could it be Neil's? Unrelated to today. Maybe he cut himself and missed these spots." Her eyes hung on the evidence in Tony's hand for a moment. "Where did you find it?"

"Exactly," he replied, returning to the body, pointing to a bathroom door that looked partially open. Noble briefly dismissed the evidence; her mind now focused on the bigger picture. "I think the killer was already in Neil's apartment and might've been injured from a prior altercation. Maybe with our other victim. Or maybe involved in something that hasn't been reported yet. There are multiple drops of dried blood in the bathroom behind the door. Like the suspect was standing behind it.

"So," Noble continued, stepping away from where she was working. Tony turned to look at the door, and Harper did the same. "Let's assume that the suspect attacked Neil when he walked into the bathroom, dragging him out here to where he tortured him, for possibly seeing Bridget's murder, or the suspect wanted some information from Neil," she stated. "The more I think about this, my gut is telling me, Billy Russell has to be involved, and he did this to Neil to get information on Tracy?"

"But how does Neil know about Tracy? Did you ever talk about Bridget, or could we possibly be looking at two different suspects? Maybe Bridget's and Neil's murder aren't related," he suggested, looking back and forth between Sergeant Harper and Noble.

"Oh, my god. What happened to Neil is all my fault!" Noble replied as she placed her hands over her face.

"What do you mean it's your fault, Noble?" Harper pinned her crossed arms over her chest.

"I spoke with Neil within the last couple weeks and was bouncing off ideas with him. He helped me a lot after Diana died, but I swear I never gave him any names or addresses. We always talked in hypotheticals." Noble worked her jaw in a tight circle.

"Well, if the suspect didn't know that when he started, then he only killed him to tie up a loose end," Harper stated evenly.

"So, the suspect left here after killing Neil, most likely with no additional information." She held Tony's gaze for a moment before looking away briefly. "And where does he go? Does he go home and try to calm himself down and regroup, or does he continue to look for Tracy?" Noble mumbled, almost like she was speaking to herself instead of Tony and Harper.

"Tracy no longer lives at the address where the actual assault happened. But she does still own her business building. And Russell knows where it's at since he had been following her before he attacked her," Tony stated.

"If I'm Russell, I would eventually go to that place looking for her, the one person who sent him to prison, and then take care of business," Noble added. "He wants to set the record straight and remove Tracy Snow from the equation. He might not realize that she lives above the bar now," Noble's face scrunched up in worry.

"Maybe killing Tracy is his final blow or act," Tony said.

As Noble continued with her working theory, Tony nodded along in agreement. "He's pissed, he might not have intended to use it, but Russell grabs the closest thing to him in the alley, the crowbar." The muscles in her throat tightened. "When Bridget fights back, his anger against women and Tracy Snow gets the best of him, and Russell kills Bridget in a fit of rage. He doesn't like the fact that a woman, Tracy, got away and dictated his life while he was away in prison. Russell spent all this time there wanting to make her pay for being the one that got away," Noble hypothesized as she offered ideas to Tony and Harper.

"And now, somehow, he's left blood at Neil's apartment that will either match him or belong to Bridget," Tony added to the working scenario.

"There is no maybe. We know his end goal is to kill Tracy Snow. The realization is how many more people will have to die for him to get to her?" Sergeant Harper nodded. "We've done everything we can, so let's head back to the office. I want to call Sergeant Blackwell over at DOJ and see if he can send some agents to help you locate Billy Russell before he strikes again. I'll see you at the office," Sergeant Harper said as she zipped toward her car.

"Hey, Noble, maybe they'll send over a hot agent you can have that coffee date with." Tony laughed as they walked to their car to return to the office.

"Bite me, Vistole!" Noble replied as they loaded their gear into the trunk of their work car.

†

"Hey, Mom L, are you checking up on me? Or is this that phone call you said I might expect?" Charlie asked as she laughed into her cell phone.

"Hey, favorite daughter of mine, as much as I'd like to say I'm checking up on you, this is work-related." She chuckled. "I got off the phone with your boss, Sergeant Blackwell, and she's assigning you and a couple of agents to my unit's current case—or, as of today, cases," Leah answered in a tired voice.

"Okay, my supervisor hasn't officially told me yet, but as soon as I get the order, you'll be the first to know," Charlie said as she looked around the office to see if Sergeant Blackwell was around.

"Great, got to go, sweetie. I'll talk to you later," Leah conveyed as she ended the phone call.

"Okay," Charlie replied.

"Matthews, Taylor, get into my office now," Sergeant Blackwell ordered from her chair.

"Yes, ma'am," they both said.

"What have you done now, Mike?" Charlie asked as she started toward the sergeant's office.

"Me? Why does it always have to be me? Maybe you did something this time, Charlie," Mike replied as he followed her. Mike looked at her and asked, "What's up with that? She usually stands in her doorway and yells at us."

"I got a heads up about a case we'll most likely be assisting on with the local police department," Charlie replied.

"Great! Maybe you can finally get asked out on a date. I mean, you've been in town like forever and have done nothing to enjoy yourself," Mike added as he traipsed ahead of her toward the supervisor's office.

"Knock it off," Charlie replied, following behind him.

"Remember the briefing a few days ago about the absconding parolee, Billy Russell, out of Region One? Well, he's the primary suspect in two murders, and the detectives believe he might go after his only surviving victim," Blackwell clipped. "Sergeant Harper, over at the Onserf Sex Crimes Unit, has requested some help with surveillance. And you two are up. So, I need you to get your gear, any information we have on Billy Russell and his commitment case, and report to Sergeant Harper tomorrow morning at 0800 hours." Blackwell gave a dismissive wave of her hand.

"Is Sergeant Harper our primary contact?" Charlie broke eye contact.

"Yes. This guy needs to be in custody. It appears he's an absconding high-risk sex offender, and we don't need anymore negative press," Sergeant Blackwell advised.

"We'd be more than happy to assist them with taking this guy down, ma'am," Charlie answered as she took the sticky note that Sergeant Blackwell handed her.

"Keep me updated, and let me know if you'll need additional bodies to help with canvassing or surveillance. Don't be late for the briefing tomorrow morning at their Northwest substation. I want updates in the morning and at the end of the shift. I've Sergeant Harper's number if I have any concerns." Blackwell rested her elbows on her desk.

"Do you want us to work on any new cases tomorrow since we'll be working on this joint operation starting Wednesday?" Charlie asked.

"No. Get to work on any prepping you need to do. That'll be all. You're both done for the day," Sergeant Blackwell replied as she returned to reading a report.

"How about you get a folder together? I'll contact Sergeant Harper and confirm where we're meeting tomorrow and what she needs for the briefing," Charlie said.

"You always want the effortless way out, Matthews. Make your call while I'm working hard on my computer to find our suspect," replied Mike. He started laughing when a pen came flying, narrowly missing his head.

Charlie picked up her cell phone and dialed Harper's number. On the third ring, an authoritative voice said, "Harper, Sex Crimes!"

"That's no way to answer a phone, Leah. I thought by now that Mom would have helped you in the manners department," Charlie replied playfully.

"Hiya, kiddo. Some things will never change. Please wait a minute, but let me guess, your team will come here to help us with our case. Your Sergeant Blackwell works fast. I should thank her in person next time I see her," Leah said.

"Yep, I'll be there with bells on, Mom L. Anything to help you out and get this pervert, or killer, off the street," Charlie replied with disgust in her voice.

"Great. Make sure to call your mom to let her know that you'll be in our neck of the woods tomorrow night. Set aside the evening for dinner," Harper said. "I've got two great sex crimes detectives assigned to this case, and I think you'll work well as a team. Is your new partner, Mike, coming as well?" Harper asked politely.

"Yes, Mike and I will help you out. Sergeant Blackwell will have two additional agents at our disposal if we need them. I'll set aside tomorrow night to see you and Mom again. It has been too long, and I miss you both. Even though I was there a few nights ago, I miss seeing you two. I love you, and I'll see you tomorrow," Charlie said.

"Sweetie, I love you too. Quick question before I hang up. Do you still drink coffee?" Harper asked nonchalantly.

"Yes, why?" Charlie replied in a questioning tone.

"No worries. I've got to run. See you tomorrow." Harper laughed as she disconnected the phone call.

"What the heck is Mom L up to?" Charlie said out loud.

"Hey, Charlie, I've got everything printed. I'm going home to relax for the rest of the day, and I'll meet up with you tomorrow. Text me the address where we need to be and the time, and I'll see you there," Mike said as he moved out the door.

"Sure thing, Mike. I'll do it now, so I don't forget," Charlie replied to an empty office.

Once she texted him the address and ensured she had all the case files loaded into her bag, she headed for the coffeehouse.

CHAPTER FIFTEEN

"It's like you know where I will be before I do. How are you doing today, Detective Gentry? Hope I'm not interrupting," Charlie said as she looked at Noble.

"Oh, excuse me. Sorry. How are you, Ms. Matthews?" *I hope she doesn't want to sit down.*

"I need some coffee for my afternoon pick-me-up, and I love coming to this place. I thought about sitting down and enjoying some downtime. I see that you're busy, so I'll let you get back to work."

"Excuse my lack of manners. Please join me. We all could use a break, it seems." *Dammit, Noble, why did you invite her to sit down? Are you a glutton for punishment or something? This may be my coffee date, and Tony will back off a little. She was protective of Jessie, so that's a plus. This won't be unpleasant; she does have a beautiful smile.*

"Don't mind if I do," she said as she sat across from Noble and smiled.

There's something about her. Maybe it's her energy, but she interests me. What better way to get to know her than over coffee casually? And with no strings attached. Let's see if she's worth that next step.

"So, Ms. Matthews, why is this your favorite coffee house? Only regulars come here," she asked as she closed her case file and focused on the woman across from her.

The woman's eyes lit up like a sparkling light on a Christmas tree, with merely a hint of mischief. *I wonder if she's like this with everyone, or maybe, with any luck, only me.*

"My mom, Elizabeth, always comes here, so sometimes she brings me with her, and I know fantastic coffee when I taste it. I am thrilled to be back in the area and enjoy it. And please call me Charlie."

"I can't argue with you about that. This is the best coffee house ever." Noble let out a genuine laugh. "When working on some of my cases, this is the place to come and work without interruptions. It allows me to focus and work on releasing some tension, if you can believe that. And call me Noble."

"Places like this keep me coming back—the ones where you can bring your work and reset after a long day. We'll probably be seeing each other a lot more. I needed a place to unwind and relax, and this was it." Charlie smiled a lopsided grin at Noble. "I'm so glad to be putting it back on my schedule. It was missing, and there was no other place like it in my last city. There's something special about returning to the town where my history and family are. I missed it."

"What made you leave in the first place? And what's brought you back to our great city? If you don't mind me asking, Charlie." *When she talks about her family, her eyes light up like the sun's rays beaming down. Her smile, with the corner of her mouth turned up, clearly shows that her family means a lot to her. That's a plus in my book.*

"I don't mind at all. Let's see, love got me to leave, and heartbreak brought me back. Growing up is great; realizing you don't have to settle is a straightforward decision." Her voice was so quiet it sounded as though lost in a gale. "Also, I could move back to work here. I work for the state, and sometimes, getting a transfer is hard. I couldn't pass up the chance to come home and be closer to my family. My parents still live here and are excited to have me back," Charlie added. "Sorry, I'm rambling. What about you, Noble? Are you a transplant to Onserf, or are you homegrown from the area?"

"Homegrown as you get. I decided I wanted to stay and make a positive impact in the town where I grew up." Noble's eyes conducted a visual sweep of the business.

"Are you waiting for a colleague, Detective?" Charlie asked.

"No, just checking the room periodically. In my line of work, you should never get complacent," Noble remarked.

"That's good to know," she said as she took a sip of her coffee.

"As I was saying, love and heartbreak are both culprits here, but deciding to stay here was never an option, as my job is important to me. My dad doesn't live here. He's out of state." Noble smiled. "It's great that you could relocate back here. Those state jobs can be a pain because of how hard it is to transfer sometimes. One of my friends' kids is in the process of that so they can move back here, too," Noble finished. *She seems interested in my life away from work. That could be a good thing. I don't think dropping everything about my life on her is a good idea. After all, this is hardly a date; it is more like a chance meeting. There is a high probability that there will be an actual date as she's checking all the right boxes for me: kind, not overpowering, upbeat, family oriented, works, will want to take this slow as someone has hurt her in a relationship, and her radiating personality might win me over.*

"Hopefully, she'll be just as fortunate as I was to relocate and be near loved ones. My family holds an incredibly special place in my heart. Despite being physically distant, they have been my unwavering support system this past year." Her gaze ensnared Noble. "They were there for me during the heartbreak mentioned earlier, helping me navigate the difficult times, and they continue to lend a helping hand today. I cherish them dearly. You might have never been honored to meet me without their presence in my life." Charlie chuckled.

"Oh yeah. And why is that?" Noble arched one eyebrow.

"Maybe she would've been worth shooting, but more things in my life are way more important than she ever was or will be. Sometimes, those thoughts creep into your mind even though you know you'll never act on them. There is way more cons than pros." Charlie hunched her shoulders.

"Then it's a good thing she wasn't worth all that drama. I can relate to having thoughts like that now and again, but I will never act on them. That's not who I am." Noble's breath snagged in her throat to contain a laugh.

"Why are you laughing, Noble Knight? Those serious cons kept me from going to the dark side. Karma will eventually visit her, and all will be right in the world."

"Note to self, make sure you never piss off Charlie. Or there will be hell to pay." She jokingly wrote it down with her finger on the outside of her case file.

"Love your deadpan humor, Noble. But on a serious note, for future reference." Charlie leaned over the table and looked her directly in the eyes. "This person you are having coffee with, who is me, is loyal. And when you disregard that loyalty, my actions will be quick and fierce in response. There is no negotiation, especially when your ex has a quickie with a coworker. I believe in fighting for true love, but when it's not reciprocated and cheating occurs, it's time to cut my losses and move on. Do you understand what I'm saying?"

Noble swallowed slowly, trying to articulate a response. But looking into those eyes told her all she needed to know. The discussion had become serious, and she needed to answer without humor. "Yes, I understand. As with my line of work, all I have is my honor and integrity. People won't talk, trust, or rely on you without either. That's how a personal relationship should also be. I don't think true love can last if you don't talk, trust, or rely on each other," Noble said. "It can also be hard to find. That kind of love blindsides you initially, allowing you to see the person putting it all out there for you. They're taking a chance and hoping that the feeling is mutual. And when it's mutual, nothing but death can end it. I understand where you're coming from. Noted for future reference as well." Noble twisted her hands together.

"I'm glad we understand each other, Noble. I hate to cut our chance meeting short, but I need to head home, as I have some work to catch up on. There will be a nice, chilled bottle of beer with my name on it and a long soak in the tub afterward."

"Thank you for enjoying a cup of coffee with me today. It was pleasurable and enlightening. Don't work too hard, and don't fall asleep in that tub." Noble stood as she always did out of respect for the person she had shared her time with.

Charlie stood, trod two steps toward her, placed one hand on Noble's hip, raised on her tiptoes, kissed Noble on the cheek, and said in her ear, "Just for future reference, I hope that we might have many more coffee dates, or maybe even a dinner date so we can get to know each other. I prefer seeing you smile, Noble, so please remember that I can be a friendly ear if you ever need to talk. Remember, I saw you with Jessie, and if she approves of you, I do too."

"This is new for me, as it's been over four years since a coffee date. There could be some rust involved, but yes, there's an extremely high probability that some coffee and dinner dates will involve you and me," Noble said in a husky voice. "So please be patient. Baby steps. But I'd like to get to know you better. Next time, I'll tell you more about me and why it's been four years." Her face twitched. "And here I thought you were annoying when I first met you. You asked too many questions at Jessie's house that day, but it seems the more we run into each other, the more you rub off on me."

"Are you trying to end this before we even start, Noble? Tsk. Tsk. It'll be fun proving you wrong about that annoying bit. And so you know, baby steps work for me, too. After all, this is only the first date," Charlie chided.

"Sorry, I'm only being honest. I want to start on the right foot. It's annoying but cute that you were watching out for Jessie's well-being," Noble said.

"Nice try on the save. But cute is progress. I'll take it any day over annoying. Remember to call or text me when you are available for our next date. I'll be waiting to hear from you. Pace yourself, Noble." Charlie cocked her head to one side.

"Yes, ma'am. Hearing from me might come sooner than later, but you'll be the first to know," Noble admitted with a nod.

Noble watched Charlie as she sashayed toward the exit. *Wait till I tell Vistole I had a coffee date with a woman. It was an unplanned one, but it was a nice one, all the same.* Noble could feel the sensation of her heart beating, forcing small waves of throbbing blood directly into her temples. When she stood, she felt her once sturdy legs crumple beneath her. Noble had to sit down or risk embarrassing herself by falling to the ground. She replayed the events with Charlie in her mind and smiled as she covered her face with the palms of her hand and said, "I'm in so much trouble." *Why couldn't she have been overly annoying, like our first encounter? At least she's okay with taking it slow, which I was teetering on or just above it.* She took out her phone and added Charlie's contact information. On a whim, she texted to set up another coffee date. *Go big or go home, right?*

Hi Charlie, it's Noble. I'm checking to see if you'd be free tomorrow, Wednesday, late afternoon for an official coffee date. I enjoyed today and would like to see you again. If you're unavailable for coffee, how about dinner at my place instead? That way, we can talk more freely and not worry about interruptions.

You had me at dinner at your place. What time would you like me to be there, and would you like me to bring anything? Other than my annoying self. 😉

Just you, and remember, I could upgrade you to cute. So, the only thing you need to bring is yourself. And 5:30 would be perfect. 😊

Touché, detective. You're a tough safe to crack. Send me your address, and I will see you then. Casual dress attire?

Let's go casual for dress attire. And Charlie, it's Noble. Please call me Noble from now on, as I don't think this is work-related anymore. Here's my address. I look forward to seeing you tomorrow night.

Casual it is. Looking forward to tomorrow, Noble.

Me too!

†

Charlie bounced into the house, peeked around the corner, and saw Elizabeth and Beth lying on the couch watching a movie.

"Hey you two, what're you watching?" Charlie fixed her gaze on the television.

"Mom, we're watching my favorite dinosaur movie. You know which one."

"Sure do. How were you for Grandma Beth today?"

"Mom, I never get into trouble, you know that." Elizabeth laughed as she skipped to Charlie and hugged her.

"Charlie, she's an absolute angel with me." Beth went over and kissed her daughter on the cheek.

"Great! And I want to make sure it doesn't change," Charlie said as she ruffled her daughter's hair.

"How was work? Is everything okay? You're home early."

"Great, Mom. They let us off early today because, on Thursday, we're briefing Mom L's unit on the case she mentioned. My sergeant is allowing us to catch up today and tomorrow on our couple of cases. As of Thursday, we'll only be working jointly on one," Charlie finished her update.

"Is that what's got you in such a good mood? I could feel your smile from across the room." Beth laughed.

"No, I had a kind of coffee date today. We kept running into each other, and she invited me to sit and join her. I had a pleasant time, and talking with someone with a life like mine was so nice. You know what I mean?"

"That's great. Especially in your line of work. Does this woman know about Elizabeth yet?"

"Does who know? About me?" Elizabeth chimed in.

"Can't get anything past you, supersonic ears. Wasn't watching your movie, now, were you?" Charlie made a tsk-ing noise with her mouth.

"I only heard my name. And yes, you know my dinosaurs are important to me," Elizabeth grumbled.

"Get back to watching them. Grandma Beth and I are going to talk in the kitchen."

"Okie-dokie. See you tomorrow, Grandma. Love you."

"Love you too, Elizabeth." The corners of Beth's mouth curled upward into a wide grin.

"To answer your question, Mom, she doesn't know about Elizabeth yet. Can you keep Elizabeth tomorrow night? She's invited me over for dinner to get to know each other better," Charlie asked.

"Oh boy, don't fall for another one like that doozy of an ex you have. And please don't even entertain the idea of sleeping with this woman until you get past the first date. Or until you find out more about her." Beth furrowed her brow.

"Mom. I'm not that hard up. She wants to take it slow, and I'm okay with that. Especially since I have Elizabeth to think about. She knows I had a nasty breakup and wants to tell me more about her life." A groan accompanied the roll of her eyes. "So, it's safe to assume we will have a heavy conversation about our lives and getting to know one another. I do plan on telling her about Elizabeth. Because we both know that this will only go further if it's a package deal. Elizabeth is the most important thing in my life, and I won't put her through hell again."

"Okay, it's the mother in me that worries. I only want the best for my daughter. Do you at least know where she works? And can you tell me her name, solely on the off chance you don't call us after dinner?"

"Of course. She's a detective with Onserf Police, and I met her at Janet Williams' house. Remember, her daughter, Jessie, had a case, and Noble was the detective." Charlie beamed. "I undeniably like her, Mom, and there's something between us. We both want to take baby steps, and we are fine with that." Charlie looked at her mom and asked. "Are you okay?"

"Did you say her name is Noble?" Beth's words trailed off.

"Yes, why?" An impish smile made Charlie's mouth twitch.

"About five feet eleven, green eyes that remind you of a forest where you can get lost, and a smile that reaches her eyes. That Noble? Noble Gentry, to be more specific." Beth's lips curled upward.

"Yes, you described her perfectly. Do you know her?" Charlie ran her hand through her hair.

"Oh, boy!" Beth breathed through her open mouth.

"What's 'oh boy' supposed to mean? Mom, can you let me in on it?" Charlie's heart pounded hard in her chest.

"Um, well, you see, Noble is our friend, Nob. She works for Leah. I can't believe it."

"I can't believe what? That she'd want to go out on a date with me, or that I'd want to go out on a date with her?" A twinge of anger laced Charlie's voice.

"I didn't see that coming from her. Do you know about her wife who died?" Beth's shoulders dropped with a sigh.

"Mike told me a little about her before I ran into her today. It sounds like she wants to talk about it tomorrow. I will also tell her that my job with the state is law enforcement. Hence, that is one reason we'll take it slow," Charlie stammered. "We both have pasts, Mom, but if she's the one, I can't put the possibility aside for something that happened in the past. It felt so natural sitting there and talking today. No expectations, and can you believe she thought I was annoying when we first met?" She pressed her hands to her cheeks.

"I don't want either of you to get hurt. You're both important to us for obvious reasons, and Noble because she and Leah are good friends. Leah stepped up and helped when Diana died. It made me love her more; I wasn't sure that was possible." A gentleness touched Beth's lips. "We want you both to be happy, whether together or with others. Please remember, she's got a bruised heart, but it sounds like you might be the right medicine to heal it. Of course, we'll watch Elizabeth tomorrow." Joy shone in her smile.

"Thank you, Mom. Now I need to let Mom L know. Can I let her know on Thursday? Tomorrow will be the day of reckoning. And we'll either end up taking the next step, or we'll remain friends."

"If she asks, I won't lie to her. And please at least call or text to let me know when you get home after dinner tomorrow. Even though you'll be with Noble, I will still worry."

"I'll text you as soon as I get into the house tomorrow. Also, you're right about her eyes. Whenever we've run into each other, I get lost in them, and I'm okay with that. They remind me of a safe place, and those eyes—that's all her. I never quite felt that with anyone before, so this is new for me, too." Charlie blushed.

"If this works, she'll love you forever. She's one of the most honorable women I know besides Leah. I will root for you both as you're two incredible women. Speaking of incredible, it's time to head home to that sexy wife of mine. I'll see you tomorrow. Love you." Beth wrapped her arms around Charlie.

"Thanks for the pep talk, Mom. Love you, too."

"Hey, Mom, the dinosaur movie is over," Elizabeth said.

"Are you ready for your bath and bedtime story?" Charlie asked as she took Elizabeth's hand and approached the bathroom.

"Yep. Love you, Mom."

"Love you to the moon and back."

"And then some," Elizabeth yelled at the top of her lungs.

Chapter Sixteen

Billy Russell stood across the street from Blade's Brewery, debating on if he should go inside to see if that bitch still worked there. *I need to find her so she can pay for what she did to me.* Russell was fidgeting in the alleyway with a perfect view of the bar. *I need to make sure she doesn't recognize me too soon, as I want to play with her a little. I don't want to waste my time if she's not here anymore.* He shuffled over, entered Blade's, and casually looked around. There were at least twenty people inside, but none looked like her. Billy strolled over to the bar and sat on a stool.

"What can I get you?" the tiny blond behind the counter asked.

"Whatever beer you got on tap. The cheapest one at that."

"Coming right up," she said as she set the stein before him.

A slight nod, accompanied by a grunt, was all he would give now. He tossed some money on the counter and took a couple of chugs from his beer. A mirror made up the entire wall behind the bar, letting him look around without being too obvious. Movement at a table in the bar's corner caught his attention. *I think that's her. I need to make sure. It sure looks like her, but a lot older than when I last saw her.* The woman left the table and started moving toward the bartender, who was mixing a drink in the middle of the bar.

"Hey, Vera, heading to the office now to do some paperwork."

"Okay, Tracy. If I need backup, I will give you a holler."

"Great, thanks."

Billy looked at her in the mirror as she proceeded right past him. She didn't pay him any attention, which was great for him. *It means that either she doesn't recognize me, or she's let her guard down. Let's hope it's both. She's making it way too easy for me. This might not be a challenge, and I hope she fights like last time. If it hadn't been for that neighbor calling the cops, I wouldn't be sitting here today.* He finished his beer and meandered out of the bar, ready to execute his plan. Pulling out a cigarette, lighting it, and taking a deep drag, Billy realized he needed to come here every night to see if she had a regular schedule and to make sure he could follow her to wherever she lived. He'd finally be able to rid the world of Tracy Snow. He took one last drag and flicked the cigarette into the street as he headed toward his motel.

†

Tracy entered the office and felt the hair on the back of her neck stand up. Knowing that wasn't a good sign, she looked at the security monitors behind her desk. Tracy saw nothing unusual in the bar area, but something wasn't sitting well with her. She made a note to check the tapes closer after closing, stuck it on the front of the monitor, and sat down to review some numbers.

Chapter Seventeen

Noble returned home in time to catch the last quarter of the football game. She loved this time of year. She could spend the evening eating dinner on the couch, reviewing her files, and watching the game. Noble hadn't realized she had stayed so long at the coffeehouse. It was good that her favorite pizza joint was only a few doors down. *Now, this is life—pizza and football.* Shoving half the slice into her mouth, she heard the text alert for her phone go off. Pulling the phone from her back pocket, she wondered who'd be texting her.

Hi Nob. Hope you had a great day at work and didn't bring it home tonight. It's been two weeks since you came to our house for dinner, and we hope you can make it Monday. Leah says you're both off that night, so we won't take no for an answer, and we look forward to seeing you. You and I need to catch up. Make sure you eat dinner tonight and get some good sleep. You'll be busy here for the foreseeable future or until you catch this guy. Talk to you tomorrow. We love you.

This was unusual. Noble wondered why Beth was texting her, as she usually called. Beth always had a way of reading her and would call her on any of her bullshit excuses for not going over there to stay connected. She'd better answer her now, or she probably would get Beth's call in the morning, wanting to know why she didn't respond.

Hi Beth, I got home from work and sat down to watch the game and eat pizza. Yes, it would be great to catch up, and I'll put dinner on the calendar for Monday with you and Leah. I've got something I want to share with you both, so this will be perfect. As always, I love you, too.

Noble wondered if Charlie was the type of girl who enjoyed relaxing on the couch, eating pizza, and watching football or other sports. She hoped so, or this might turn into a great friendship instead of anything more. No, Noble was sure she and Charlie were alike except for being annoying occasionally, and she seemed to be a breath of fresh air, unlike Noble. She laughed out loud, causing her to laugh even harder. *She'll be good for me, and that's exhilarating and scary at the same time. Before you're ready to prance down the aisle and get married, let's see how tomorrow night goes. Remember, baby steps.* Noble put the remaining pizza in the fridge, threw the trash away, and headed to bed.

Chapter Eighteen

"Hey sweetie, before I head into work, can we set up dinner sometime next week with Noble?" Leah asked. "It's time she meets Charlie since they'll work together soon. They'll make an effective team and are good at brainstorming in such cases."

"Well, Noble said she was coming to dinner Monday night if you don't have her working too hard." A glint touched Beth's eyes. "I texted her last night asking her to come over as it's been too long. She said she had something she wanted to talk to us about."

"Why text? You usually call her. Are you trying to switch up your attacks on her to get her to come around more?" Leah said, laughing at her attempt at a joke.

"Something like that. I worry about her. She needs to be happy like us, and that won't happen if she's working crummy hours and going straight home," Beth said. "It'll be good to introduce her to Charlie. They both need friends in their lives for various reasons. And since they're both important to us, I hope they hit it off and become great friends," she continued. "I need to tell you something, but Charlie asked me not to say anything. At least until she's ready to tell you. It'll be sooner rather than later. I don't like it when she puts me in this position."

"When you say it like that, I agree. They'll be good for each other. I saw your note about Elizabeth staying the night tonight. To what do we owe the pleasure of her company?" Leah's eyes broadcast surprise. "And honey, if nothing is wrong with Charlie, I will respect her wishes and not ask questions. Unless, of course, you want to share a 'hypothetical' scenario with me," she gently prodded.

"Leah, it sounds like Charlie has met someone, and they're having dinner. She says she feels a connection with this one, and that's never happened before," Beth stated. "We'll both approve of this one. I told her she needed to text me when she got home so we know nothing has happened to her."

"Hmm, I hope she's careful. Her ex is a crackpot, and another one like that might destroy her." She exhaled. "Whoever this new gal is, she better want a package deal, or I'll tell her to get packing myself. Elizabeth must be a priority. If anyone hurts them again, they'll answer to me." Leah squeezed her hands into fists.

"Agreed. However, you should line up after me, babe, as I'll be in an ass-kicking mood. I might even go hands-on this time." Beth waggled a finger at her.

"I love it when you get all tough like that, babe. Makes me wish work weren't on the schedule today, as I'd love to spend some quality time with you," Leah said as she kissed Beth on the lips and pinched her ass.

"There should be some quality time coming up for you in the next couple of days," Beth said as she lifted Leah onto the kitchen counter, stepped in between her legs, and planted a searing kiss on her lips.

Leah wrapped her legs around Beth and brought her closer. She kissed the side of her neck and whispered, "This will never get old. I love you, but you pick the worst times sometimes, babe." Leah rested her forehead on Beth's and took a deep breath.

"I know. I want you never to forget what's waiting for you at home. Now get to work, and I'll see you tonight," Beth said as she helped Leah off the counter and walked with her to the door. "Be safe, I love you."

"Ditto, sweetie. See you tonight."

†

"Knock, knock. Mom, it's us," Charlie said as she used her key and opened the front door.

"In the kitchen."

"Grandma Beth, I brought my favorite movie and my sleepover jammies for tonight. When is Mimi going to be here?"

"She's on her way right now. Even something about wild horses wouldn't keep her away tonight," Beth said as she hugged Elizabeth.

"Mom, it's too bad you can't watch the dinosaurs with us tonight. Next time. Grandma, can I put the movie in now? That way, it's ready when Mimi gets here. Bye, Mom. I love you."

"Love you, too, sweetie, and I'll see you when I get off work tomorrow."

"You ready for your big date tonight? Are you going dressed like that? Are you trying to kaput this before it even starts?" Beth gestured at Charlie's sweats.

"No, and what's wrong with sweats? Noble said it was informal. I take it to mean sweats are okay. If she said casual only, that would mean jeans to me. And if wearing sweats is a deal breaker, then it is better to know this now," she stated. "That way, we don't have to invest too much time in anything other than friendship. We got this under control. Now, I'm worried about how she'll react to me having a daughter, and how it'll go when I mention who my moms are." Charlie traded a glance with Beth.

"Well, as someone who knows Noble, they'll both scare her, but she'll rise to the occasion. She won't want to make any mistakes. If she thinks you're worth the risk, she'll be fine taking it." Beth slanted her head. "She and Diana wanted a family; it never happened. So, there shouldn't be a problem," she continued. "Don't get upset if she gets quiet. She's a thinker, so she'll need to visualize everything in her mind quietly and think it through carefully. So don't be that obnoxious person she met the first time. Let her come to these decisions on her own," Beth said.

"Boy, that's a lot to remember. I'll let you know when I get home tonight. Wish me luck," Charlie said as she kissed her mom goodbye.

"No luck needed. Be honest, and the rest will have a way of working itself out. And most of all, have fun learning about each other. I think you'll each surprise one another." Beth hugged her.

"That's what I'm banking on. Well, and that I look forward to her kiss." Charlie imagined herself melting, just sliding onto the floor in a puddle of hormones and liquid lust.

"Stop, I don't need nor want to hear anymore. After all, you're still my daughter," Beth said, her eyes closing for a lengthy blink.

"I'm keeping it PG for you, Mom. I don't want you to think poorly about me because I want to rip all her clothes off and spend the day in bed with her. But I figured you didn't need to hear it." Charlie laughed as she closed the door on her mom before she could reply.

Chapter Nineteen

"Shit, I better not be getting called in to work tonight," Noble said as she picked up her phone. "Gentry."

"Hey, Noble Knight, can you open your front door? My hands are full."

"Um—"

"Noble. Are you there? I'd hate to have anything break out here." Her words fell dead and brittle like oak leaves in the fall.

"Oh yeah, sorry about that." Noble opened the door, and all she could see were flowers—a beautiful variety suddenly thrust in her direction.

"Can you please take them? I wasn't sure what to bring, so I hope these are okay," Charlie said as she thrust the flowers toward Noble.

"They're beautiful. Thank you. Come on in," Noble said as she took the flowers from Charlie.

"Don't mind if I do. I hope you had a good day. I spent the day at home finishing up the last of the unpacking," Charlie said.

"Yes, I did a little work, but only a few phone calls. I had the day off scheduled for a few weeks. Sometimes, it's good to self-reflect."

"It is. Once a month has always been my motto," Charlie said. "Now that I'm back in Onserf, I can enlist my parents to help me. I've missed some of those self-reflecting days." Charlie looked up into Noble's eyes.

"You look adorable in your sweats." Noble's inspection lingered. "I'm glad you're okay with eating in and being casual tonight. I'm not one for always going out to fancy dinners." She gave a nervous laugh. "Some would say I'm an introvert, but a conversation between two people getting to know each other is always better in a quieter, relaxing climate."

"You look cute yourself, Noble. Although there probably isn't anything you look shoddy in, and that could include you in a burlap sack."

"Thanks, I think. You don't mince words, do you?"

"This is me in all my glory, flaws and all," Charlie blurted.

"That's good to know. So far, your glory looks surprisingly nice." Noble smiled. "Pizza for dinner, is that okay with you? Have a seat on the couch, and I'll bring over the box, plates, and napkins. What would you like to drink? I have beer, wine, water, or soda," Noble offered as she walked toward the kitchen.

"How about some water? I will only have an alcoholic beverage if I'm not driving or have a designated driver. Habits from seeing too much on the job and because alcohol was a negative factor in my life when I was with my ex."

Noble brought everything out and sat next to Charlie on the couch. “Dig in, and if you’re still hungry after this box, there’s another in the kitchen. I don’t drink too often either.”

“A woman after one’s own heart. Pizza is my favorite food. I’m sorry you had any negatives in your life,” Charlie replied.

Noble took a big bite of pizza and said, “It’s my favorite, too. So, I remember you saying that you worked for the state. What exactly do you do?”

“I’m a special agent. To be exact, I work in the Sexual Predator Apprehension Team. Are you familiar with it? We usually refer to it as SPAT.”

Noble stopped mid-chew and was pondering her question. In the meantime, some cheese was hanging from her chin, and the tickling sensation brought her back to the present.

“Noble, you’ve got some cheese on your chin,” Charlie said as she handed her a napkin.

“Thank you. Yes, I’ve worked a lot with the SPAT team over the years. My partner, Tony Vistole, is a close friend of Mike’s.”

“Wow. It’s funny that you mentioned Mike. That’s my partner. Great guy.”

“So, a cop, huh? I have to admit that never crossed my mind. No wonder you were grilling me at Jessie’s. I can’t believe I missed that; I must be slipping,” Noble said, a worried expression marring her face.

“Is me also being in law enforcement going to be a problem?” Charlie’s face fell the slightest bit. “I’d understand, well, not admittedly understand it, but I’d have to accept it if you didn’t want to go down that road.”

"No, being in law enforcement isn't a problem for me. I need to give you a little background about me," Noble explained.

"Isn't that why we're here tonight? I expect to learn a lot from you. If I hadn't had any interest, tonight would have never happened. You only get to see a few cards in my hand." Charlie gave her a subtle wink.

"Is that right? Thanks for the sneak peek." Noble snickered.

"Anytime. And if you play your cards right, you might see the full hand. So, tell me about Noble."

"Well, my actual title is a widower. My wife, well, she died four years ago. I'm not quite ready to go into all the details, as it would make me extremely uncomfortable crying in front of you on our first date." She lowered her head. "She worked for Onserf police as well. Therefore, baby steps work for me." She spoke slowly. "I haven't wanted to go out on a date since Diana died, but then you came along, and I am interested in slowly entering the dating realm. Specifically, I'm the type of person who only invests in one person at a time in the dating world." She resumed, "I want to date only you to see where this may lead. I'm too old to be dating multiple women and would rather invest in the quality of a relationship than have a quantity of women in my life."

"Technically, this is our second date, so keep up." She grinned. "Second, I'm deeply sorry for your loss, and I mean that with sincerity. It's never easy losing someone that's especially important to you. Particularly when you've no control over the outcome." Charlie put her hand on Noble's forearm and squeezed it lightly. "And if I haven't been clear, I'm also interested in dating only you. Whenever you're comfortable, please know that you can tell me about Diana. I know she was an important part of your life, and it would be an honor to hear more about her."

"And to think I wasn't too sure about you when we first met," Noble said as she leaned forward and looked Charlie directly in the eye. "Thank you. If it's alright, I'd like to kiss you."

Charlie nodded and slowly closed her eyes as Noble's face came closer. Their mouths connected for the first few seconds, which felt like a lifetime, but they didn't move. It was like trying to keep the excitement in the kiss alive forever but allowing that first touch to be imprinted on her brain for life. Noble slowly opened her eyes to find Charlie watching her with a smile. Charlie's lips were so gentle. Suddenly, Noble felt the chill of the air against her lips as Charlie disappeared. She reached out and tenderly touched Charlie's cheek before moving in closer, gazing at her lips, then locking eyes with her before their lips met. Charlie hesitated momentarily, but Noble took the lead again and kissed her back.

Holding their kiss for an eternity, Charlie finally pulled back and said, "Oh my. You made my toes curl up and gave me decent-sized goosebumps."

"You never cease to amaze me, Charlie. We need to talk. So please get back to your corner. These baby steps are going to be tough. I'm letting you know that now."

"Okay. It's safer if you stay on that end of the couch and me on this end," Charlie stated. "Whew. Okay, so I have a couple of things to talk with you about, and we probably should have done that before the kiss." Her breath stalled.

"All ears. Tell me what's going on in that head of yours."

"Well, I refuse to use the term divorced, but I am. We rushed into marriage way too fast, and it turned out to bite me in the ass," Charlie confessed. "She said everything right, and

I thought we loved each other. But saying those words means nothing if you don't have the actions to back them up," she added. "Come to find out, she'd been cheating on me with multiple women. And the kicker was that in the end, she didn't care about us or how it devastated Elizabeth," Charlie declared.

"What a bitch. Committing to someone means you're committed to them through good times and bad," Noble commented. "I'm so sorry you had to go through that. I never understood people who think the grass is always greener on the other side. Don't they know they're supposed to nurture and love their grass to have it green and happy?" she added. "Charlie, who's Elizabeth?" Noble's voice was a shred of a whisper.

"She's the important thing I wanted to share with you. Elizabeth is my four-year-old daughter. She's my life, and we come as a package deal," Charlie revealed. "I'd understand if you weren't ready for a child in your life, but she's the most important thing in my life, and if we move forward, you need to know that it would involve both of us being present in your life, not just me. I need to know that your commitment would include us both. It's a lot to take on, so I understand if you only want to be friends," Charlie said in carefully spaced words.

"Oh." Noble's chest vibrated with her pounding heart.

"Excuse me, Noble, may I use your restroom?" Charlie whispered.

"Oh, sure, it's down the hall, first door on the left." She pointed her finger toward the hallway.

†

"Thank you. I'll be back in a moment." Charlie disappeared down the hallway. She stepped into the bathroom and shut the door behind her. She couldn't help but wonder if the absence of a response was a positive sign. Her mom said Noble tended to take her time when thinking things through. Hopefully, that was the case now, especially since she felt a strong bond with Noble. *Alright, Charlie, let's find out what she thinks. On second thought, since you're already here, you might make sensible use of the facilities. In case you and Noble need to have a serious conversation. You don't want to interrupt it on another trip to the bathroom.*

†

"Hmm. She has a child?" Noble said as she sat alone on the couch, awaiting Charlie's return. *She let me in and bared her soul about her daughter; it was clear she was the most important thing in her life. How can I not respect that Charlie would put her child first but still give me an option to opt out and abandon ship? Do I want to bail? It is an enormous responsibility but worth the risk, especially with someone fierce and loyal like Charlie.*

When Charlie returned to the living room, Noble was no longer sitting on the couch but pacing back and forth in front of the fireplace.

"Noble, everything okay?"

"Yes. Yes, it is."

"Great," Charlie said as she sat back on her assigned couch corner.

Noble drifted over, sat beside Charlie, pulled her onto her lap, and said, "Yes. I know this is our second date, as you reminded me, but yes, you both are worth the risk. I love and want kids, and having you both in my life would be an honor." Noble took a deep breath. "But I still need baby steps for some of the other things that go hand in hand with a relationship. Namely, not rushing into bed but thoroughly getting to know each other. And getting to know Elizabeth. You could say I'm old-fashioned, and things must be done properly." Noble felt the heat of a blush on her cheeks.

Charlie placed her arms around Noble's neck and replied, "I was worried that might have been a deal breaker," she stated. "My mom said you were a thinker, and I needed to give you a little time to weigh your options, and then you could decide."

"Who's your mom, and how does she know me? Because I only know of one person who's ever described me like that, and she's an extraordinary woman. So is her wife." Noble tilted her head.

"The funny thing is, yesterday I found out you're friends. They're both incredible women, and thanks to them, they raised me right." Charlie spoke calmly, resembling a tranquil lake untouched by any breeze. "Beth is my biological mom, and Mom L is exceptional. But only my mom knows where I'm at tonight. I haven't had time to talk with Leah yet," she expressed. "You did, however, get a glowing endorsement from Mom. The jury is still out with Leah until I talk to her."

"You had me when you put your daughter first. It wouldn't have mattered who your parents were. Because they're usually innocent victims in relationships involving adults. You have my word that I will do nothing on purpose to hurt you or Elizabeth," Noble vowed. "We will take this slow, and I believe that as a mother, you can decide when we take it to the next phase, where I meet your daughter." She gently squeezed Charlie's thigh above her knee. "Remember when I said I was rusty at relationships? Children have been nonexistent in any of my prior ones so it will be a learning curve. Pointers from you will be welcome," she told Charlie.

"And one of us needs to talk with Leah, so her feelings don't get hurt," Charlie said.

"We probably need to talk to her before Monday, as Beth invited me to dinner. And the word no is not in her vocabulary, so I see where you get your outgoing personality from."

"Aren't you the sweetest? I will show you every facet of my being and let you learn to love… I mean to like them all."

"It will be my pleasure, and I will be your best pupil," Noble said as she kissed Charlie on the nose.

"How about I let you talk to Leah tomorrow at work? There will be plenty of backup who could save you if your talk goes south," Charlie teased. "Or we can go to their house before dinner and talk with them both on Monday. With Elizabeth there, Leah won't act up. I'm giving you fair warning that Leah has always been protective of me, so be ready." She tipped her head back and hooted.

"Gee, thanks for the warning." Noble shook her head. "I'm going in early tomorrow to prepare for our joint meeting later that day," she said as she caressed Charlie's cheek. "Are you going to be there? I assume you and your partner will be part of the team since Billy is an absconding parolee," Noble stated.

"Yes, Mike and I'll be there. I've been reading up on this guy, and we need to get him off the street as soon as possible," Charlie said as she planted a kiss on Noble's wrist.

"Yes, we do. His victim, Tracy Snow, was my case. It's ironic because my assignment was sex crimes, but I was working overtime on patrol. There was a rash of rapes at the time, and dispatch sent both Diana and I to a suspected rape call. That was the last call Diana responded to when she died," Noble said as she lowered her head.

"Again, I'm so sorry for your loss, Noble," she said as she brought Noble's head to her chest and kissed the top of it. "When you're ready to talk, I'll listen."

"Thank you, Charlie. That means the world to me."

"Noble, she was an important person in your life. I hope you'll share her with me at some point. Again, no rush. It needs to be when you're ready."

"That's not the way to spend a second date. I'm sorry. I was hoping to spend some real quality time, well, any time with you." Her shoulders slumped.

"Oh, Noble, believe me when I say this has been the best second date ever. Scout's honor."

"Scout's honor, huh? Why do you think this has been the best?"

"When I first met you at Jessie's, you looked drained, not only emotionally but tired. And then I watched how you were with Jessie." Charlie revealed a slow smile. "You give everything you have to something that indeed matters to you. And for me, that matters. If you're like that with victims, people you work with, and absolute strangers, I think you'll be off the charts in a personal relationship," she continued. "And you're someone I'm willing to invest in, Noble."

"Thank you, Charlie. When I look at you, I see someone fiercely loyal, willing to lend her voice to someone in need, and someone who'd complement her partner, girlfriend, or whoever you decide to invest your time in. Looking back at our first meeting, I didn't think in a million years that we'd be sitting here talking—and on a date, no less." She chuckled.

"Noble, I look forward to many more dates with you, including Elizabeth, and last but not least, getting together with my mom and Leah."

"Whenever you're ready, let me know." Noble smiled.

"Maybe you can come by my house on Monday for a couple of hours, meet Elizabeth, and then drive to my mother's house together," Charlie suggested. "This way, you can relax and get to know us as a mother-daughter duo. When I introduce you, it could be as my new friend. What do you think about that?"

"I think I'd like that idea. Can I say that I'm glad we kept bumping into each other, and you took the lead about going out on a date?" Noble acknowledged. "Charlie, I'm not sure we'd be here right now if I were calling the shots."

"Noble, don't worry. We can give you a little oil to loosen up your rusty parts," Charlie said as she fell back onto the couch, laughing hysterically.

"Oh really? You should be careful not to tease me, because I have no problem making you pay." She playfully tickled Charlie's sides, making her squirm with laughter.

"Okay, okay, okay. Uncle. I give up." Charlie gasped for air.

"I believe someone is ticklish," Noble remarked.

"On no, you don't. You have to erase this little incident from your memory. Forget about it, or better yet, let me help you forget." Charlie pulled Noble close and kissed her, awakening new sensations. Starting slowly and gently, then with more passion, Noble and Charlie sank deeper into the couch, finding stability in each other.

"You know we need to slow this down," Noble said as she looked into Charlie's eyes. "But before we do, I need one more kiss." Noble kissed Charlie on the forehead before claiming her mouth again. Her tongue slid inside Charlie's mouth, gentle but demanding, causing Charlie to tighten her arms around Noble's neck. As Charlie pulled her closer, she felt like her heart would explode—feelings she hadn't felt in a long time. Noble wanted to keep kissing Charlie, tasting her, and nibbling her lips, which tasted like warm vanilla sugar. But she knew that if they continued, she didn't know if she could stop. And the first time needed to be much more special than on a couch.

Charlie put her hands on Noble's chest and slowly pushed her away. "Okay, now we need to stop. Whew, you pack quite a kiss. My temperature must be off the charts."

"Well, we're only as exceptional as our partner," Noble said as she sat up and extended her hand to Charlie, helping her sit on the couch. *I now understand why people have described kissing as a slow-burning sensation that goes to your toes. It's like standing near a campfire and letting the heat surround your body, making you all toasty warm inside and out.*

"Then we make an outstanding team and I'm looking forward to more team-building exercises with you soon."

"So do I. But we should remember those baby steps. I'm sure you're younger than me, so those baby steps will be useful," Noble blurted. "I don't want to end it before it starts because I can't keep up. I think more cardio needs to be added to my workout routines," she grumbled.

"Out of shape. Noble, you look like you're in excellent condition, so you won't get any complaints from me."

"Ahem—" Noble muttered.

"What, cat got your tongue?" Charlie came back with.

"Maybe," Noble admitted.

"You're adorable when you blush. Don't enjoy receiving compliments, do you?"

"It's been a while, so it'll take some getting used to. Thank you."

"I'm happy to help you out anytime. I should probably get going," Charlie added as she slid off Noble's lap beside her on the couch. "I promised my mom that she'd get a text from me when I got home. There's no need to keep her up late since she has Elizabeth," she explained.

Noble reached for Charlie's hand, stood, and gently pulled Charlie to her feet. "I'll be expecting a text from you to ease my mind that you made it home safely."

"Of course. I live smack dab between you and my mom's. I might have to try walking it one day. It can't be more than half a mile," Charlie replied.

"It's only about a mile from here to your parents' house. Sometimes it's easier to use your feet and get your steps in, so you don't have to search for a parking spot in their popular neighborhood," Noble said.

"Maybe I'll leave my car at my mom's and have her drop me back at the house when you come over on Monday," she suggested. "We can walk back over there with Elizabeth. How does that sound?"

"That would be perfect. An enjoyable stroll to work out any remaining kinks of nervousness will be perfect for me," Noble added. "But leave your car at your house, and we can walk from there. It'll be less than half a mile. And if Elizabeth gets tired, I can return to your house and get my car, and I will pick you up." She shrugged her shoulders like it was nothing.

"Well, it's not like you're going into battle with the boogeyman, Noble. It's only my mom and Leah. I'm sure everything will be alright." Charlie laughed. "And if we walk, you can't abandon us at my mom's."

"Easy to say, as you're not the woman meeting the parents and dating their daughter." Noble raised her eyebrow in a challenge. "Have you ever seen your mom or Leah mad? I have, and it's not something I want directed at me," she challenged. "And no, I won't abandon you."

"Oh, come on, Noble. You have no reason to be worried. They know you, and based on that alone, you should be okay. You'll probably even get their blessing on Monday." A chuckle quaked its way out.

"If you say so. Make sure you have your phone handy tomorrow. Remember, I'll let Leah know, and I might need reinforcements," Noble said, looking skyward as if saying a silent prayer.

"It will be on. Walk me to my car, or you might have an overnight guest tonight."

"After you, let's go," Noble said as she opened the front door and waited for Charlie.

"I love seeing you blush. I can't wait until it's from a little extracurricular activity between us," Charlie said as she patted Noble's stomach and walked out of the house.

"You will not make this easy for me, will you?"

"Nope, you're going to crave me something fierce, Noble. You can take it from me on that. I'm telling you, I'm in it for the long haul," she purred. "There's something about you that sets off all my positive spidey tingles, and I know it might scare you, but for me, I know everything will work out," Charlie declared.

"You got all this from one date? I'd hate to see you interviewing a suspect. Your conviction rate must be off the charts." Noble beamed. "You stir something inside me, too. I want to go slow. You know what they say? Slow and steady wins the race." She nodded in agreement.

"Yes, it does. Please kiss me quickly so I can get in my car and get home safely. I have calls and texts I need to make."

"Yes, ma'am," Noble said as she leaned over and kissed Charlie on the cheek, opened the driver's door for her, nudged her to get in, and watched her drive away.

†

"Best night ever," Charlie said to the empty car as she pulled into her garage and clicked the button. Once closed, she got out and entered the house, turning off the alarm and putting her bags on the kitchen chair. Grabbing bottled water, she headed to her bedroom and got ready for bed. Before turning off the light, she texted Noble.

I'm home and getting ready for bed. I had a fantastic evening, and again, thank you for taking the chance on me and Elizabeth. I can't wait to see you again.

I'm glad you made it home, and I look forward to spending time with you both. Get some sleep, sweet dreams, and I'll see you at the briefing tomorrow. I'll also talk with Leah.

Sweet dreams to you, too. See you tomorrow. You got this Noble Knight? I've got complete faith in you.

Thanks for the vote of confidence. Text your mom and let her know you're home.

Will do. Charlie replied, and then texted her mom.

I hope she doesn't ask many questions, as I'm ready for some profound sleep.

Hi Mom, I'm home now and am crawling into bed.

Please tell me you're in bed alone.

Oh come on, yes, I'm in bed alone. It was only our second date. I'm not some cheap floozy. That might change by the third date, as she's as tempting as a candy cane at Christmas.

Okay, young lady, that's too much information. Glad it went well. I'll talk to you tomorrow. Love you.

Love you, too, Mom. Good night.

Chapter Twenty

Noble sat at her desk, thinking of how she would tell Leah about her and Charlie. She hoped Leah would be okay with the recent development but would understand if she weren't. Noble would not stop seeing Charlie. It had been four years since Diana's death, and she was ready for another shot at happiness. *You never know what'll happen until you take the chance. I hope Leah doesn't make me transfer out of the unit. Shoot, I didn't think about that. It might be patrol-bound. Slow down, Noble, don't rent the U-Haul before you win the girl. Give it a minute and wait till you talk to her. There's no sense getting worked up until you know what you're up against.*

"Hey, Noble, can you please come to my office for a second?" Sergeant Harper said from the doorway.

"Yes, coming that way."

"Close the door and take a seat, please."

"Okay," Noble said as she sat in the chair in front of Sergeant Harper's desk.

"Change of plans regarding the briefing today involving Billy Russell. I have canceled it."

"Why? This guy needs to be taken off the street. Whose idea was it to cancel the meeting? This is ridiculous," Noble said as she stood and paced back and forth.

"Take a deep breath, Noble. Russell has been sighted in Nevada. Boots are on the ground searching for him now. I'm waiting for an update from the sheriff in that jurisdiction as we speak," Harper said as she lifted her hand in the air. "They want to postpone the briefing until further notice or proof that Russell is not in Nevada and that he's still here in Onserf. They're merely doing their due diligence and covering all their bases."

"Shit, there's no way he's in Nevada." Noble exhaled. "That son of a bitch is hunkering down here in Onserf, waiting for the right time to come after Tracy. It's a smoke screen. Where did they get the information that he was in Nevada?" She slammed the palms of her hands on Harper's desk.

"They've received multiple calls from those who live across the border inside Nevada in a small town named Beatty. You know they need to check every lead, Noble."

"What do you want us to do? Do I need to notify the SPAT team?"

"No. I want you and Vistole to continue working on both homicides, which are probably his handy work. We need to link him to one or both," Harper directed. "Also, you need to monitor Tracy, whether going to her establishment or calling her on the phone. We want to know if there's been anything unusual around the bar or if new customers have come in that have given off a weird vibe. And of course I let the SPAT supervisor know. Don't worry, he'll slip up, and we will arrest him," Harper continued. "You're smarter than he is, Noble.

Work on his prior cases, get into his head, and figure out his next step before he does. I've got complete faith that you'll nail this guy."

"Thanks for that, Leah. Can we talk off the record?" Noble's breath stalled.

"Yes. What's up? Everything okay?"

"Everything is fine. Great. I've been out on a couple of dates with someone I met while I was doing a follow-up on one of my cases." Noble gave a nervous laugh. "We kept running into each other before she subtly hinted that we should go out on a date. She came over to the house, and we hit it off, if truth be told. We're going to try dating. I told her I needed to take baby steps, and she was more than okay with that." Noble fiddled with her earring.

"That's great, Noble. I think taking it slow will be fine for you. Remember my motto: slow and steady wins the race," Harper said.

"That's what I said to her. I told her about Diana and explained that I wasn't ready to share everything," she conveyed. "She understood and consoled me. What kind of woman would console a person she wants to date about her deceased wife? I feel a connection with her. I can't explain it, but it's there. Diana and I had a connection, but this one is different, stronger, and it's scaring me."

"If it scares you, things are going in the right direction. Take your time, get to know her, and see where it all leads. I want you to be happy. You deserve to be happy, Noble. I'm only glad that you're finally realizing it for yourself."

"There's something more I need to tell you, Leah."

The shrill of Leah's desktop phone echoed inside the office. "Sergeant Harper. Yes, ma'am, I'll head to your office now. I've got to go, Noble. It's the chief, and you know we can't keep her waiting. On Monday night, you can fill me and Beth in on this new mystery woman who's caught your attention. I'm happy for you."

"Okay, I'll see you Monday," Noble said as she stood and followed Sergeant Harper out of her office.

"Hey, Tony, we've had a change in plans," Noble said as she walked up to his desk.

"Oh yeah, what's that?"

"There have been multiple calls placing Russell in Nevada. Everything with the SPAT team is on hold until they can confirm or deny that information, but I call bullshit. They've agents in the area, so Sarge says we keep working and helping with the two homicides. She wants us to link Russell to one or both. So how about we split his cases and work on some theories?"

"That sounds like a plan. I'll take them home with me, as it'll be quiet this weekend, so I'll work on timelines, etcetera. I want to nail this bastard."

"Funny, I said the same thing to Sarge."

†

Noble and Charlie texted and talked on the phone for the next few days. There were no plans to get together until Monday. Noble needed to read her cases, create a timeline, and put it inside a binder. She liked to be prepared for every case she was working on. It was much easier in court when Noble tabbed, highlighted, and wrote specific notes about each case.

What does a four-year-old like to do? She needed to be ready for this, and, like everything else Noble did, she wanted to be ahead of the curve. What she liked at four was probably way different from what Elizabeth liked. Noble googled every toy that involved dinosaurs, sharks, and sloths. She had loved all three and earned the label of a tomboy for playing with boys' toys, but dolls didn't interest her unless they were action figures. She also loved to read, so maybe she'd get a book for Elizabeth. The phone ringing brought her back to the present.

"Gentry."

"Hey, Noble, I'm checking to see how you're doing with the cases," Tony said.

"Getting there. I was going to take a break and run a couple of errands. I will also run by and check on Tracy at the bar. Do you want to meet me there at about four?"

"Sure. I could use a break, and we can brainstorm what we have so far."

"Okay, see you soon," Noble said as she disconnected the call.

"Bye."

†

Noble arrived at the Spectrum Mall and headed to one of the toy stores. She was walking up and down the aisles until she stopped in her tracks when she saw a dinosaur set that included a plastic mountain and twenty-five dinosaurs, and it said for 4+ years of age on the box. *Wow, it was almost like the one I had growing up. One down, one to go.* She picked up a book on sharks and one on sloths. This should be good. She hoped she wasn't off base, and Elizabeth didn't like dolls. She'd have to do some significant make-up if that was the case.

†

Noble walked out to her car and drove a couple of blocks to Blade's Brewery. Parking about six businesses down from the bar, Noble exited her car and started walking. As she approached the bar, she saw a white male at the entrance to the alley across the street and down from the bar. She didn't want to stare, so she slowed and looked at the business she was passing. Each time she turned to walk, she'd casually turn and look across the street. The guy was still there. It seemed odd, but she wasn't close enough to see him well. She stopped outside the bar, pulling her phone out, acting like she would make a call. Noble tapped the camera button and pretended to make a video. The man didn't move, but she saw she caught his attention. She turned around like she was talking to the phone and took several screenshots, hoping she could get the man. She tried not to make it evident that she was trying to get his picture. She turned around again and felt a firm hand on her shoulder.

"What the hell!"

"Sorry, Noble, it's only me."

"Tony, you're lucky you didn't lose a hand."

"What were you doing when I walked up?"

"Don't be obvious, but there's a guy across the street in the alleyway entrance. He looks suspicious, and I was trying to see if I could get a photo of him."

Tony pointed up the street and said, "He walked into the alley. That alley goes to the next block, and cameras are mounted on the telephone pole. Remind me to pull the video when we return to work next week."

"Sounds like a plan. It doesn't feel right, which means something is going on."

"Let's go in and see if Tracy has noticed anything out of the ordinary this last week."

Noble held the door open and said, "After you."

They entered the bar, and two tables had patrons. Tracy was helping pour drinks for her customers when she looked up, acknowledged their presence with a smile, and said, "I'll be right with you."

Noble and Tony walked over to a table in the corner and sat down. Tony had his back to the door, and Noble made sure he understood she wanted to face it. Noble recognized he hated sitting that way but knew to pick his battles.

"Hi, Detective Gentry. How can I help you and your partner today?"

"We were coming by to see how everything was going. Has anything unusual happened lately? Any odd mail, phone calls, or patrons that rubbed you the wrong way?"

"One day, after I passed a guy sitting at the bar, I felt uneasy—like the hair on the back of your neck standing up. It made me so uncomfortable that I locked the office door. I made a note to myself to pull the tapes. They're on my desk for that day. I haven't had time to look at them. There hasn't been any mail or phone calls I've answered or were noticed by my employees."

"Any chance we can take those tapes to review them?"

"Sure, let me grab them from the office."

"Thank you. Tony, this could be something. I'll take home the videos and start reviewing them. If I get anything, I will call you. When we leave here today, drive by the alley and see if that guy is still hanging out. Call dispatch and have a patrol unit respond to do a Field Interrogation card if he is. If we can add or mark him off, that will help us out in the long run."

"I can watch the tapes, seeing as you bought a gift for someone and might be busy."

Noble laughed and said, "I can still multitask, Tony. The gift recipient won't get it until Monday unless I make some accommodations for Sunday."

"Here are the tapes, Detective Gentry. Also, have you got anything back on that cigarette butt that I gave you. Remember when I told you about that night I saw the man with the cigarette, it gave me the same feeling as the guy at the bar. The funny thing is that I only saw the ember of a cigarette since it was night. Do you think it could be Billy Russell?"

"That's why we're here checking. I think he's still in town, but we're waiting for confirmation that he isn't in the state of Nevada. I'll call and update you once we get a yay or nay. In the meantime, we've requested extra patrol and one officer to be assigned to the bar. You'll be seeing more of Detective Vistole and me during the week. Even if we need to come in after shift, we will do everything we can to get him, Tracy."

"Thank you, Detective. That gives me some comfort."

"And here is my card if Detective Gentry is unavailable. I also put my cell phone number at the bottom. We're here to help you in any way we can."

"Thank you both. I won't let him scare me or control my life. I'm not his victim anymore, but a persistent survivor. People like him don't deserve to breathe our air, but we can't sink to their level, or they'll win. I'm delighted you're on my case again, Detective Gentry."

"Tracy, we'll get him. If it's not today, then it'll be tomorrow. He belongs behind bars, and we look forward to the day when that's where he'll be. Don't take any unnecessary chances and call us if you need to, regardless of the time of day or night."

"I can do that. Vera is staying with me, which makes me feel a little safer. We try not to turn on any lights in the apartment at night. Same with the television. I don't want anyone to know that someone lives up there. I've additional security cameras on the staircase going up and on the roof. They're on every entrance, exit, and window, too. The police department also monitors them, so if someone does set off the alarm, your department will respond."

"Great. Well, we will let you get back to work. I'll call you when we're done viewing the tapes."

"Thank you, detectives. Have a great rest of your evening."

"We'll be in touch."

Tony and Noble stopped outside the bar, and each scanned the street.

"I don't think he's over there anymore."

"Good. I'll let you know if I spot anything on the tapes or if I can get anything on my video from earlier. He's nearby. I can feel it."

"Whenever you get that feeling, you're always spot on. For me, there might be more frequent nights here at the bar. As a single guy, hitting two birds with one stone never hurts. Of course, I won't drink any alcohol, but I want to get a feel for the clientele and see if anyone seems out of sorts."

"You realize that this is a gay bar, right? And you're not gay."

"Yes, I realize that, but I have a couple of guy friends who are, and they won't mind coming with me. And before you ask, yes, they're cops, too. The more of us there are, the sooner we can get this guy."

"Great idea, Tony. I'll see you on Tuesday."

"You will. And on Tuesday, you can tell me who the gifts were for."

"I think I can do that," Noble said as she walked to her car and headed home. She hoped something on that tape was another piece of the gigantic puzzle.

CHAPTER TWENTY-ONE

"Why does it feel like that chick standing out front keeps looking over here? Might need to take a photo and see if I know her or if she's some nosy broad like that bitch." He pulled out his tiny camera and waited for her to look in his direction again. Pushing the zoom focus button, he snapped countless pictures and put the camera behind his back when some dude walked up and started talking to her. He then took some photos of the guy, too, in case they were cops. Billy wanted to know who they were if they began to hang around the bar. "Let's hope the quick trip to that small town in Nevada throws the cops off where I'm at. I don't want any distractions when I finally get my hands on that bitch, Tracy. She's going to wish she never identified me the first time," Billy said as he watched the business from the alley again. Once he saw them entering, he walked out of the alley and down the street in the opposite direction.

"Oh, excuse me." Billy looked up as he almost ran into a lady walking down the street. "Sorry about that, ma'am," Billy said as he continued walking.

"It's okay, young man. I wish more people your age were as considerate. What's your first name?"

"It's Billy," he said as he slowed his pace. "And you have a nice day yourself."

"Why, thank you."

"Goodbye," Billy said as he walked the three blocks to his hotel. "I wonder if I should go back and kill her since she's seen my face. Women are always nosy. She's lucky I've bigger fish to catch. Me being nice shouldn't throw up any red flags."

Entering his hotel room, Billy looked at all the stolen property on one of the two beds. People were stupid. Leaving their cars unlocked and their house windows wide open, it was easy to get around town and have some cash. Billy sat down and took the camera out of his pocket.

"Let's see who that chick was." As Billy turned on the camera and zoomed in on the picture, he said, "Shit, I think it's the damn pig that put me away—the one that worked that bitch Tracy's case. I need to break the password on this laptop here and see what I can find out about her. Might need to take her out as well." He turned on the computer and typed in 1234 for the password, and the computer allowed him access. "Someone stupid probably thought of that easy code. 1234. Wow, that was way too easy. The laptop must have belonged to a child or a woman. It's obvious no man with a brain would choose that as a password."

He entered the hotel wi-fi passcode and connected to the internet. Typing in his name and Tracy Snow, several articles came up. Clicking on the first article, Russell started laughing.

"They got it all wrong. What shitheads." He backed out, clicked on the next one, and repeated until he reached the bottom of the list of articles. He opened it, and it caught his attention. "Well, I'll be damned. This payback is going to be fun." As he continued reading, he exclaimed, "Shit, I did not know. But now that I do, things will get a lot more interesting down the road."

CHAPTER TWENTY-TWO

"Charlie said casual, so casual it will be," Noble said as she looked at herself in the mirror. "Jeans and T-shirt, it is." Noble grabbed a sweatshirt, backpack, and keys, and headed out the door. It took her about fifteen minutes to amble over to Charlie's house. Her heart was thudding, and it felt like it wanted to break out and cross the race's finish line. "Come on, Noble, take a deep breath and knock on the front door."

"Hi, Noble; I saw you at the door hesitating and decided to put you out of your misery. Come on in."

"Hey, Charlie, I figured since I was a couple of minutes early, I'd catch my breath before entering the lion's den."

"Get in here. Elizabeth won't eat you outright, but she might experiment with you before she eats you for dinner. I'm only kidding, well, maybe. I'm hoping she's on her best behavior."

"So, you're telling me you're unsure how this will go? Whew, I feel so much better. Not!"

"Come on, live dangerously," Charlie said as she got on her tiptoes and kissed Noble.

"Okay, that makes me feel much better," Noble said as she turned and connected with Charlie's lips in a quick kiss.

"Mom! Is she here yet?" Elizabeth yelled from the kitchen.

"We're coming. Hold your horses."

Noble could hear Elizabeth's laughter from the other room, which put a big smile on her face.

They entered the kitchen, and Charlie said, "Elizabeth, come on over here and meet—"

"Noole. I told my mom what you said that day we met when you were in uniform," Elizabeth said as she got down from the chair, ran up to Noble, and embraced her legs.

"Well, hello. It's great to see you again," Noble responded as she crouched down and looked at Elizabeth directly.

"How do you know my daughter?"

"We were at the coffeehouse after the police memorial. We, I mean, Leah had left a few minutes before, so it was only me. Elizabeth approached me to tell me that her family were officers, too. She was with a babysitter who chastised her for talking to a stranger."

"Can I hug you because we're not strangers anymore?"

"Yes, you can—"

"Yay. I'm glad you're here tonight," Elizabeth said as she launched herself at Noble, causing her to fall onto her back.

"Oh, my goodness, Elizabeth. Be careful and try not to hurt Noble."

"It's okay. She's a future linebacker but also a good hugger. It will take a lot more to hurt me than a hug."

"Will you watch my dinosaur movie with me later?"

"We're going to your Grandma Beth and Mimi's house tonight. When we come back here, it might be past your bedtime, young lady."

"Would another night work?" Elizabeth asked as she dropped her lower lip in a pout.

"Yes," Noble said.

"Can I have some input in this conversation?" Charlie piped in.

"Absolutely," Noble said as she grabbed Charlie's hand and tugged her down to the ground with her and Elizabeth.

"Wee, isn't this fun, Mom? Did Noole scare you? Noole, when my mom gets that look, it usually means someone is in trouble. You might be in trouble. I hope you don't get a timeout."

"Your mom wouldn't give me a timeout. We wanted her to join us, right?" Noble said as she brought Charlie and Elizabeth up to her chest and hugged them with each arm.

"The night is still young, ladies. How about we get off the floor and sit on the couch?"

"Okay, last one there's a sweet potato," Elizabeth said as she got up and ran toward the living room couch.

"Sweet potato? I don't understand that one. Can you give me some insight into it?" Noble inquired.

"Not sure to tell you the truth. Elizabeth has some odd sayings. But it's okay with me. Take my hand, and I'll help you up, OG."

Noble grabbed Charlie's hand, got yanked up like a kite raised by the wind, and was off the floor in a flash. "No timeout, right?"

"Not tonight. When you get put in a timeout, it will be because there will be plans to include you, me, and adult time," Charlie said, winking.

"Oh. Okay," Noble stammered.

"I love seeing you blush, Noble. I'm sorry. I'm unpolished and, in practical terms, say what comes to mind."

"Still getting used to it, but it's growing on me."

"Mom. Noole. When are you coming in here?"

"Coming, sweetie," Charlie bellowed.

Noble picked up the backpack she had set on the floor when Elizabeth plowed into her legs. Grabbing Charlie's hand, she said, "Lead the way."

Noble and Charlie sat on the couch while Elizabeth sat in her bean bag near the television.

"What's in your backpack, Noole?"

"Well, I brought something that we could play with."

Elizabeth jumped out of the beanbag and approached Noble to help her unzip the backpack.

"Go slow, Elizabeth. You can help Noble, so listen to what she says."

"Okay, Mom."

"Are you ready?" Noble traded a glance with Elizabeth.

"Yes."

They both slid the zipper open, and a wrapped box appeared. Elizabeth's eyes widened, and she waited until Noble nodded and helped her remove the box.

"How about you take the wrapping paper off?" Noble hitched her thumb toward the box.

"Okay," Elizabeth said as she slowly started peeling the paper off the box.

"Does she always take her time opening gifts?"

"Yes. She didn't get that from me. But if you tell her to rip it off, she will." Charlie laughed.

"Can you go any faster, Elizabeth? Then we can play with it until we have to leave." Noble laughed.

Elizabeth tore the paper off so quickly that Noble and Charlie laughed. She looked at her mom once the paper was off and screamed, "Dinosaurs! Look at all the dinosaurs. Can we play with them now? Please?"

"Only for a bit."

Elizabeth jumped up, threw her arms around Noble's neck, and said, "Thank you, Noole."

"You're welcome, sweetie. Let's open the box so we can get to the dinosaurs."

Elizabeth stood quietly, fidgeting until Noble opened the box and laid all the dinosaurs and the plastic mountain on the table.

"Here you go. You can play with them now."

"Oh boy, look at them. They're pretty," Elizabeth said as she got on her knees, picked up a dinosaur, and started playing.

Charlie reached over, squeezed Noble's forearm, and whispered, "Thank you. You didn't have to get her anything, but you scored some points with the dinosaurs."

"Her face lit up like mine when I got my first dinosaur set when I was little. It was well worth the investment. Look at how happy she is."

"Thank you," Charlie said as she leaned over and kissed Noble quickly.

"What was that for? Let me rephrase. I did not expect that. But thank you."

"You took the time to go out and get something for her. That means you care, and that's huge in my book." Charlie smiled.

"Well, she's likable, and anyone who thinks otherwise is an asshole," Noble scoffed.

"You're not supposed to say bad words, Noole. Remember, Mom will put you in a timeout."

"Sorry. Can you help me work on that? I might slip up repeatedly, but I will try hard not to use hurtful words," Noble admitted with a nod.

"Mom, she said sorry. Please don't put her in a timeout."

"She gets one free pass, but if it happens again, Mommy will put her in a timeout."

"Thank you, Mom," Noble said as she winked at Charlie.

Charlie leaned closer and whispered in her ear, "I'll be whatever you want me to be, but Mom has never crossed my mind. That's so far out of the atmosphere, you need to rethink that comment."

"You're so right because what I'm feeling for you is not motherly," Noble stated, sustaining eye contact and licking her lips.

"Hello, remember Noble, a child is present, so don't look at me like that."

"What're you two doing up there? Noole, will you play dinosaurs with me?"

"Saved by the bell. I will," Noble said, kissing Charlie quickly and then sliding to the floor where Elizabeth was.

"You two play nice. I will be in the kitchen finishing up a couple of things. If you two are good, you'll get a snack.

"Do you like snack time, Noole? I love snack time. Since you're here, we will get cookies. My Mom's cookies are the best. Does your mom make them for you?"

"I only get snack time on the weekends. She used to bake them for me when I was your age. After she died, my dad started making them for me."

"Sorry, I hope I didn't make you sad thinking about her," Elizabeth said as she jumped up, walked over, and hugged her.

"Thank you, sweetie. Mentioning her didn't make me sad. Instead, your hug made me happy."

"Why is that?" Elizabeth asked, a worried expression marred her face.

"Well, it shows me you care about people's feelings. That's an outstanding trait to have. You probably got it from your mom. Those are the people we should always surround ourselves with."

"Are you and my mom getting married?" Elizabeth asked. "My other mom is not nice. She always makes Mom cry, and that's mean. Mom makes me still see her, and I don't want to. Does that make me mean, too?"

"No, that means you love your mom a lot and don't want to see her hurt." Noble gave Elizabeth a subtle wink. "As for the next question of are we are getting married, not right now. We want to see each other and ensure everything will work before we take such a big step," she tacked on. "And what if you didn't like me? Your mom needs to agree because you're also an important puzzle piece. Do you understand?" Noble smiled.

"Yes. I know you're what we need. You'll keep us both safe. I knew it the day I saw you. You'd never be mean to my mom and me. I hope you like her and want to stay forever," Elizabeth replied.

"We're off to a good start. And yes, I do like your mom a lot. Even though this is new to us, I won the game before it started."

"I don't understand."

"Well, I will have your mom in my life, and you'll be there too. I plan to do things with you, and with you and your mom. How does that sound, Elizabeth?"

"Oh, so like you win because you get to spend time with me and Mommy?"

"Yes. That's the best part. Getting to know you both."

"So maybe we can go to the zoo and ride the rides at the playpark."

"We will talk with your mom about putting it on the calendar. Do you like the rollercoaster at the park, Elizabeth?"

"No, the one time I rode it, I thought my stomach would run out of my mouth. I wouldn't say I liked it. I love going out in the boats or on the train ride."

"That sounds like fun. I look forward to going with you and your mom."

"Me, too. Here, you can play with this dinosaur," Elizabeth said as she handed Noble a brontosaurus.

"I will be right back."

"Okay," Noble said.

†

Charlie stood outside the living room around the corner and listened to the entire exchange between Noble and her daughter. She turned her back and wiped a tear from her cheek. Taking a deep breath, she turned around and walked directly into a wall. *How the heck did I hit a wall? I wasn't that close to it.*

"Sorry about that. Are you okay?" Noble asked. Concern pinched her forehead in the middle.

Walls rarely had a conversation with you. Awe, man, I hope she didn't see me crying. What kind of cop cries?

"Charlie. Are you okay?"

"Yes. Sorry about that." She stepped back from Noble and looked her in the eyes.

"Come here." Noble tugged her back for a hug. "You heard our conversation, didn't you?"

"I was getting ready to come around the corner when I heard Elizabeth ask you about us. And the nosy part of me stayed put until I heard your answer. Besides, I didn't want to interrupt your deep conversation with my daughter." Charlie gave a partial smile. "I knew she didn't like her other mom, but I did not know she didn't enjoy going to see her. Now I feel like a terrible mom for making her go."

"I hope I didn't overstep my bounds by telling her I'd like to spend time with her. You could never be an awful mother, but now that you know, you should find out why she doesn't enjoy going." Noble fixed her gaze on Charlie. "Since your ex hasn't been nice to you, I'm okay if Elizabeth doesn't want to see her. What's this ex's name?" Noble asked.

"You didn't overstep, and I'm happy you both like each other. This relationship is all new to everyone involved." Charlie smiled. "So far, it's smooth sailing, but there will be blips, I'm telling you right now. And as far as the ex goes, her name is Naomi Bridgeport."

"Excuse me. Charlie, did you just say Naomi Bridgeport?"

"Do you know her? Please tell me you didn't date her?" Charlie stepped back and tilted her head up to look at Noble.

"Oh, hell no. That woman hit on Diana when we were dating and didn't care that Diana wasn't available. That's until I had a chat with her. I had to think out my response to her so she wouldn't try to get me in trouble at work. Sometimes it sucks to be deemed 'the thinker,' but luckily Diana calmed me down, and I spoke to Naomi a few days later."

"So, how did you meet her?"

"Diana and I were attending a police training conference out of town, and she set her sights on Diana in a class. Later that evening, we were in the hotel bar, and she hit on Diana. Mind you, I was sitting beside her with my arm around her.

She's lucky she got the courtesy of a conversation and not a busted jaw," Noble said, her nostrils flared with anger.

"Everyone sees me as 'the doer,' but she did a number on me, and it took me a while to realize that my loyalty to her was over after the second indiscretion," Charlie admitted. "We were probably together when she did that. Thank god my mom and Leah helped me, or I'm not sure I'd have recovered. And thank goodness you didn't punch her; she's not worth getting into trouble over," Charlie said as she pressed a hand to her mouth to stifle her giggles.

"Naomi and I are night and day. I treasure anyone willing to be in a relationship with me. I only do monogamous and expect the same from the person I'm seeing," Noble declared. "I never understood why someone would treat the person they love like that. You'll never have to worry about that with me. And your mom and Leah can attest to my character."

"That's good to know, but I'm a way better judge of character these days, and you'll get the same from me. One woman only for me."

"Let's make sure you're all cleaned up. No need to have Elizabeth see you like this," Noble said as she took a folded napkin out of her back pocket and dabbed Charlie's face to dry up any leftover tears.

"Mommy, are you okay? Why are you crying? Noole, you weren't being mean, were you?"

"Oh, Elizabeth, Noble was helping me dry some good tears from my face. She was being sweet."

"Okay, just making sure she wasn't being mean, or I might have kicked her in the leg to stand up for you. No one should ever hurt you. That's not nice."

"Hey, Bug, violence is not the answer. Remember what I said earlier about not being like mean people? Always be better," Noble said as she kneeled to look Elizabeth directly in the eyes.

"I will try, Noole, but sometimes it can be hard. Why did you call me Bug?"

"Since you gave me such a cool nickname, Noole, I thought Bug would work for you. Is there another name you want me to call you?"

"No, I like Bug."

"Okay, honey. It's past snack time, but it's time to go to Grandma and Mimi's house. Please go use the restroom, and we'll leave when you return."

"Be right back," Elizabeth yelled as she skipped to the bathroom.

"Don't forget to wash your hands," Charlie hollered.

"I won't."

"Bug, she'll love having her nickname. Oh, Noble Knight, what will I do with you?"

"That's me. Take it or leave it. Bug needs to know that violence is not the answer. On rare occasions, it can be, but she doesn't need to know that yet." Noble lifted her shoulder in a half shrug. "But if Naomi starts anything with you two, she'll also have me to answer to, although I'm sure I will be in line with your mom and Leah."

"Thank you for wanting to stand next to me in battle and not in front of me. I don't like to think of myself as weak, especially being in law enforcement," Charlie whispered, her eyes soft and filled with an inner glow. "And you're right; you'd be third, if not fourth, in line behind Elizabeth. I'm lucky to have you in my corner."

"Never in front, as you're a skillful warrior. But I will always be by your side or covering your back," Noble said as she kissed Charlie's forehead.

"Ready. Grandma and Mimi, here we come."

†

Leah was driving down her street when she saw two women and a small child walking. The child was in the middle, and each woman held her hand and swung her in the air. As her car approached closer, she recognized Charlie. "Oh, I wonder if she's bringing this new gal she's seeing." As she passed them, she saw that the other woman was Noble. "What the heck. Did they get here early and take Elizabeth for a stroll to wear her down? I hadn't thought they'd met. I'm on time, so they must have shown up early to visit with Beth." She pulled into her garage, and once she opened the door to the house, the aroma of a perfectly cooked meal filled her nose. "Honey, I'm home."

"Good. I'm glad you didn't get held over today. That means that Noble should be here on time as well," Beth said as she kissed Leah and took her briefcase.

"I saw Noble, Charlie, and Elizabeth walking here. They should be at the door any second. Did they come over early? Noble wanted to talk to me a few days ago about something, but I had to be somewhere, and with everything happening I figured we could talk tonight at dinner."

"Oh well, I can't wait to see Elizabeth," Beth said.

"You get to see her every day; I miss her fiercely. Maybe I can take her to the zoo this week," Leah grumbled.

"Maybe. If it's not during my time," Beth shot back as she snorted through her laughter.

"Wow! How about, if you're nice, I will let you go to the zoo with us," Leah said as she grabbed Beth, pulled her close, and kissed her.

"Didn't you hear us knocking at the door, Grandma and Mimi? Ew, what's with everyone kissing?" Elizabeth said with a windy sigh.

"You know Grandma and I kiss, so who else have you seen kissing, Elizabeth?"

"Mom and Noole. I like Noole. We played with the dinosaurs she brought me today. She's nicer than Mom Naomi. Noole's fun, and she makes Mom laugh."

"Noole? You mean Noble?" Beth inquired.

"Yep. Only I get to call her Noole," Elizabeth said.

"And you said your mom and Noole have been kissing?" Leah arched a questioning eyebrow in Beth's direction.

"Uh huh? They look all mushy, like you and Grandma."

"Hey, Mom. Hi Leah," Charlie said as she hugged each of them.

"Hello, sweetie. Elizabeth has been filling me and Beth in on some things."

"Oh. And what information did my baby girl divulge?"

"You and Noble have been kissing and being all mushy like her grandma's."

"Hi everyone. It smells delicious," Noble said as she walked into the kitchen, eight wide eyes staring back at her.

"Oh. That's a good thing. Thank you for helping Mommy out, Elizabeth."

"Did I miss something?" Noble said as she trained her gaze on Charlie.

"You didn't talk to Leah, Noble?"

"No, I tried a couple days ago, but she had to attend a meeting, so I figured I'd talk to her here. I probably should have let you know that I wasn't able to connect with her," Noble added apologetically.

"Oh boy. Sounds like Elizabeth filled them in on us being mushy with each other."

"Noole, I'm sorry. I think I got you into trouble with Mimi. It must not be good because I've never seen that look on her face. Sorry," Elizabeth said as she looked down at the floor, dejected.

"Bug, it's okay. You did nothing wrong. I think your grandmas are surprised, not mad. It will be alright. I promise. Come here," Noble said as she picked her up and hugged her reassuringly.

"Noble is right, sweetheart. Grandmas were surprised. How about I take you into the living room, and you can tell me about your day? I might even put in your favorite dinosaur movie to watch until we get the table ready for dinner," Beth said as she lifted her out of Noble's arms and into her own.

"Can I chat with Leah, just the two of us? I promise to come find you as soon as we have chatted," Noble said, holding her hands loosely behind her back.

"Okay, I will go hang with my mom and Elizabeth." Charlie nodded, a smile taking over her face.

"Before you say anything, Leah, I did not know who she was until technically our second or third date," Noble said as she threw her hands in the air. "I like her and want to spend time getting to know more about her and Elizabeth. I haven't felt this way since Diana, yet it feels different." She smiled a lopsided grin at Leah. "A good kind of different. Charlie stirs something in me, and I'm willing to go to the mat with you on this." Noble shifted her weight between her feet and rocked from side to side, like a boxer keeping her muscles warm before the bell.

"That's reassuring, as I'd hate to kick your ass for hurting my little girl. What's it about Charlie that's different from Diana?"

"Charlie exudes a breath of fresh air, and I appreciate her unwavering loyalty, candidness about the status of our relationship, and determination to fight for genuine, true love." Noble took a deep breath. "She also said that she and Elizabeth were a package deal. That sealed it for me—her love for her child and how she put her first. You don't see that too much anymore. And I want the package deal. I couldn't imagine anyone not wanting Elizabeth in their lives," she said, a wide smile spread across her face. "Don't even get me started about Naomi. You know me, and I'd never act the way she did. Cheating is not in my DNA. She knows my heart got hurt in the past, but she's not demanding to know everything right now. She wants me to feel comfortable to tell her when I'm ready. And believe me, it will be soon, as I need to trust her like she's trusted me with Elizabeth."

"That was what I wanted to hear. But let me reiterate, Noble, that I will make your life miserable if you hurt either. They're mine and Beth's lives. I won't see them go through what they went through with Naomi again. Do you understand where I'm coming from?" Leah warned.

"Absolutely. But you should know one thing—"

"What's that?" Leah stretched out the last word for emphasis.

"When and if this becomes serious, and knowing me, it probably will. Marriage is serious; I intend to ask you and Beth for her hand in marriage. I'm old school that way and feel the parents deserve that respect, even you, Leah," she said as her chin notched up a few inches. "You saw that respect when I was with Diana. I know Charlie isn't Diana, but she will get that same respect. And besides, there's something special about Charlie, and I look forward to discovering what that is."

"That's good to know, but don't you dare call me your mother-in-law? I'll kick your ass on that point, too," Leah said, laughing.

"Oh, good lord, never."

"Everything okay in here?" Charlie asked as she entered the room.

"So, why didn't you tell me instead of making Noble?"

"She offered, and I didn't think it would be a problem, Mom L."

"You both have my blessing, but I'll tell you what I told Noble. If she hurts you, she'll answer to me."

"My god, you know I can fight my own battles now." Charlie shook her head.

"I do, but it never hurts to have reinforcements." Leah shrugged.

"Thank you, but I don't foresee a problem like what happened last time."

"I know, sweetheart, but we moms must watch out for our little girl, no matter how old she is."

"Thank you. And I love you for that, but be here for both of us," Charlie said as she kissed Leah.

"Look at that. You'd have thought I stole your lunch money, Noble," Leah said as she snorted through her laughter.

"It will never happen. I'm not worried about it, but facing a Leah Harper firing squad deserves something, too. Just my two cents." Noble waggled a finger at Leah.

"You two, will you stop it? And when I look at you, Noble, it's more like looking at all the candy in a store and finding the right one to feed your craving," Charlie said as she kissed Noble.

"Whoa, I didn't need to hear that. Moms shouldn't hear anything like that at all. Beth, is it time for dinner?" Leah asked as she walked toward the living room.

Both Noble and Charlie broke out in laughter as Leah covered her eyes and ears. Noble looked down at Charlie and lowered her head, claiming her mouth in a deep kiss that promised their future together.

"Wow, Noble, I love how you kiss. You make my toes curl, and my entire body gets the tingles. Mmm, I love that feeling."

"Stop. It would be best if you behaved yourself. Especially at your parents' house with Elizabeth in the other room."

"Spoilsport," Charlie said as she grabbed Noble's hand and walked toward the living room where everyone else was watching dinosaurs.

"Charlie, why don't you, Noble, and Elizabeth prepare the table for dinner? That way, we can be mushy for a couple of minutes."

"Grandma, ew. Let's go, Noole and Mom," Elizabeth said as she jumped up and ran into the kitchen.

"Ew is right, Bug, wait for me. Come on, Charlie."

"I'll be right there," Charlie said as she walked over to the couch, bent down, and hugged her mom and Leah. "Thank you for your support. I may have gotten it right this time."

"You did, Charlie. Time will show that. I'm not sure why Leah or I never set you two up, but you both were happy and in relationships, so it didn't cross our minds. I'm so glad you've found each other now. You both deserve happiness, and Elizabeth is one fortunate girl."

"I agree, Beth. Now scram, kiddo, while we spend a few moments together. Just yell when it's time to sit down."

"I can't believe my parents are sending me out of the room so they can make out on the couch. Wait a minute. It is because you two haven't changed one iota, and I hope to have this someday."

"Oh, believe me, you will. Have you not seen the way Noble looks at you? Get ready to be treated like the princess you are. You'll think, 'Why the hell did I waste my time on Naomi when Noble has been waiting in the wings,'" Beth said.

"I look forward to it. And I'm pretty sure Elizabeth does too."

"Charlie, we could use a little help in here," Noble called out.

"I'm coming."

†

Beth and Leah lay on the couch next to each other and giggled like two schoolgirls as they kissed and whispered sweet nothings in each other's ears. When Beth rolled on top of Leah and pushed her hips down onto Leah's, a small moan escaped her mouth. The friction of their jeans sent both their arousals into overdrive.

"Sweetheart, we need to slow this train down, as we have company in the other room." Leah inhaled a stuttering breath.

"You love to torture me, don't you?" Beth exhaled.

"We can pick up where we left off when our company leaves." Leah had a mischievous look plastered on her face.

"Can we send them home now?" Beth tapped her fingers on Leah's chest.

"No, that would be rude. Are you ready? Let's sit on the opposite ends of the couch until they call us for dinner."

"You're kidding, right?" Beth said but moved to the other end of the couch.

"Coming in, heads up."

As Noble and Charlie entered the living room, they laughed when they saw Beth and Leah sitting at opposite ends of the couch.

"What's so funny?" Beth asked as she looked at Leah with a questioning look.

"On second thought, I don't think we want to know. Let's go eat," Charlie uttered.

Once everyone sat and started serving themselves, the talking ceased.

"Thank you for having me over, Beth. I've missed seeing you and missed your cooking." Noble relaxed into a smile.

"I'm glad you're back, Noble. It's been a long time, and with today's news, we hope to see you more frequently." Beth leaned forward at her words.

"Thank you, Beth, and you will."

"Noole, when can you do a sleepover at my house?"

Noble's eyes doubled in size.

"When your mommy says so," both Beth and Leah replied.

"Elizabeth, this isn't the type of conversation for the dinner table."

"Sorry, Mom, I'm excited to make a fort with Noole and sleep in it."

"It's okay, Bug. We can talk about it later," Noble said. "If you still have one, maybe devise a plan to make the fort right before your nap time on the weekend. That way, we can all build it. Only if it's okay with your mom," she suggested.

"Can we make a plan, Mom?"

"Yes, honey. We can plan," Charlie replied.

"Now that it's settled, how about Elizabeth and I watch a movie while you three talk shop?" Beth proposed.

"Thanks, sweetie. We'll make it quick. After all, Charlie needs to clear the table, and Noble will wash the dishes before they head home."

"You know we don't have guests doing the dishes. And that's your job since I do the cooking." Beth shot Leah a look.

"Since when did family become categorized as guests? No worries, Charlie and Noble will be happy to help, right, ladies?"

"No problem at all, Leah. Seeing as I'm not one hundred percent family yet."

"Oh lord. Mom, spend some time with Elizabeth, and I'll keep these two on task."

"Okay, okay. I will do the dishes after our talk," Leah said as her eyes rolled skyward.

"Mom L, stop rolling your eyes."

†

"Charlie, did Noble fill you in on this Russell character?" Leah moved her plate to the side, leaned forward, her fingers laced before her on the tabletop.

"Yes, she did, and we can't wait for the joint briefing. The quicker we get this guy off the street, the safer the citizens of Onserf will be."

"I don't think we really need to talk about this since you've been filled in," Leah said.

"Good. Now, let's get the table cleared and the dishes done. Your moms probably want to spend some quality time together, and we don't want to keep Bug up too late," Noble said as she carried dishes into the kitchen. They spent the next fifteen minutes washing and cleaning up.

"Charlie, why don't you let her stay the night, and your mom will bring her back to your house sometime tomorrow?" Leah said as they walked back into the living room. Beth and Elizabeth were asleep on the couch, snuggled under a blanket.

"Okay, although I hate to leave her here. You both have helped me out already."

"That's what grandparents are for. Now, you both get on your way and be careful on your short trek home. Let me know when you get to your house so I won't worry," Leah said.

"Thank you and tell Mom I'll chat with her tomorrow morning. Love you."

"Good night, Leah," Noble said as she followed Charlie out the door.

"Love you too, Charlie. And Noble, I will also expect your text when you get home."

"Message received, boss," Noble groaned as she and Charlie walked off the porch toward the sidewalk leading them back to Charlie's house.

†

Leah walked in and gently kissed Beth on the forehead. "Come on, let's get you and Elizabeth to bed. She can sleep with us tonight."

"Sorry, we fell asleep. It was a long day," Beth mumbled.

"It's okay. It happens to the best of us. I'll grab the munchkin after I turn off all the lights. Head up and turn down our bed so we can all collapse and sleep."

"You're such a keeper," Beth whispered as she stood.

"Ditto!" Leah mouthed as Beth walked past her toward their bedroom.

After turning off all the lights and doing a quick walk-through, Leah picked up Elizabeth and headed to their bedroom. As she entered, she saw Beth smiling at her.

"What're you smiling at?"

"Seeing you with Elizabeth brought back some wonderful memories of when Charlie was that age," Beth admitted.

"They're two peas in a pod. Especially with spilling information about mushy stuff." Leah grinned.

"I thought Noble handled it extremely well tonight."

"I agree, Beth. But if our dear friend Noble hurts our girls, she knows we won't only kick her ass but make life as she knows it unbearable."

"You'll have to wait your turn because there might not be much of her left after she answers to me," Beth said as she shrugged. "Now kiss me so we can sleep before the munchkin wakes up. And yes, you owe me a raincheck from earlier. I hope to collect soon." Her lips brushed Leah's ear, raising goose bumps across her skin.

"Yes, ma'am," Leah said as their lips met.

†

"It's clear now," Charlie whispered.

"What?"

"If you want to hold my hand, it's clear now. In case you were afraid of Leah seeing us."

"Sorry, I was checking out the neighborhood. I got a little preoccupied, especially with it being nighttime and all. Even if I were afraid of Leah, I would always hold your hand," Noble proclaimed as she squeezed Charlie's hand.

"It's good to know that I'm not the only one who scans an area they're walking through. Do you see the car at the end of the block?"

"You mean the one with the dome light that just dimmed?" Noble said, using a quiet voice so that Charlie was the only one that could hear her.

"That's the one—just a little Frank Yellow Ida. You know, for your information only. I've never seen it on my block before. Looks out of place."

"Duly noted. I'll see if I can get a picture of the plate as we go by."

Noble put her arm around Charlie's neck as they continued up the block and took her phone out. They stopped on the sidewalk under the streetlight and touched their heads together as Noble put her phone up so they could take a selfie.

"Can you see the plate yet? Charlie whispered.

"Almost. We need to get at least one car closer since they parked outside the streetlight range."

"Okay, honey, whatever you say. I want to get a fantastic picture of us," Charlie broadcast, presumably hoping the person in the vehicle would not mind them taking a picture.

They walked about ten more steps when Noble pulled out her phone, pulled Charlie closer, and started taking photos of the car.

"This is the last one, or we'll be out here all night. I want to get home."

"Thanks, honey," she said as she raised up on her tip toes and kissed Noble on the cheek.

"It looks like we can check on this tomorrow. Here's a nice, clean shot of the license plate," Noble stammered as her startled eyes swung Charlie's way.

"Let's go, spoilsport. I don't want you to turn into a pumpkin since it's almost after your bedtime." Charlie tugged Noble's arm, pulling her forward until they walked side by side. They passed the car and continued walking down the street. They heard the engine start once they crossed the street and were about five cars away.

"Charlie, I don't think we should go into your house. If this person is up to no good, they don't need to know where you live," Noble said.

"I agree with you completely. Let's get in your car and go around the block. If they follow us, we know something is up. If they go another way, maybe we spooked them, and they won't return to the area again."

Looking toward the suspicious car, Noble opened her vehicle's passenger door, waiting until Charlie was securely inside before shutting it. She walked around to get into the driver's seat. She started her car, looked in the rearview mirror, and drove away from the curb. Noble noticed the vehicle make a U-turn and head in their direction. Once she reached the stop sign, she turned right onto a major street, driving under the speed limit. Charlie was looking behind them and saw the other car's headlights as it turned left onto the same street they were on and went in the opposite direction.

"Well damn, maybe it was another criminal since it doesn't look like he's following us," Charlie said as she faced Noble.

"That's a good thing. Now I feel a little better driving you back to your house. Hopefully, it was some random person visiting a friend and was leaving when we were walking by," Noble said.

"I might contact my neighbor and see if they had anyone over last night. And if they did, ask what kind of car they drive."

"I'll call dispatch now and have them run the vehicle. I don't want to wait until tomorrow in case something happens," Noble replied as she gathered her phone to make the call.

"This is Shelley. How may I help you?" the dispatch supervisor answered the phone.

"Hi Shelley, it's Detective Gentry, badge P as in Paul 577. Can you run a vehicle plate for me?" Noble asked.

"Hi, Noble, give it to me," Shelley replied.

"It's 7V14598. Should come back to a GMC pickup," Noble stated.

"Noble, it comes back clear and is registered to a Kelsey Cooper in Onserf."

"Can you send me a copy of the printout with all that information, in addition to any calls at that address, and let me know if the registered owner has ever been contacted by anyone at the department?" Noble asked.

"Will do. It'll be on your desk in the morning. Good night."

"Thank you. Have a good night," Noble said before ending the call.

"Now that we've done all we can on this, I think the evening went well with Mom and Mom L tonight."

"One thing I've always loved about Leah is her fierceness and loyalty to her family and close friends. And I truly believe she'd kick my ass."

"You're right, Noble. They both would. My mom had to use everything in her arsenal to keep Mom L from destroying Naomi. I believe she had her transferred to some crappy detail for a while."

"I remember that. Leah's entire shift wanted to kick her ass, including me. However, Leah's and my reasoning were completely different," she said as she kept her tongue in check. "You for Leah and Diana for me. And now that we're together, all bets are off if she messes with you or Elizabeth." Her fingers coiled into tight balls.

"I was onto something when I named you Noble Knight. It fits you perfectly," Charlie said, a gleam in her eyes. "But please don't waste your time thinking about her. She's not worth it. Pull over right here, and you can escort me to my door."

"Yes, ma'am!" She exited the driver's side, walked around the car, opened Charlie's door, and extended her hand.

"Thank you." Charlie grabbed her hand and got out of the car.

Noble pulled Charlie in for a hug and a quick kiss. Using what little leverage she had, Charlie turned them both around and lightly pushed Noble up against the now-closed car door.

"I want to invite you in, but the rules of going slow would be out the window. So, I will settle for some kissing out here where it's safe."

As Noble's lips hungrily met Charlie's, she whispered, "I can't help but wonder how safe it is for us to be out here, appearing as one person or two, indulging in our naughty desires." The intensity of their connection was undeniable, as their bodies seemed fused in that moment.

Charlie tried to get closer to Noble, but she could only pump her hips into Noble's thigh. She slowly inched her hands under Noble's shirt and growled as the kiss intensified.

"We need to stop," Noble gasped as she enclosed Charlie's hands and brought them out from underneath her shirt.

"Wow! We got a little carried away."

"Just a little." She kissed Charlie on the forehead.

"I think we need to go to our ends of the couch, so to speak." Charlie laughed as she stepped away.

"Well, as soon as I get home, I will have a fantastic dream." Her gaze fell onto Charlie. "I'll text you when I get there so you know I made it. Meanwhile, you've about five minutes to get inside and check your house and ensure the whole house looks okay, or I'm coming in." Noble pulled a slow smile.

"Okay. And I will see you at the briefing tomorrow. Good night, Noble," Charlie uttered as she walked away, unlocked her front door, and entered her home.

Noble stood, feeling like five minutes was an eternity until her phone beeped.

All looks fine in here. Sweet dreams, and I'll see you tomorrow.

Sweet dreams, Charlie, and I'll text you when I get home.

Noble pulled away from the curb and headed home. Along the way, she noticed the car from earlier parked in front of a business less than a block from her house.

"Well, that's odd. Something doesn't seem right. What are the odds of this car being here?" Noble said to no one as she slowly drove past the vehicle.

The vehicle had someone in the driver's seat wearing a baseball cap which was pulled down, partially covering their face. It was hard to see inside since they were not parked under a streetlight. After she passed the vehicle, Noble looked into her rearview mirror, and she saw the red ember glow of a cigarette and the driver flicking the cigarette butt out the window. Noble made a mental note to do more digging on that license plate once she got into the office tomorrow. *Something doesn't feel right.* As she turned onto the side street near her house, she looked in her side mirror and saw the exact vehicle pulling away from the curb, heading in her direction. Noble had about a block to make it home. Her garage, connected to the back of her house, opposite where she entered. She hit her clicker to open it, sped up the half block, pulled into her driveway and garage, and clicked the button to close it. Noble exited her vehicle, walked through her backyard, and looked through her fence to see if the car was following her.

"Shit, this is more than a coincidence," she decided as she saw headlights coming down the street from the direction she'd just come. She didn't dare move as she didn't want to set off the floodlights near her. "It's the same damn car," Noble declared under her breath. The car was almost past her house when her phone started blaring, one of her favorite ringtones, letting her know someone was trying to get a hold of her. "Fuck…fuck…fuck!" Noble slowly reached down and hit the button to silence her phone. Praying to all the gods, she hoped no one heard it other than herself. But she was sure one other person heard it as the car stopped in the middle of the road for what felt like a lifetime. Then the driver revved the engine and sped down the street out of sight.

Noble removed her phone and saw that the missed call was from Charlie. She quickly dialed her number and waited for her to answer the phone. Unlocking the back door, Noble entered, closed it, and locked it behind her. She avoided turning on any lights, in case the person decided to drive by again.

"Are you okay? You should be home by now. I wanted to ensure you're alright, and I missed your voice." Charlie peppered her with questions.

"Can I say something now?" Noble said as she chuckled.

"Yes! I suppose you can now, sorry."

"It makes my heart smile that you're worried about me, so no more apologies. I spied the car we saw earlier when we were walking home and noticed it parked a block from my house," Noble stated. "Although I couldn't see who was inside, I managed to park my car in the garage, hoof it to the side of my house, and witness it drive by."

"What the hell? It has to be related to one of your cases, Noble."

"It stopped when my ringtone went off. I don't think the driver saw me, but you, my dear Charlie, had crummy timing through no fault of your own."

"Oh boy, I'd have loved to see your face. We need to make sure we rerun that plate tomorrow to ensure that it wasn't an unreported stolen vehicle. Something is going on, which is not leaving a good feeling in my gut."

"Agreed. We need to let Leah and Beth know. Get some sleep, and I'll see you tomorrow."

"You as well, Noble."

Noble laid her phone down after the call ended and got ready for bed. *There has to be a connection between this car and Billy Russell. If that's the case, the idea of me staying with Charlie needs to be brought up with Charlie, Beth, and Leah.* When Noble's head hit her pillow, she fell fast asleep.

†

Russell couldn't believe his fucking luck. He only needed to find out what houses those bitches lived in, although he was sure that fucking ringtone going off was at the house he stopped in front of. She must've been watching to see if he was following her. Russell had to exercise caution to ensure the successful completion of the task without getting caught.

He anticipated that leaving the car in the vicinity would sufficiently unsettle her, preventing her from noticing his approach when the time came to eliminate her. Maybe he'd even leave her a little surprise gift. *They're going to pay for what they did to me. No man should be in prison for taking what is rightly his.* Russell parked the stolen car and made his way back to his hotel. Tomorrow, he'd steal another one and figure out his next move. He took one final drag of his seventh cigarette that night, flicked it onto the pavement, and walked away.

"Every last one of them will pay. And they will pay with their life!" Russell spat out into the crisp night air.

CHAPTER TWENTY-THREE

Noble was looking out the driver's side window at two women sitting on a bench and they appeared to be involved in a conversation. The women were holding hands and smiling at each other. *Oh, Diana, I think I found someone. You'd like her. You two would be best friends. According to you, she'd like you, too! If anyone had asked me a month ago if there could ever be anyone to care about again, my answer would have been, I don't know if I ever could because it hurts too hard losing you. I still miss you, yet I am thrilled I've found Charlie. You will always be my first love, but like you used to say, my heart can hold much love from many people.* A horn honking brought Noble back to reality. Noble blinked, looked up, and saw that the signal light had turned green, and she proceeded through the intersection. Noble had to make it to a briefing on time or else she'd buy pizza for the entire district.

Noble pulled into the district station parking lot, exited her vehicle, and headed for the back door. As she entered the building at a full sprint, she collided with a body small in stature, fit, and most likely belonging to a woman. Two lovely-sized breasts cushioned Noble's fall outside the women's locker room. This body felt familiar. They fell to the ground, and Noble began an apology when she looked up into the most beautiful blue eyes she'd ever seen. Yep! That body sure felt familiar. Those intoxicating eyes, daring her to say something, caused Noble to stop midsentence. Noble couldn't help but get lost in Charlie's mesmerizing beauty, all thanks to those breathtaking eyes. If Noble didn't know any better, she would have sworn she caught a glimpse of a mischievous twinkle in those eyes.

Noble's eyes slowly lowered. She saw long blonde hair, gorgeous full lips, a soft, delectable neck, and two lovely breasts hidden behind clothing. Her skin became erect with goosebumps as her eyes rested on Charlie. Even when they collided, their bodies fit perfectly.

"Noble."

Noble blinked, looked up, and saw Sergeant Harper looking down at her.

Oh crap, I need to help Charlie up off the ground. Am I never going to hear the end of this from Leah? She wanted to laugh, but always the professional, she didn't. Noble's mind was running on overload and, for once, was at a loss for words. *I shouldn't be ogling Charlie like this at work.* She needed to keep it professional.

Noble stammered, "Sorry," and put her hand out to assist Charlie in getting up off the ground. Once Charlie was standing, Noble realized she was the perfect height, as Charlie's head only came up to Noble's chin. She loved being able to rest her head on top of Charlie's.

Noble turned to Sergeant Harper and realized that she'd yet to say something. Noble put out her hand and stated, "I'm

Detective Noble Gentry," she said, trying to make it appear that they'd never met and keeping it professional.

Charlie responded by taking Noble's hand in a firm handshake and replying, "Special Agent Charlie Matthews." She followed it up with a wink in Noble's direction.

Noble felt a shock that sent her pulse racing throughout her body as their hands intertwined. She looked into Charlie's eyes and presumed she could feel it, too.

Noble smiled. "Nice to meet you, Special Agent Matthews."

"Please, call me Charlie, and may I call you Noble? Formalities are better used with rank, right, Sergeant Harper?"

Sergeant Harper nodded as she let out a booming laugh.

Noble thought she must have missed something between those two. Sergeant Harper would never act like this with a stranger. Oh my! Leah is getting in on the ruse. Wait till Beth hears about her wife's acting skills.

"Leah is my stepmother," Charlie replied.

"Your stepmother," Noble enunciated with shock.

Leah let out another booming laugh when she saw Noble's unfamiliar look. "Okay, you two, let's put this to rest and head on into the briefing room. People will soon know enough about you two based on how you look at each other. Let's finish this so we can focus on Billy Russell."

Noble watched Charlie and Leah hug each other, and all three headed into the briefing room.

Tony Vistole met up with Noble as the briefing started.

"Do you think SPAT is trying to save face after Russell absconded parole?" Noble asked Tony.

"We would if we were in the same position," Tony replied as he shrugged his shoulders.

Noble felt the hair on the back of her neck rise like someone was watching her, so she slowly lifted her head and panned to her left and right. She saw nothing unusual, so her radar must be off. Noble couldn't shake that feeling and looked up again. And across the room, her eyes made contact and locked with Special Agent Matthews. There was that twinkle she had seen earlier in Charlie's telling eyes. Noble knew she was in trouble. She had quickly fallen for Charlie and was happy about it. But she wondered if she deserved to be this happy.

Charlie smiled and raised one eyebrow as if boldly declaring, "I like what I see," to Noble. Noble slowly tried to control her breathing and nodded as if agreeing with Charlie's assessment. *What am I doing? I don't flirt! And not with someone while at work!* She was becoming sure that she was ready for whatever this was.

Tony and Leah smiled when they saw Charlie and Noble's silent interaction. Tony had told her repeatedly that he believed it was time for Noble to date again. It had been a long time since Tony had seen her like this, not since Diana. Noble knew Tony wanted the best for his work partner and would do anything to help Noble be happy again.

†

Leah knew she was taking a risk with Charlie and Noble but believed they'd be happy together. She figured that continuing to break the ice would put them in a situation where they would have to rely on each other's instincts and training.

Sergeant Harper assigned details to all agents and detectives involved in the operation. They'd pair Tony up with Special Agent Mike Taylor, and their job would be to sit in a van in the parking lot and watch the business where the victim, Tracy Snow, worked.

The SPAT team believed Russell wanted to get to his last victim, Tracy Snow, and either rape her again or kill her. Leah sensed that Noble was anxiously awaiting her assignment when she advised Noble she'd be working with Special Agent Matthews.

†

Noble and Charlie snapped their heads up, looking directly at Sergeant Harper. Other than a chuckle or two, you could have heard a pin drop in the briefing room. Noble saw Tony and Mike give each other a thumbs up, probably because they were best friends. She looked at Tony and shrugged, unsure if they already knew she and Charlie were dating.

Sergeant Harper advised Charlie and Noble what their assignment would entail. They'd be a couple that frequented the bar regularly. That way, they could monitor Tracy Snow or work at the bar. The guys started hooting and hollering with some whistling while Charlie and Noble were at a loss for words.

The operation was to commence officially next Friday night. Today was only Wednesday, and Noble had to entertain half the thought that Charlie was her 'work' girlfriend, which she already was. Noble took a deep breath and closed her eyes.

"Noble, are you okay?" Leah asked as she walked toward her.

Opening her eyes, she mumbled, "Breathe in, breathe out, come on, girl, it will be okay!" Noble nodded and turned toward Charlie. She noticed that she had a smirk on her face.

Noble thought, *damn, she'll be the death of me, and we haven't even done anything more than kissing yet!*

"What're you laughing at?" Noble asked Charlie.

Charlie responded, "At least you're much better looking than my partner, Mike Taylor."

Noble immediately blushed. *I never blush, so the guys will know that something is up.*

"I'd take offense to that, Matthews, if it weren't the truth," Agent Taylor replied as he jerked his shoulders in a shrug.

"You know you're my only partner at work, Mikey," Charlie said as she tossed him the side eye.

Noble noticed Tony watching her as she shrunk in the corner and turned a lovely shade of red.

"Hey, Mikey, let's go to Patrick's Pub for a drink at the end of the shift, and it's even on me."

†

Charlie smiled and felt like this would be a great crew to work with and even better for her as she got to work with Noble. *Something about her makes me want to declare my eternal love for her, yelling from the highest mountaintop worldwide.* That Elizabeth already adored her was risky enough for her to take it as far as they were both willing. *Mom L initially said to stay away from her officers, but I'm not sure it will be that easy with Noble. Thank god she and Mom already gave us their blessing.*

"Hey Noble, would you and Tony like to join us? Leah said she might catch up with us later after she finished her paperwork in half an hour," Charlie asked, a mischievous look plastered on her face.

Not giving Noble a chance to decline the invite, Tony replied, “Yes, we’d like that. Thank you.”

As Noble and Tony were walking out of the substation, Noble looked at Tony, who had a massive grin, and said, “Don’t even go there!”

CHAPTER TWENTY-FOUR

Leah rushed into her office and dialed her wife's number before either Charlie or Noble could corner her and ask her a billion questions.

"The keeper of my heart. What do I owe the pleasure of receiving a phone call from you?" Beth cooed as she sounded out of breath.

"Oh my, I'm not sure what you were doing, but if I can assist you, let me know, and I can be home in ten minutes," Leah purred into the phone.

"I love you so much. You can take care of that later when you're off the clock for the day." Beth chuckled. "I was doing housework, but I'd much rather do what you had in mind. Anyway, how did your briefing go?"

"Well, Noble plowed into Charlie; they both hit the ground. It was awkward for all three of us. We pretended not to know who each other was, especially because it looked like our good friend Noble wanted to skip right on to dessert." Leah gulped down a steadying breath. "So, I decided during the briefing to pair them up as a couple on the Billy Russell case. I thought Noble was going to bust an aneurysm on me," Leah said as she released a drawn-out exhale.

"Oh boy, you like to play with fire, my dear. I hope Charlie and Noble can keep their heads in the game long enough to arrest that shithead, Russell," Beth replied.

"Don't worry, I've a plan. I will be inside the business. It may be as a patron or a worker. That way, an extra set of eyes will be there if anything goes wrong inside."

"Leah, please be careful and take care of not only yourself but the girls as well. Noble is getting to a place she hasn't been in a long time, and we need to guarantee nothing derails that."

"Always careful, as I have you to come home to. Speaking of coming home, the group is going out for a few drinks. Can I go? It would only be for a couple of hours," Leah said, her voice sweet and smooth like syrup.

"Yes, have fun with the crew, and I'll see you when you get home. If you need me to pick you up, call me. I love you. And Elizabeth will be staying with us tonight. Charlie called and asked, since everyone is going out tonight."

"Will do. I love you, too! That'll be good for Charlie, to get out and relax. Goodbye."

†

They all sat down in the booth at Patrick's and ordered their drinks. Both Noble and Charlie were sitting across from each other in the booth. Noble was never this quiet, and she was always the one who did the pursuing. That was until she found Diana. Diana was a breath of fresh air and didn't take too kindly to Noble's pursuit. It took months before Diana would go out with Noble. After the first date, they were inseparable. Diana made life worth living, and that all came to a halt when an unknown suspect who'd tried to rape a woman ran her over, killing her, as he fled the scene. And now Charlie. She found that her heart slowly swept up into Charlie's, and for the first time, she thought she might head to forever. And the bonus was not only Charlie's breath of fresh air but Elizabeth's.

Noble blinked, looked across the table at Charlie, and felt like a cradle robber. The funny thing was that Noble had done nothing except kiss Charlie! But she couldn't wait to take the next step. "I honestly shouldn't be having thoughts like this about my friend's daughter. But she feels like the main character in my life story. The one that saves the day and gets the girl. I need to stop worrying about Leah and Beth. This is between me and Charlie. Four years have passed, and I need to move on. That's what Diana would have wanted, but I'm afraid to let anyone get close for fear of losing them," Noble mumbled. Noble knew it was only a matter of time before something would happen between her and Charlie. The thought of it not only excited her, but it also terrified her at the same time.

"I beg your pardon. Were you saying something?" Looking up from her drink, Charlie gazed into Noble's eyes.

"Oh, I apologize. I'm just talking to myself," Noble replied with a smile, feeling the intensity of her passion. *I wonder if Charlie can sense my desire when she looks at me. Perhaps Charlie's imagining my eyes igniting after a night of fiery, raw intimacy. She might be pondering that based on her expression.* A warm, rosy blush tinted Charlie's cheek. Noble met her gaze, causing her blush to deepen into a full scarlet hue.

"Excuse me, I need to use the restroom. When I return, Gentry, get ready to play some darts," Charlie announced as she walked away.

"Shit, I don't know how to play darts," Noble replied to a laughing Tony and Mike.

"Well, she's a natural at it. All I can say is don't bet against her because you'll lose every time," Mike answered. "Get ready, here she comes."

"Let's go, Gentry. I'll be gentle with you, I promise," Charlie said as she chuckled.

"Alright, Matthews. I'll try to be as gentle with you," Noble replied with one eyebrow raised.

Noble shouldn't be worried; she knew that. How hard could it be to hit the dart board? She had a plan that always relied on her natural ability to be accurate, coupled with distraction and alcohol. Noble had confidence and the basic knowledge of how to play darts. Darts was a more relaxing extension of her day job. The precision of the dart as she aimed at the cork felt as steady in her hand as her firearm during qualifications at the range. Noble only needed to focus, follow her game plan, and try not to think about Charlie. Easier said than done. She closed her eyes and silently prayed as she turned to Charlie.

"Do you want to warm up or get started on a game?" Charlie asked as she handed Noble three darts.

"Let's play one practice game; it's been a while since I last played. I need to get the cobwebs out of my arm, and I'll be ready to go," Noble replied.

"I'll go first," Charlie answered as she sank all three darts in the bull's eye in under twenty seconds. She turned to Noble and said, "Your turn."

"You've got to be kidding. You're some professional dart player on the side, right?" Noble looked at Charlie.

"No, I played darts while working stressful cases in my house. It helped me relax," Charlie replied with a wink.

Noble threw her first dart, which landed beautifully on the wood wall behind the dart board. Her second and third darts had the same fate.

"Shit, it's good we didn't wager a bet. I have a feeling I'll be no competition for you," Noble answered, looking at Charlie.

"First off, you're standing wrong. Why are you leaning backward like you're afraid of the board?" Charlie said as she came and stood right behind Noble.

Noble tensed, her body going on high alert. Charlie placed her hands on Noble's hips and turned her to face the dartboard. She got on her tiptoes and whispered to Noble, "Always turn and face the board. Put one of your legs back about six inches."

"Yes, ma'am," Noble replied as she stepped back with her left leg. She accidentally bumped into Charlie, causing her to lose her balance.

"Gentry! You better not let me fall," Charlie pleaded as her body started to gain momentum away from Noble.

"Shit. I'm so sorry," Noble said as her hand jutted behind her, grabbing and connecting to what she hoped was Charlie's belt buckle to keep her upright. With a firm grasp, Noble helped Charlie regain her steadiness.

"No worries, Noble Knight! I have no problem with you trying to yank my pants off. But how about next time it's not in public." Charlie chuckled as she put her arms around Noble's waist.

"Um, what's next, boss?" Noble inquired while trying to focus on the board, not the body molded to her backside.

"Well, you need to be upright and keep your back straight," Charlie replied as she took Noble's hand and placed a dart in it. She raised her and Noble's hand. "It would help if you started by focusing on the bullseye, taking a deep breath, and then releasing the dart when exhaling. Hopefully, it will result in a bullseye," Charlie said as she pressed her body against Noble while holding her hand.

"Do you need help with anything?" Noble asked as she noticed Charlie appearing flustered. Two could play this game.

"Yes, I do. Taking baby steps might be the death of me." Charlie smiled.

"Excuse me for a moment; I need to hit the restroom, and when I come back, I'll give you some pointers regarding those baby steps." Noble grinned as she walked away.

"Yo, Noble," Mike and Tony said, each sporting giant smiles.

Noble nodded to the guys still at the table when she walked past them toward the restroom. *I wonder if they know about us or if they see a power struggle between their two friends who happen to be women. My money is on them, and I bet they think they're setting us up tonight.*

As Noble neared the restroom, she heard footsteps behind her. She turned and saw Charlie right behind her.

"I figured I should go as well, so I wouldn't need to interrupt you giving those baby pointers you were going to give me," Charlie said as she walked past Noble, who held the restroom door open for her to enter.

Once they were in the restroom with the door closed, they turned and faced each other. Noble was glad she had a little height on Charlie and smirked when she saw her put one hand on her hip and point the other toward Noble's chest.

†

As Charlie's finger contacted Noble's chest, she knew Noble was a goner. Charlie saw that and continued her assault on Noble's chest. Charlie backed Noble into a corner, and when Noble came to a stop against the wall, Charlie didn't. When Charlie's body touched Noble's, the electricity in the air felt like sparks flying on the Fourth of July.

Noble let out a growl as she claimed Charlie's lips in a spine-tingling kiss. The kiss was commanding yet tender, letting Charlie know Noble wanted her. Charlie caressed Noble's lips in her assault. She opened Noble's mouth so that her tongue could enter heaven. Their tongues were in a duel as the temperature rose.

Charlie mumbled, "May the best woman win!"

Noble put her arms around Charlie and drew her closer, not that they could get closer to each other than they already were. Noble put her knee in between Charlie's legs and pressed gently. Charlie groaned, and her hips rocked.

She's making me excited and feel like this after only knowing each other for a short time, Charlie thought. The banging on the bathroom door brought them back to the present. Noble had locked the door, presumably anticipating this encounter with Charlie, not in the bar bathroom but in the encounter itself.

Noble rested her chin on Charlie's head and yelled, "Hold on a minute!"

They both tried to gain their composure and straighten their clothes. As Charlie opened the door, the woman said, "Get a room next time." Both Charlie and Noble left the restroom in silence.

When they returned to the table, they noticed Tony and Mike playing pool with coworkers. Noble slid into the booth, and Charlie sat next to her.

"After what happened, I didn't think sitting next to you would be too forward. We probably need to tell the guys that we're dating." Charlie shot a glance at Noble from the corner of her eye. "We don't need to have them thinking they'd a hand in it at all," Charlie said.

Noble smiled and held her beer up for a toast. "Here's to second chances and new beginnings." Both their mugs clanked together.

"What're we toasting?" Leah asked as she walked up to them with a beer.

"Second chances, new beginnings, and to getting Billy Russell off the streets once and for all," Noble and Charlie answered in unison.

"Hear, hear," Leah answered as she took a long drink of her beer and sat down. "Have you let the guys know yet that you two are together?"

"No, we will before we leave tonight. Hey, Leah, does Beth know how to play darts?" Noble asked as she avoided looking at Charlie sitting next to her.

"Charlie kicked your ass, didn't she?" Leah stated as she laughed.

"I take that as a yes," Noble replied.

"Take it from a person who has had their ass kicked by both mother and daughter on multiple occasions. You always want to be on their team," Leah stated in a matter-of-fact tone.

"They're good and highly competitive. You didn't bet on anything."

"Uh, no. We never got past the first set of practice throws," Noble answered.

"Oh, come on, I even gave you a free lesson. You left the game and went to the bathroom," Charlie said as she turned to Noble and stared her down with a wink and a smile.

"Well, when nature calls, you can't ignore it," Noble replied with a smile of her own.

"I've got your nature calls right here, Noble Knight," Charlie said as she nudged her with her elbow.

"Yes, you do, Ms. Matthews!" Noble said as her face turned red and she shifted in her seat.

"Well, now that you two have all that cleared up, how about dinner tomorrow night before we have a briefing for the first night of the op? How about five o'clock?" Leah asked both Charlie and Noble.

"Sure, that sounds like a plan?" they both answered.

"Okay, kids, I'm going home to see my wife. See you tomorrow," Harper said as she left a tip on the table, walked to the guys, and exited the establishment.

"Are you ready to blow this joint?" Charlie asked Noble. "We can go to my house to work and devise a strategy for this undercover assignment."

"Sounds good. Let's tell the guys we're leaving," Noble replied, leaving enough cash to cover everyone's drinks.

They walked over to the guys and said good night. Charlie suspected Tony and Mike had figured out what was happening between them because they looked like two proud brothers watching their sisters go on their first date.

†

"I'll drive since I had nothing to drink," Noble stated as she grabbed Charlie's hand and led her towards the door.

"And since I beat you at practice darts, I'll let you." Charlie chuckled.

As they exited the bar, they headed toward Noble's car. Noble stopped dead in her tracks and quickly pulled Charlie to a stop about twenty feet from her vehicle and said, "Hold on a minute," Noble barked as her eyes did a quick scan of the parking lot and surrounding area.

"What's wrong, Noble?"

"Something is on my windshield, and it wasn't there when I got out to come in tonight."

"Maybe some advertisement. All these businesses in this area do it."

"Hmm, I don't want to know how you know that, and two, they rarely put it in an envelope. It's good that I always have a spare set of gloves. Stay here for a second, Charlie, please."

Noble put on her gloves and slowly approached her car. She walked counterclockwise around her vehicle, looking for anything else that might not belong. Noble knelt and looked under her car to ensure it looked okay. Once satisfied, she stood and approached the front where the envelope was. Using her thumb and index finger, she gingerly took hold of the envelope and lifted the windshield wiper with her other hand, allowing her to remove it. The sealed envelope had no writing on its exterior.

"Does it say anything on the outside?" Charlie asked as she took a step toward Noble.

"No, but there's some type of paper inside," Noble said as she looked at Charlie.

"Well, open it up and see who's interested in you."

Noble opened the flap and removed a piece of paper and two pictures. As she read the paper, her body tensed, and when she looked at the pictures, her head shot up and looked directly at Charlie. "What the hell," Noble mumbled.

"What's wrong? What does it say? Talk to me, Noble," Charlie begged as she closed the distance to Noble.

"'I'm coming for you, bitch. Stay out of my business,'" Noble said as she pinched the bridge of her nose.

"Such a ladies' man response. Do you think it's Russell, Noble?"

"Most likely, but whoever it is, they sent me some pictures. One was during my time on patrol, and the other was at Neil's crime scene." Noble swallowed to clear a knot.

"You know we need to let Leah know. We need to document this, and we need to book these items as evidence," Charlie said as she looked up to Noble and caressed her cheek.

"Yeah, can we let her know in the morning?" Noble uttered. "Can you call and have a Crime Scene Unit tech respond to take pictures and document the scene? I'll take photos of these on my work phone so we can look at them at the house."

"We'll get the bastard." Charlie softly squeezed Noble's forearm.

CHAPTER TWENTY-FIVE

After Noble pulled the case number, and the Crime Scene Unit photographed the scene and collected the evidence, they headed to Charlie's house. As they exited the car and walked up to the front porch, Noble took a deep breath. Noble could smell Charlie's sweet perfume as Charlie unlocked the door. It smelled like vanilla with a touch of lavender. Noble's senses were on high alert and begged for release. As Noble leaned in, the aroma of Charlie's neck made her entire body break out in goosebumps. Noble closed her eyes and prayed to make it through tonight. Diana was the last woman that Noble had been with, and it'd been four long years since anyone had piqued her interest.

"Hey, are you okay, Noble?" Charlie had turned around and was watching Noble, who had an intense look of hunger on her face. Taking a moment, Noble closed her eyes, and when she reopened them, she stared into those beautiful blue eyes again.

"Yes, I'm fine. I'm trying to figure out how to make it through tonight without breaking my rule."

†

Charlie smiled, grabbed the front of Noble's shirt, and pulled her into the house. After shutting and engaging the deadbolt, she turned and pushed Noble toward the door until they both collided. Charlie looked up at Noble and noticed her breathing heavily, which reminded her she wasn't. Charlie was so caught up in this intense moment that she'd forgotten to inhale. Their lips met, and the moment her tongue pressed against Noble's bottom lip, Noble parted her mouth like a freshly split-open peach, inviting her into the warmth of Noble's mouth. Charlie's tongue sensuously entered Noble's insistent mouth. Noble's lips tasted like summer. Sweet and refreshing, like warm days and lazy afternoons.

What seemed like a lifetime later, Noble's hands slipped from her neck as Noble's fingers clinched her hair. Her hands felt like warm embers, igniting and raising a fire from within Charlie. Her hands slowly reached Noble's waist, and Charlie's chest pressed against hers. Finally, Noble slowly pulled away, and Charlie groaned loudly. She kept her eyes slightly shut, not wanting this moment to end but savoring it all. The last thing Charlie wanted was for Noble to pull away. Her hands dropped from Noble's waist. She struggled to come to grips with the world spinning before her eyes as time seemed to stop. How could she ever let Noble go now?

"You damn well know how to keep me wanting more. You're a lethal combination, lady. Heart, integrity, loyalty, and your looks aren't terrible either," Charlie replied.

"And I could say the same about you. I want to leave my comfort zone, and you're helping me with that. You bring something out in me that hasn't been out in a while," Noble said with a smile.

"Bring out, like you wanting to devour me," Charlie said.

Noble burst out laughing and said, "Something like that." Charlie pulled Noble's head down and kissed her again. Tongues intertwined, and Charlie pushed her body into Noble's as they both moaned.

†

Pausing, Noble broke their kiss and nibbled on Charlie's right ear, earning her some deep sighs from Charlie. Noble visibly saw Charlie's pulse pounding on the side of her neck like it was ready to take flight. The sighs continued when Noble switched to Charlie's left ear. Charlie ran her fingers through Noble's hair and pushed her head down, signaling she wanted Noble to kiss her harder. Charlie began rocking her hips into Noble, and Noble let out a growl. Noble started nibbling from Charlie's throat to her lips again. A soft sigh escaped her, and the kiss intensified.

"I want to take your clothes off and feel your body," Noble said as her lips danced around a smile.

She took Charlie's shirt out of her jeans and pulled it over her head. Noble moaned when she saw the nice, lacy bra with two gorgeous breasts hiding beneath. Lowering her head, she brushed her lips against Charlie's left breast, the fabric of her bra between them. Noble slowly brought her hands up and unclasped the bra in the back. Charlie tilted her head back and moaned.

"You're driving me crazy," Charlie groaned.

Noble lifted her head and smiled at Charlie before removing her bra. Noble stood transfixed by the two most beautiful breasts she'd ever seen. She cupped the left breast and tweaked the nipple, causing it to pucker.

"No more! We need to take this into the bedroom right now before I explode," Charlie said as she was gasping for breath.

"Which way? I'm ready to move on from baby steps," Noble declared as she lifted Charlie off the floor, causing her to wrap her legs around her.

Charlie pointed toward the bedroom, and Noble made it there at the speed of light. Noble slowly laid Charlie on the bed and helped her remove her jeans and panties.

"You're beautiful," Noble said.

Charlie blushed and said, "You've got too many clothes on! But first, we must ensure you're ready to take this to the next step. What's between us isn't casual for me, Noble."

Noble removed her shirt, bra, boxer briefs, and jeans and stood before Charlie. "I think you've got my answer. I want all of you—the good, hopefully not too much of your bad, the friend, the lover, the mother—all of it. Is that clear enough for you?"

"I know. And yes, I do. Just touch me, please." Suddenly, Charlie pulled Noble down on top of her. Noble automatically slid her knee in between Charlie's legs and zeroed in on her right nipple with her tongue. Noble was sucking and slowly nibbling on the nipple, causing it to pucker and become hard. Charlie started rocking her hips into Noble and wrapped her legs around Noble's waist.

"Not so fast. I want to sample your entire body before you come!" Noble said.

"Well, you better hurry because my body is on fire right now, and I'm close to losing it," Charlie replied, goosebumps clothing her bare skin.

She chuckled and started kissing Charlie down her stomach. Noble made her way to a nice patch of blond hair and placed her hands under Charlie's butt to help control her when she devoured her.

"Please hurry, you're torturing me!" Charlie said in a husky voice.

Noble slowly brought her tongue down and slid it gently over Charlie's folds.

"Oh, for the love of god! Keep going," Charlie yelled as her hips bucked and rose off the bed.

She slowly did it again, this time her tongue slipping between Charlie's folds, merging with the wetness. Noble's tongue continued inward and found Charlie's clit, rubbing it in small circles.

"Yes!" Charlie cried out as her hips were rocking faster. Her back bowed, shivers nipped her spine, as the orgasm worked its way through every nerve ending in her body.

The smell, taste, and feel of her against Noble, skin to skin, brought only one word to mind: home. Charlie felt like home. The past had no meaning anymore. Only memories of Charlie were in the here and now.

"Please, no more! If I didn't know any better, I'd say you're trying to kill me," Charlie said, laughing as she was gasping for air.

Noble slid her body next to Charlie's and kissed her hard. Noble brought Charlie into her arms and held her tight. "I would never want to harm you, but I did want to show you exactly how I feel about you," Noble said as she grabbed Charlie's hand and brought it to her mouth, pressing a soft kiss on her knuckles.

"I think it's your turn for some torture," Charlie said. Charlie rolled onto Noble and straddled her hips as she brought her mouth to Noble's and kissed her. As the kiss intensified, their tongues became one as their rhythm synchronized.

"That was something new that we will have to do again. I've never had a partner willing to do that before, and I have to say it's hot! I can't wait to find out what you taste like!" Charlie said.

"It was my pleasure, and you tasted like pure home," Noble said.

Charlie moved down to Noble's breasts and slowly licked and sucked on each nipple, causing them to become stiff and stand tall. Noble was running her hands through Charlie's hair and moaning as the exquisite sensual activity was playing out on her chest.

Charlie began slowly kissing her way down Noble's stomach. It was a pure, uncensored Noble. Noble's hands were now grabbing hold of the bedsheets in anticipation of Charlie finally contacting her clit. Charlie kissed the small triangle of brown hair, continuing down to Noble's thigh, and started nibbling her way up to where the treasure was.

"You're not playing fair, Charlie, and you'll pay for that later!" Noble stated.

"I want to sample your entire body before I feast on the main course," a smiling Charlie said.

"You'll miss out on that main course if you don't hurry, and hurry fast!" Noble said as she gasped to breathe.

"Your wish is my command," Charlie said. Charlie slowly ravaged Noble's clit like a fire burning out of control. Charlie started licking Noble's clit, causing Noble to rock her hips and lift them off the bed. Noble placed her hands on Charlie's head and pulled her closer to intensify the friction.

Noble let out a loud moan as Charlie started sucking her clit and using her hands to massage her breasts. Tremors took hold of Noble's toes and spread throughout her body. As Noble felt her body explode, she saw stars bursting as she screamed from the most powerful orgasm that she'd ever had in her entire life. Charlie licked up and devoured all of Noble's juices and continued sucking on her clit, bringing Noble to the height of multiple orgasms. Noble finally said, "No more. I can't breathe, and I don't think I can walk or leave the bed today."

"I wanted to ensure I ate all my dinner and cleaned my plate!" Charlie said.

"I think you ate the plate also! I'm not complaining because I like a woman who likes to clean her plate." Noble laughed.

"You surprise me, Noble Knight. I love your quirky sense of humor in the bedroom."

Noble admitted, "I want to clarify that I'm not normally this aggressive and haven't been with anyone since Diana." *I can't believe I said that out loud. She'll think I'm a loser now,* Noble thought.

"I don't make it a habit of sleeping with women this early on in a relationship, but there's something about you," Charlie replied.

"Charlie, I couldn't agree more with you than I already do! And that quirky sense of humor has been dormant for many years. Thank you for breathing life back into it," Noble said as she hugged Charlie, brought her mouth down to Charlie's, and kissed her. "As much as I'd like to stay in bed with you all night, I think we need to get up, shower, eat, and go over this case so we can review the case files," Noble said.

"Okay. We also need to look at the letter on your car's windshield tonight. Let's shower, and we'll go from there," Charlie replied.

Charlie got towels, showed Noble where the bathroom was, and said, "Get in, and I'll put some coffee on for us."

Noble got under the hot shower spray and let the water run down her body. *I've been with other women. Why does this feel different with Charlie? I don't know, but I want to see where this leads because I know I can lose my heart to her and might have already.*

The most beautiful hands lathering her back with soap suddenly brought Noble to reality.

"Well, stranger, imagine seeing you here," Charlie said.

Noble turned around, letting the spray hit her back. She kneaded Charlie's shoulders, pulled her back against her body, and replied, "I was hoping you'd come and help me wash my back, seeing as I'm your guest."

"Oh yes! I can help you with anything," Charlie replied.

Noble wrapped her arms around Charlie and kissed her on her neck. Noble's left hand stayed wrapped around Charlie's stomach as her right hand reached its goal: the treasure in the blond triangle. Charlie arched her back into Noble, causing her to step back and lean against the shower wall for support. As Noble found Charlie's clit with her fingers, she teased it with a circular motion.

Charlie snuck her left hand around for greater access to Noble's clit and initiated the same routine. When Charlie's hand touched Noble's clit, it caused her to gasp in pleasure. Noble was bringing Charlie to climax first when she felt her body stiffen and shake uncontrollably against Charlie's. Noble followed moments later when she let out a scream and slowly sank to the shower floor with Charlie wrapped in her arms.

Charlie let out a small scream, as she ended up in Noble's lap.

"Whoa, are you okay? Are you hurt? Open your eyes," Charlie demanded.

Noble slowly opened her eyes, a broad smile appearing on her face. "I think I died and went to Heaven," Noble said.

Charlie slightly poked Noble in her ribs and said, "You scared me!"

"I didn't mean to. I was relishing how you made me feel, and I needed to sit down before my legs gave out," Noble replied. Noble pulled Charlie against her and hugged her fiercely. "Thank you," Noble whispered.

Charlie responded by saying, "For what?"

"For taking the chance on me," Noble said as she closed her eyes briefly.

"It was all my pleasure, and don't think for one moment that I haven't thought about this happening between us," Charlie stated as she looked Noble in the eyes. "I watched you with Jessie and noticed you long before yesterday. I didn't know if you'd have a problem seeing me, as you thought I was obnoxious when we first met," Charlie remarked, her tone carrying a slight chuckle.

"Believe me, you're all woman, and I'm looking forward to spending a lot of time with you away from work," Noble declared. "Charlie, you make me feel things I haven't felt in a long time, and as much as that scares me, it makes me believe that you're in my life for a reason; whatever that reason may be, I hope to find it with you and only you," Noble murmured as she reached out her hand to brush a lock of wet hair away from Charlie's face.

"How about we get off the shower floor and away from the lukewarm water, grab something to eat, and talk about our case and your note?" Charlie suggested.

"Works for me. And what do you mean that you've watched me with Jessie?" Noble inquired, her eyes sparkled with a smile.

"When I visited, I always heard her talk about you. Well, I saw you once but stayed in the other room. Using the trusty internet, I thoroughly researched you. I guess you could say we're both ready to see what happens, and I don't plan on staying away again," Charlie stated as she kissed Noble on her forehead.

Noble and Charlie got up and helped each other dry off, which led to another round of kissing and heavy petting before they left the bathroom and headed into the kitchen for lunch.

†

"Noble, wake up!" Charlie whispered as she gently shook her shoulder.

They'd both fallen asleep on the couch with open case files on Billy Russell. It was well after two in the morning, and Charlie sat looking at Noble and smiled. She had beautiful brown hair and the smoothest skin. A slight frown formed on her face, and Charlie smiled. Noble slowly opened her eyes while Charlie smiled down at her.

"What're you smiling at, gorgeous?" Noble asked.

"You're the most beautiful woman I've ever seen," Charlie said as she stroked Noble's cheek slowly.

"I beg to differ, as I'm looking at her right now," Noble declared.

"I think we need to go to bed and get some sleep so we're ready for our family dinner and an assignment tonight," Charlie stated.

"Okay, let me grab my keys, and I'll be on my way," Noble replied as she started to gather her case files.

"Oh, no, you don't. You're not leaving this house tonight," Charlie stated. "You'll sleep with me, and yes, I mean sleep because we need to be fully alert to catch this guy. And we need to have our sleep when we let Leah know about your letter. The one we didn't even get to talk about last night," Charlie ended as she took Noble's case files from her and laid them down on the table.

Charlie and Noble walked down the hall, removed their clothes, and crawled into bed. Noble pulled Charlie into her and kissed the back of her head. Almost immediately, they were both asleep with smiles on their faces.

†

"For the love of god, who's calling me this morning?" Noble mumbled. She reached over, picked up her cell phone, and said, "Detective Gentry."

The line was silent until she heard Leah's voice. "Hello, Noble; how are you today?" Leah asked.

"I'm fine. I was up late studying case files on Billy Russell," Noble replied.

"That's great because we need to get this guy off the street quick. Can I talk to Charlie?" Leah asked, a gentle laugh tickled her throat.

"Why did you call my cell phone and not hers?" Noble asked as she rubbed the sleepy time out of her left eye.

"Um, I called Charlie's cell phone, and you answered," Leah said as she bit back another laugh.

†

Charlie grabbed her cell phone from Noble's hand and said, "Hi Mom L, how are you this morning?"

"I don't think I'm doing as well as you, but I've no complaints." Leah snickered.

"Hilarious, Mom L. What's up? Are you okay? Is something wrong with Mom or Elizabeth?" Charlie asked in a frantic voice.

"Calm down, child! I'm fine, and the other two are good. She, meaning your mom, directed me to call you to ask if you could bring some macaroni salad to dinner tonight. Can you stop by the store, or is your calendar full till dinner?" Leah replied with a question of her own.

"Ha, ha, you're funny. We'll be happy to bring some salad. I think we can squeeze a little time in to get to the store before dinner," Charlie gave a snappy comeback.

"Great. Your mom and I thank you. Don't forget to rest before tonight and tell Noble to take her vitamins. Love you, princess," she said. "Oh, and one last thing: you both will have to explain why neither of you told me about the letter left on the windshield of Noble's car last night. Did you think that the patrol sergeant on duty last night would not notify me?" Leah said, her voice laced with irritation.

"I'll make sure she takes all her vitamins, Mom L. We will talk to you both about it tonight. Love you too, and I'm hanging up now," Charlie replied as she hit the end call button.

"Holy cow," Noble said with her hands over her face.

"Don't worry, my mom will keep Mom L in check at dinner tonight," Charlie replied, removing Noble's hands from her face and kissing her gently.

"Are you sure I'm not dreaming?" Noble asked.

"No, but we will try to catch a couple more hours of sleep before we hit the store. So, close your eyes and relax. And the cat is out of the bag regarding the letter you got last night," Charlie replied as she cuddled beside Noble.

Chapter Twenty-six

As the sun sank toward the horizon, it painted the sky in warm colors, and outstretched shadows reached out across the street, resembling fingers searching for something just out of grasp. Billy Russell seethed as he glared at the building, his fists clenched tight, knuckles white against the peeling vinyl of the steering wheel. He was certain that the woman he despised was inside, and the thought ignited a fire in his gut. Memories of their twisted past flooded his mind, each one a reminder of the betrayal that had landed him in prison. He was done playing nice; this time, he would make her suffer. The satisfaction of ending her life would be his, and if that damn female cop dared to interfere, she'd find herself in his crosshairs sooner. She had no idea about the dark history they shared, but soon she would learn just how ruthless he could be.

He needed to figure out Tracy's routine. There had to be a weak point, a moment when he could catch her off guard. He fished out the newly stolen phone from his front pants pocket, scrolled through the handful of articles he had saved until he found the one named "Gentry." The detective had been relentless in her pursuit of him during his trial, a constant thorn in his side. Maybe she'd be the perfect bait. He laughed, imagining the chaos it would cause. First, he'd get to Tracy, then he'd turn the tables on Gentry. It would be a fitting twist of fate, with the hunter cop now finding herself in the role of the prey. As he sat there running scenarios through his head, he felt a familiar nudge, the thrill of the chase igniting his senses.

†

Tracy stepped outside the brewery, she felt the cool breeze on her face, invigorating yet unsettling. The street was quiet, and her instincts screamed at her to be careful. Just as she began to sweep the sidewalk, the noise of tires crunching on gravel drew her attention. She glanced over her shoulder, heart pounding. A car was parked too close, its engine idling, a silhouette behind the wheel. She quickened her pace, feeling the weight of unseen eyes on her back.

"Hi, Ms. Snow," a woman's voice spoke.

Her name being used caused her to stop as she reached for the brewery door. When she looked, she recognized her neighbor.

"Hi, Maria. Off and running I see. Where are you headed tonight?"

"Sorry if my ride scared you. He was supposed to park in front of my business. Well anyway, I'm off to visit family and go to the farmer's market in the morning. Have a nice evening, Ms. Snow."

"You as well, Maria."

After waving to Maria, Tracy walked toward the brewery, pushing through the door and shaking off the feeling of dread. She saw Vera wiping down the counter and forced a smile. "Hey Vera, are you about done?"

"Yes. Tracy, you look a little pale. Everything okay?"

"Yeah…it's just unnerving not knowing where Russell is. Poor Maria's friend probably thinks I'm crazy."

"That's it, Tracy. I'm staying tonight. Let's lock up and head upstairs and we can have some tea. Or something stronger if you need it."

"That sounds great. I've already locked everything up, so let's head up now."

Tracy felt a momentary sense of safety locked inside, but the gnawing unease lingered, a reminder that her past wasn't just a shadow; it was Billy Russell, a predator, waiting to strike again.

†

Russell watched as Tracy swept outside the business. A smile crept across his face when he saw her frantic attempt to retreat into the building as the car stopped in front. He relished the thrill of the chase, sensing the electric pulse of her fear in her response, a rush so exhilarating it was almost palpable. This wasn't about revenge anymore; it was about asserting his dominance. The City of Onserf had treated him like a criminal, but soon, he would show them who truly held the power. That bitch might think she was safe for now, but he would make sure she knew nowhere was safe. Not anymore.

Russell started the engine, when a loud backfire happened. Looking toward the business, he noticed the blinds on the second floor above the bar catch his eye. *Well, I'll be damned.*

He hadn't even thought about there being an apartment above the bar. No wonder he couldn't find an address for her. Putting the vehicle in drive, he slowly drove past and headed back to his hotel room. *Now that I know she lives there, I need to check if there is a back door off the alley or if the front is the only entrance to the business. This is shaping up to be fucking fantastic.*

†

In her apartment, Tracy paced as Vera prepared their tea. A loud bang interrupted her thoughts. Startled, Tracy rushed to the window, her breath catching in her throat. Outside she saw a group of teenagers walking. They must have hit one of the metal trash cans that lined the street for morning trash day. Relieved but annoyed, she started to lower her hand from the blinds she had cautiously moved aside, when her instincts kicked in and she spotted an unfamiliar car slowly driving down the street in her direction. "2RDM345, 2RDM345, 2RDM345," she repeated as she wrote it down on the notepad she kept by the window. She noticed wisps of smoke curling from the driver's side. *Something about that car is not sitting right with me. I need to let the detective know, in case it turns out to be related.*

"Did you see something outside?" Vera asked as she wiped her wet hands on the dish towel.

"What do you mean?" Tracy replied, looking puzzled.

"Tracy, did you see something? I saw you writing something down quickly and you were mumbling. You also look a little rattled," Vera pressed, clanking two coffee mugs together as she set them on the counter.

"Sorry, Vera. Yes, I did. There was a car driving by slowly. I was able to get the license plate, and now I'm going to call Detective Gentry and leave it on her voicemail."

"After you call, come sit down and have some tea," Vera stated as she poured the hot water for tea.

"Thank you."

"Get to it or I might go pour us something a little stronger," Vera replied, turning her back, grabbing the mugs, walking into the living room, and placing them on the coffee table as she sat.

"Hi Detective Gentry. This is Tracy Snow. I know you're not in the office, but I wanted to give you a license number of a car that was slowly driving by a few minutes ago." She cleared her throat. "Not sure if it's related but I have a bad feeling about it. Well, anyways, call me back or come by when you can." Tracy ended the call and went to join Vera in the kitchen. *The sooner they find this monster, the sooner I can live without fear. I never asked for this, and I'm tired of looking over my shoulder.*

CHAPTER TWENTY-SEVEN

"You know what? Let's meet up later after dinner. That way, we can avoid any unnecessary drama from Leah tonight," Noble suggested with a smile as they pulled up to Beth and Leah's house.

"No can do, Noble Knight. Don't let her get to you. We've done nothing wrong. It was all terrific," Charlie replied with a wink and a smile.

"Okay, let's do this, only for you. Let's go." Noble squeezed Charlie's hand.

"That's the spirit, Noble Knight," Charlie declared, lifting the salad to her lap.

Noble got out of the vehicle and walked around to open Charlie's door. She grabbed the salad and offered her hand.

"Thanks," Charlie whispered as they walked toward the front door.

†

"She opened the door for her and acted appropriately. How cute is that!" Leah stated as she and Beth watched from the kitchen window.

"Stop it, sweetheart. We both love Noble, and it's time for her to see someone. As a bonus for us, it's Charlie, which means we'll see both a lot more." Beth kissed Leah.

"I know! But I'll still worry as a parent and friend." Leah ran a hand through her hair.

"We're here. Stop making out in the kitchen, and make sure you're presentable for your daughter and her date," Charlie shouted as she and Noble walked through the house.

"Hey, sweetie." Beth hugged her daughter.

"Hi, Mom and Mom L." Charlie grinned at Leah who stood slightly behind.

"Hi, Noble, it's good to see you again." Beth grabbed her hands, leaned in, and gently kissed her on the cheek.

"It's great to see you, too, Beth." Noble squeezed her hands and smiled.

"Hey, Noble, I hope you got some sleep today since it will be an interminable night." Leah smiled and crossed her arms across her chest.

"She did, Mom L. She even had her vitamins," Charlie replied as she put her arm around Noble protectively.

They all looked at Noble, presumably waiting for her to say something as her face turned red.

"Well, I got some sleep in between my multiple workout sessions. So, thank you for asking." Noble grinned as she looked at Leah.

"Okay, that's enough! I need not know any more information about my daughter's sex life." Leah waved her arms in the air.

"Good to know." Charlie squeezed in as she kissed Noble.

"Mommy, Noole. I missed you," Elizabeth yelled as she raced over to them and hugged their legs.

"Hey, sweetie, you're coming home with me tonight so Grandma and Mimi can have a day off. I've missed you so much."

"And, Bug, how about we go to the zoo tomorrow?"

"Yay! Mommy, can we go? Please."

"Yes, we can. We're both off the next few days, so we'll have lots of fun."

"Elizabeth, why don't you help me get things ready? Mimi needs to speak with Mommy and Noble." Beth held out her hand.

"Okay. Come on, Grandma."

Leah walked to the living room and sat in her recliner. Noble and Charlie followed and sat on the couch.

"First off, tell me about the note. Any ideas?"

"No, although we both believe it could be Billy Russell," Noble stated. "And Tracy left a message on my work phone. She gave me the license plate number, 2RDM345, of a suspicious car she saw drive by her business," she added. "I did some research, and it's another dead end now. My gut is telling me it's all related to Russell."

"Noble, do you have any history with him besides the Tracy Snow case?" Leah asked as her fingers drummed on the arm of the recliner.

"Not that I'm aware of. I have yet to have time to discover the location of the other picture. It was during my patrol days." Noble cast her eyes on Leah. "I'll take some time tonight to look on the internet and find the attachment to the news article. It might give me a clue if we can get it narrowed down."

"We've less than a week before the official start date. The department hasn't had any more tips about Russell, and I think he's still here in Onserf. Especially if that letter left on your car's windshield is his doing." Leah methodically flipped through her notepad.

"Listen to me," Noble emphasized. "Russell thinks he's smarter than us. There is no way he left town."

"So, if we can take care of Russell and this letter guy, we can get back to work on our regular caseloads," Charlie stated.

"You spoke like a true SPAT agent, Charlie. Oh, Noble, you're in for the ride of your life with this one," Leah teased.

"I'm seeing that." Noble laughed a hearty, genuine chuckle.

Charlie's head whipped around so fast she heard a crack. "Hey, this isn't fair. Two against one. Noble, hasn't anyone ever told you that you're obligated to side with your girlfriend and not her parents?"

"Yes. But there should be a little give and take when that parent is also my boss," Noble responded with a wink and nod of acknowledgment.

"I'll have to think about that one. We can disagree," Charlie huffed.

"Will you two knock it off? I feel like the only adult in the room, and we don't have time for this. Now kiss and make up before dinner. I'm heading in to see if Beth and Elizabeth need any more help." Leah stood and walked toward the dining room.

†

"She's right, Noble Knight. You can make it up to me later. Agreed?"

"Agreed," Noble replied as she stood, extended her hand, helped Charlie up, leaned in, planted a quick kiss on Charlie's lips, and guided her toward the dining room.

"Did I mention I love how we handle our disagreements?" Charlie quirked her lips.

"If that kiss was your selling point, you did."

†

"Another fabulous dinner, Beth. We need to have more of these nights with friends and family."

"I'm glad you liked it, Noble. Yes, it's been a while, and I hope we can do many more. Phooey, all I see here is family. We suggest you get used to it, as you've been part of ours for years."

"Roger that, Beth. Thank you." A lump formed deep in Noble's throat.

"Noole, are you going to be my other mommy?"

Leah laughed so hard that she snorted, and it was almost impossible to understand what she was saying. "So, please answer the question, Noble."

"Leah Jayne Harper, mind your manners," Beth chastised as she arranged her mouth in a stern line.

"Mom L, You're so embarrassing." Charlie leveled a glare.

"Mimi, you're not being nice right now," Elizabeth chimed in.

"Any chance I can answer Bug's question?" Noble asked.

"Yes, please do. I'm sorry for my outburst. Continue." Leah cocked her head to one side.

"Well, Bug, your mommy and I are getting to know each other. Sometimes, it's okay to take your time. "We want to make sure no one gets hurt, including you. And besides, when I become your other mommy, you'll be one of the top three people that know. Do you have any other questions?" Noble concluded, keeping eye contact with Elizabeth.

"Will you do a sleepover with us and help me build a fort tonight?" Elizabeth's smile swung free.

"If it's alright with your mom, we can build a fort." Noble looked at Charlie.

"Absolutely!" she answered. "How about we clean up so we can all head home?"

"Yay, come on, Grandma and Mimi. I want to build the fort before my bedtime."

"Just a second, Elizabeth. Charlie, will you help your mom and Elizabeth clean up while I speak with Noble?"

"As long as you're going to be nice, then yes, I will." Charlie glanced directly toward Leah.

"I promise. Noble, will you walk outside with me?" Leah directed.

"Sure." Noble stepped onto the porch first and heard the front door shut behind Leah.

"I'm sorry about my outburst earlier, but if you could have seen the look on your face, you'd have done the same thing." Leah flashed a huge grin at her.

"I can only imagine what I looked like. I was not expecting Elizabeth to ask that question." Noble snickered.

"None of us were expecting it, but we must all be ready for many questions ahead. Elizabeth, a vibrant little firecracker, never fails to impress. Thank god Charlie carried her and not the ex." A laugh broke from Leah's chest.

"Speaking of that ex, she better hope I never run into her." Noble held her gaze briefly before she quickly looked away, holding back any further comments.

"She's not even worth the energy," Leah remarked, her tone filled with disdain.

"True, but Charlie is," Noble declared.

"Okay, Casanova, simmer down. Karma will catch her eventually, which will be a sweet thing to witness."

"Once again, you're right. Simmering down now."

"We're more concerned with the letter you received, Noble. Please look at it more closely and see if you can narrow down the time and place of both. Because of the print on the paper, I've already elevated this case."

"After we finish building a fort and Elizabeth goes to bed, I'll start working on it."

"Although I hate to admit it, we believe you and Charlie are good for each other. You've both experienced loss, different losses, but loss." Leah watched and studied Noble. "And you both will benefit from your time together to move forward in life, knowing that you deserve happiness."

"Thanks for the ringing endorsement, Leah. I think Charlie is my now, and I can't wait to spend the rest of my life with her and Elizabeth."

"Take your time, and don't rush it." Leah pursed her lips together in a faint smile and nodded.

"No need to worry. After my first date with Diana, I knew I wanted to spend the rest of my life with her," Noble stated. "And I know that I want to do the same with Charlie and Elizabeth. I will do everything I can to cherish them and keep them safe as long as I'm alive," she declared, her gaze locking with Leah's.

"Hopefully, you won't take this second chance at love lightly," Leah admonished Noble. "You always wear your heart on your sleeve. It's one of your most endearing qualities, and your fierce loyalty."

"So you know, after this Russell case, you can expect me to sit down with you, Beth, and Elizabeth to make this official," Noble vowed. "Hands down, I like her. I love her. Who am I kidding? She's everything checked off my list for a partner—a wife. I haven't been this happy in forever." Noble smiled.

"Okay, I guess we need to catch this guy quick." Leah clapped her hands together.

The sound of the door creaking open brought their attention to Charlie, who'd stepped out.

"Are you ready to go? Not sure how much longer Elizabeth can stay awake."

"Let me go say goodnight to Beth, and we'll head home," Noble replied as she headed back inside the house.

"Don't worry, Charlie, we had a good family talk," Leah stated. "You both haven't been this happy in a long time. We're glad you found each other, as you are both important to us."

Noble picked up Elizabeth, who was sound asleep. "You ready?"

"Yes. Goodnight, Mom L."

"Goodnight. One of you, please text me to let me know you made it home and are secure in the house."

"Will do. See you at work in a couple of days, Leah."

†

Elizabeth was down for the count when they arrived at Charlie's house. Noble carried her to her bedroom, laid her down, removed her shoes, and put on the covers.

"I hope you plan on staying the night. It's late, and we promised to build that fort tomorrow with Elizabeth."

"Yes, I'll stay. Will it be better if I stay in the guest room?" Noble asked, maintaining strong eye contact with Charlie.

"Uh, not happening! Elizabeth is smart enough to understand that we're a couple. So, you'll be staying in my room tonight."

"I didn't want to assume, but that's the best news I've heard all day."

"Let's go to bed, Noble. I'm exhausted," Charlie stated.

"Lead the way. A good night of sleep will do us both well."

As they headed to the bedroom, Noble couldn't shake the feeling that something was off. It had been with her since someone left the letter and pictures in her car. It was like hair standing on the back of her neck. And those were the worst kind.

"Where are you going, Noble?" Charlie murmured in a whispery low voice.

"Was only going to check all the doors. Something feels off, Charlie."

"What do you mean? It feels off."

"You know that hair on the back of your neck standing up type of feeling?" Noble described as she pointed to the backside of her neck.

"Yes. Oh boy, that's happened to me twice in my career. Is it pointing you in a particular direction?"

"I've had it, too, and I can't ignore it now—not with you and Elizabeth, and not since that note got left on my car's windshield. My gut is telling me it's Russell."

"You're likely right. Check the doors and hurry back so we can get some sleep. Or do you need me to come help?"

"I'll be right back. You can crawl into bed."

"Okay." Charlie turned and continued to her bedroom.

Noble checked the locks on the back doors and walked toward the front entryway when she heard the earsplitting metal of what she believed was a hubcap hitting the curb. She changed direction slowly, heading toward the window. Using her memory and groping for the back of the couch, Noble took a step in that direction. However, she'd have a bruise on her shin because she hit the couch with her leg before her hand found it. "Dammit, that hurt!"

"Are you okay?"

"What the fuck? It would be best not to sneak up on people like that. Especially people like me. You know, police." The tendon in Noble's neck twitched.

"I didn't sneak up on you. For the obvious reasons of not getting hit by you and not wanting you to scream. You took a long time, and I wanted to help," Charlie grunted.

"I heard a car trying to park, but they scraped their hubcap along the curb. I was trying to make it to the window so I could look out and see if it was a neighbor."

"Noble, I'm going to take your hand. Follow me, and we can look out of the blinds." Charlie led them through the darkened room. "They won't be able to see us move the slats because we have some coverage with the bushes outside."

Hand in hand, they walked to the window. Once there, Noble used her index finger to lift the blind slats to look outside.

"When we got home, a car at ten o'clock wasn't there. Let me drop this side, and you can look." Noble cast her eyes toward Charlie.

"That doesn't belong to any of my neighbors, and I've never seen it in our neighborhood. Do you think we should have a patrol unit drive by and at least get a plate number?" Charlie asked in a firm voice.

"Yes. You go make the call, and I'll keep an eye out," Noble directed as she lifted the blinds slat again and looked outside. "This is another suspicious vehicle, and it's got my spidey senses going. Something isn't right."

As Noble quickly focused on the car outside, Charlie disappeared into the pitch-black room. Noticing an amber glow in the driver's seat, Noble surmised someone was still in the car, and they were smoking. *What the hell are you up to?*

"We're in luck. A patrol unit in the area should be here in under five minutes. My work radio is on, so we'll know when a unit arrives."

"Great. Now, we will wait and see. I need to put a bell on you to know when you're coming my way."

"5Adam22, arriving on that suspicious vehicle call." The voice of an unknown male officer came through Charlie's work radio in her hand.

"Copy that," dispatch replied.

"Great, I see car lights coming."

Noble watched as a vehicle approached. Since the spotlights checked cars on both sides of the street, she guessed it was a double unit.

"Let them know we don't want contact at our front door. In case it's Russell, we don't need to let him know the exact address." Noble pointed toward Charlie and her radio.

"Special Agent 15 to 5Adam22, FYI, contact reporting party via phone only. The number is in the call."

"5Adam22, copy that."

"Looks like they've stopped behind that car and are going up to make contact."

Noble watched the two officers approach the vehicle in question. They'd correctly placed the spotlights on the parked car's driver's side and rearview mirror. Each flashed their flashlight inside the back seat and kept going until they and their flashlights were at the vehicle's hood. She noticed one officer engage his lapel mic and heard his voice through Charlie's radio.

"Did anything come back on the vehicle that I entered into the computer?" 5Adam22 asked as he looked up and down the street.

"Affirm. Are you clear for info on that plate?" dispatch replied.

"FYI, the vehicle is unoccupied. Go ahead," the officer stated.

"It is a stolen vehicle. Northeast patrol officers took the report earlier tonight. I've already sent him a message."

"5Adam22, copy. We're going to dust and contact the reporting party. I'll let you know when to start a tow."

"Where the fuck did the driver go? They must have gotten out when we weren't looking. They're out there somewhere right now, presumably watching," Noble hissed as she rubbed the back of her neck.

Noble saw Charlie's face illuminated as she answered her cell phone. "Agent Matthews."

"Agent Matthews, this is Officer Justin. We're out front, and it appears the vehicle is empty. Were you able to see which way the driver went?"

"We didn't realize the occupant left. Is there any additional information on the stolen vehicle?" Charlie demanded as she tugged at the hem of her shirt.

"No, ma'am. Other than someone stole it earlier tonight. My partner is dusting it for prints, and we'll inventory and tow it. If we find anything, I'll call you back."

"Thanks, Officer Justin. Be safe out there."

"You, too, Agent Matthews."

"Son of a bitch. No one was in the car. They took it earlier tonight." Charlie growled her frustration. "They're going to dust, inventory, and tow it. He'll call back if they find anything." Her voice cut an angry swath through the air.

"Damn, he's got to be out there watching. Good thing they didn't come to your door." A hushed tone marked her words.

"Let's sit here on the couch, in the dark, to wait and see if Officer Justin calls back," Charlie said. "If we turn the light on now, we might as well walk outside and scream, 'We were the ones who called. Come and get us.' You know what I mean?" she spat out the words.

Noble sat at the end of the couch nearest the window. It was easier than trying to find the middle. Charlie had the same idea but landed on Noble's lap because she wasn't quick enough.

"Well, hello, Ms. Matthews."

"Oh, I'm not sorry. You were a little quicker, but you won't hear any complaining from me. This is a magnificent spot to be."

"I concur. Should we call Leah?" Noble asked.

"Let's wait to see if the officers find anything in the vehicle when they fill out the tow sheet."

"Okay," Noble replied as Charlie's phone lit up the room.

"Hello, Officer Justin. Did you find anything in the car?"

"Yes, ma'am. We found pictures of one of our officers, Noble Gentry. Do you know her?"

"Yes, I do. Only pictures, or was there anything else? What do the pictures entail?" Charlie asked Officer Justin.

"Well, Officer Gentry is attending her wife's funeral and is at the scene where her wife was killed. There's also a note." Officer Justin carefully spaced his words.

"Okay. What does the note say?" Charlie asked as she slid off Noble's lap but kept hold of her hand.

"It says for Gentry to stay out of his business, or he'll take care of her like he took care of her wife."

"Oh shit! I need you to dust every inch of that vehicle to get a print. Please go slow and have your Crime Scene Unit tech take photos of everything, including the pictures and handwritten note. I'm going to have Sergeant Harper respond and contact you," Charlie stated. An icy panic started to creep up her extremities and into her chest.

"Will do. I'll wait to hear from you or Sergeant Harper."

"Thank you, Officer Justin."

"Anytime. We need to get this guy before the asshole can get to Gentry," he stated

"Since she's here with me, that won't happen tonight. I will fill her in." Charlie ended the call.

"What will you fill me in on, Charlie?" Noble asked.

"I will fill you in. Let's go upstairs to the bathroom, where I can turn on a light. Dammit, this has the potential to be bad, Noble." Charlie spat out the words through gritted teeth. Frustration and disdain were wrapped up in her instruction.

"Why? Can you tell me here?"

"I need you to see me when I tell you what they found. And I need to see you. Take my hand," Charlie whispered as she led Noble toward the bathroom.

"Okay, spill it," Noble said as they entered the bathroom.

"There were a couple of pictures of you in the car with another note," Charlie replied as she looked at Noble directly and placed Noble's hands in hers. "They found one picture of you at Diana's funeral, and the other was at the scene where she got hit and died."

"What did the note say?" Noble asked as she closed her eyes, sat on the edge of the tub, and leaned her head onto Charlie's stomach.

"It suggested you should stay out of his business, or he'd take care of you like he took care of your wife," Charlie answered, taking a small step back in case Noble jerked her head up.

"What the fuck!" Noble yelled as her head snapped up, eyes locking with Charlie's.

"Oh, Noble, I'm sorry. That's all the information I have right now. Whoever left those items in the car did so to get to you."

"I need to go out and look at the photos," Noble replied as she stood and stepped toward the bathroom door.

"No. If you go out there now, he'll will know where I live. And Elizabeth. I need you to stay here. Please," Charlie pleaded as she gripped Noble's wrist to keep her from leaving the bathroom.

"I need to know," Noble replied, tears streaming down her cheeks and dropping onto her shirt.

"And we will, honey. I promise to move heaven and earth to get you the necessary answers. But right now, I need to call Leah and have her respond." Charlie gently wiped the tears from Noble's face.

"Okay," Noble said as she closed the toilet lid and sat.

Charlie stepped into the hallway and closed the door. "Leah, sorry for waking you up, but I need to fill you in on some recent developments."

"Are you, Elizabeth, and Noble, okay?" Leah asked, sounding concerned.

"Physically, yes, but I need you to come by my house. I have some officers outside processing a car. There were a couple of photos of Noble and a note left. The suspect must have left the car when we weren't looking. I'm not sure if he's still around watching."

"Shit. I'm getting dressed now and will be there in under five minutes," she retorted.

Charlie could hear the rustling of sheets as she imagined Leah sitting in bed and shaking Beth's shoulder to wake her up.

"Leah, the note said that if Noble didn't back off, they'd do to her what they did to her wife," Charlie replied, choking back tears.

"Fuck! Do you want Beth to come with me?"

"No, as it is, you can't come into the house either. Contact Officer Justin. He's outside on the street processing the car."

"That's a good point. If the suspect is still around, I don't want him to know where you live." Leah hissed out a breath.

"Thank you. Call me after you check out the scene. I love you, Leah. Tell Mom I love her, too."

"Talk to you in a few, sweetie. We both love all three of you."

†

"What's the matter? Are they okay?" Beth asked Leah, her eyes inquiring about the phone call Leah had ended.

"A suspect has fixated on Noble and possibly is responsible for Diana's death," she explained as she pulled Beth to her. "I need to go to Charlie's and see the photos and note without going to her house in case the suspect is still there."

"For goodness sake. Tell Charlie that she, Elizabeth, and Noble can come to stay here tomorrow until we catch this asshole," Beth replied as she sat up in bed.

"I will. I don't know when I'll be home, but it shouldn't surprise you if you see a marked patrol outside the house." Leah kissed Beth on the forehead. "We should assume he'll be looking to hurt people in Noble's life if he can't get to her."

"Way to scare me, babe. Especially with you leaving," Beth remarked with a lopsided grin.

"I'm more worried about what you'll do to an intruder than what they'll do to you. Get some sleep, and I'll call you as soon as possible. I love you," Leah replied as she kissed Beth goodbye.

"I love you, too."

†

Charlie opened the bathroom door and saw Noble sitting on the floor, knees up, hands covering her face, and leaning against the bathtub. *I can't imagine the pain and shock that she's going through right now.*

"Is Leah on her way?" Noble asked in barely a whisper.

"Yes, she is," Charlie replied as she got on her knees, gently removed Noble's hands from her face, and placed them in hers.

"I feel like I hit rock bottom right now. There's no wrapping my head around this. Anyone can find that information about Diana and me on the internet. If this is Russell, I'm going to fuck him up when we catch him," Noble vowed.

"Officer Justin is having the car processed. Could Russell be involved?"

"It would be one hell of a coincidence. Diana and I were working patrol when he committed his crime against Tracy Snow, but oh fuck…" Noble squeezed her eyes shut and shook her head.

"What is it, Noble?" Charlie begged.

"A suspect fled from a rape case around the same time as Tracy's incident. He was being chased by Diana on the day she got killed. It's possible that both are tied to Russell," she mumbled. "When he fled the apartment building, he must have pulled his ski mask down. As the second unit on scene, I only saw her patrol vehicle and heard the radio traffic."

Charlie sensed that Noble's whole world seemed to be moving in slow motion. She imagined that it felt like Noble was walking in a dream world, a horrific, nightmarish world.

"Noble, you've been grieving for the last four years. There was no way you could have known." Charlie's shoulders slumped as she spoke.

"There was DNA from Diana's scene. Why didn't the detective that day refer to her case as possibly related to Tracy Snow's since both incidents occurred around the same time?" Noble snapped. "Russell might still be in jail and not out on some 'good behavior' bullshit."

"Remember, there was undoubtedly a lot of chaos and grieving from your coworkers. Many at the department loved Diana." Charlie sought to console Noble.

"I let everyone down. Diana, Tracy, and the department because I was so consumed in my grief that I couldn't put two and two together," Noble stated as she removed her hands from Charlie's and slammed them against the tub.

"Noble, stop it! You did nothing wrong. Look at me," Charlie pleaded as she lifted Noble's face and made eye contact.

The vibration of Charlie's cell phone on the bathroom counter caused both women to break eye contact and look over at it. Charlie stood and grabbed the phone.

"Hello!" she barked into it.

"Everything okay in there?" Leah asked.

"Not really. It's been a long night. Any current info?" Charlie asked in a croaky voice.

"Take a deep breath, Charlie. We processed the vehicle. The officers could only lift about five decent prints." A sigh escaped Leah's lips.

"How soon till they can get checked?" Charlie's words trailed off.

"Per my instructions, the tech is heading back to headquarters now to see if we can get a match." Leah's tone brooked no argument. "I took photos of the pictures and notes using my work phone. I'm sending them to you now."

"We'll look at them and see you in the morning to form a game plan. Thank you, Mom L. Love you." Charlie started looking for the pictures.

"I love you, too. Take it slow with Noble. This new information is a lot to digest for anyone. Both of you, be at my office by nine."

"Well? What did Leah have to say?" Noble barked.

"We're to meet her at the office tomorrow at nine o'clock. They got some decent prints, and she instructed the tech to work on it when they get back to the station," Charlie replied in an even tone.

"Thank you. I'm sorry I snapped at you. There's a lot for me to take in right now." She hung her head.

"Understandable. Let's get some rest so we're ready to get this bastard tomorrow," Charlie replied as she helped Noble from the bathroom floor.

"Okay. But this son of a bitch is going to pay when we catch him," Noble mumbled as she followed Charlie to the bedroom.

CHAPTER TWENTY-EIGHT

As he parked his car at the end of the street, he could see which house they'd pulled into.

"These bitches are so stupid," Russell snarled to no one in the empty car. They had no clue who was following them. He would kill them if they kept interfering with Tracy Snow.

After writing down the address, he waited until all the lights were out and pulled closer to the house to get a better view. Starting the car, he drove slowly down the street without the headlights on. As he pulled into an empty spot near the house, he heard the metal of the hubcap scrape against the concrete curb, creating an awful screeching sound.

"Fuck! I should've had my lights on. There can be no mistakes. The mission is too important," Russell snarled as he turned on the portable police scanner he had stolen to see if he would have company.

After a few minutes of silence on the scanner, Russell finally heard that a unit was coming to check a suspicious vehicle. Not knowing how long it would take, he knew he needed to leave the car and hide in the shadows to avoid getting caught.

"Fuck…fuck…fuck!" Russell mumbled as he climbed out the open window, ensuring no interior dome light would come on and light him up in case they were watching.

An approaching car turned at the end of the block and lit up each side of the street with powerful spotlights. Russell knew he couldn't cross the street, so he hunched over and got behind a car near the one he abandoned. He crept alongside four cars and hunkered down till the police vehicle passed. Russell figured he could cross the sidewalk, hide in some shrubs, and hear everything the officers talked about.

"Bitches. Come on out! I want to see their faces when the officers show them the pictures and the note I had left. I wasn't ready to show them those things, but the fucking bitches sped up this game, and I'm going in for the juggernaut."

After about an hour, Russell was getting restless and crawled through the shrubs near the side of the house. He climbed the fence and was down on the ground by the time the spotlight automatically went on. He continued to the back fence line, jumped it, and made it out to the street on the next block without incident.

"Shit, I need to steal another car so I can drive by and see if there is any movement at that bitch, Tracy's address. It won't be long till I end her once and for all. I can get out of this fucking shitshow of a town and move on with my life. Once I leave this city, they won't be able to track me down," Russell declared to no one.

As he moved farther away, he took the run-down-looking car on the block as he was getting tired. Luckily, he tried the door handle, and the owner had left it unlocked. *What's the chance this dumbshit left the keys under the mat?* Russell got in the driver's seat and reached under the mat, feeling around for keys. His hand hit something, and when he picked it up, he saw it was a set of keys. *I'm sure a woman owns this car. Only a stupid bitch, would leave her keys under the mat, and it looks like the house keys, too. I'd visit her if I weren't on a mission.*

"I'm coming for you, Tracy," Russell snapped as he put the key in the ignition and started the car.

Russell parked near the alley entrance so he could see Tracy's business. He figured this was the safest spot to get away by driving or running into the alley. Turning the car off, he kept a vigil on the business until he slowly tired.

"In another ten minutes, I'll head back to the room and firm up my plans," Russell mumbled as his eyes closed.

CHAPTER TWENTY-NINE

"How much longer till you're ready to head into the office and meet with Leah?" Charlie asked Noble who sat opposite her at the kitchen table.

Looking at Charlie, Noble casually placed her hands in her back pocket. Noble knew this would be the hardest thing she'd ever had to do. But she needed to protect Charlie and Elizabeth.

"Noble. Talk to me. I need to know what's going on in your head," Charlie stated, fear dripping from the edge of her words.

"I have some things I need to say," Noble replied, leaning on the kitchen counter with her arms crossed over her chest.

Charlie stood and made her way over to Noble to kiss her, and Noble put her hand out to stop her. "Noble, what's wrong? Again, you need to talk to me. If I don't know what's wrong, I can't help you fix it." Charlie took a step back from Noble.

"I don't think I can do this anymore; I'm sorry," Noble stated. Her heart stuttered, and she had this falling, spinning-down feeling.

Charlie looked through Noble with a blank stare. Noble saw how Charlie attempted to keep her composure and not blink, holding back the floodgate of tears. "You can't do what anymore?" Charlie burst out as if Noble's words grew legs, kicked her hard in the gut, and drove all the breathable air from her body.

Noble moved away and leaned against the kitchen sink. She looked outside and sighed. "I'm too afraid of something happening to you or Elizabeth because of me, and I don't think I could survive if something happened to either of you because of the job. There! I laid it all out for you," Noble exclaimed as her breath exploded from her mouth.

Charlie approached Noble, turned her around, and put her arms around her. "I refuse to let you end what we have. I love you, and that will never change," Charlie vowed. "If you run away from me, you'll devastate me! And what about Elizabeth?" With tears, Charlie looked up at Noble. "You have me, always and forever. Please don't turn your back on us because it scares you. Take a chance on me and let me love you completely!" Charlie uttered.

"I can't have something happen to either of you because of me. It took me four years to let go of Diana, and I'm not sure I'd ever be able to get over you or Elizabeth getting hurt, or god forbid, killed because of me." Noble closed her eyes and let the tears flow down her face.

"There are no guarantees in this life. I could walk out, get into my car, and die in an accident," Charlie spoke with a quivering voice. "The only guarantee I can give you is that I love you, cherish you, and will occasionally disagree with you.

I will hold you in good times or bad, and I will spend the rest of my life showing you how important you are to me."

Noble separated her body from Charlie's and walked toward the front door. "I need some time to think. Please give me that." Noble held Charlie's gaze for a bit before looking away without another word.

†

Noble exited and closed the door. Once Charlie heard the door click, she slid to the ground in tears. *Why is this happening to me? Things were going great. What the hell happened?* After a while, Charlie got off the kitchen floor, locked every door, and headed to her bedroom.

"Mommy, why are you crying?" Elizabeth asked, her face filled with concern.

"Come here, sweetie. It's been a long night. Climb into bed with me, and we can watch some television," Charlie spoke, her voice heavy with suppressed sorrow.

"Okay. Where's Noole? Did she make you cry? That's not nice if she did."

"Yes, she did. It's going to be okay. Noble is afraid. She didn't mean to make Mommy cry." Charlie took a deep breath.

†

Charlie slowly lifted her head from the bed because someone was attempting to knock her front door off its hinges. She slowly got up and made her way to the front door. Charlie yanked the front door open and yelled, "What?"

Leah and Beth were standing there with their hands on their hips, looking at Charlie like she was a madwoman. "Charlie, what the hell is going on? You missed our nine o'clock meeting this morning!" Leah exploded. "You better have a good reason why. We are behind schedule to get this killer off the street."

"Leah, check that temper right this second," Beth snapped. "Let's go inside and finish this conversation."

"Okay." Leah pinched the bridge of her nose in frustration.

"I'm sorry." Charlie choked out. "Noble—"

"Ah sweetie, what's wrong?" Beth wrapped her arms around Charlie.

"She's scared, Mom. She'd willingly walk away rather than fight for our relationship. I don't know what I will do; my life is nothing without her!" Charlie cried out.

"Let's all sit on the couch. We want to tell you something. Where's Elizabeth?" Beth's eyes locked on to Charlie's.

"She's sleeping in my room."

"Diana had already arrived and was chasing the suspect when she lost him. What Noble didn't know was that the suspect had stolen a car and was speeding away from the scene when he hit Diana, killing her." Leah's expression was drawn in agony.

"Take your time, honey, I know this is hard." Beth squeezed Leah's hand.

"Noble was two blocks away when I picked her up in my patrol car and took her to the hospital. Noble blames herself for Diana's death, and I'm sure she's afraid of losing you, too!" Leah explained. "Dispatch sent Noble and Diana to the same call."

"This is a knee-jerk reaction! Life is unpredictable, but it's preposterous to abandon everything out of fear of what might occur." Charlie pressed her fingers to her lips. "Moreover, I know some of the events of Diana's case. How can I convince Noble that we belong together? I feel completely lost without her." She shook her head as if that would bring her clarity and end this nightmare.

"You'll need to give her space and let her work through this herself." Leah's eyes locked onto Charlie's. "Only she can realize that you're worth the risk. But she's on my shitlist for missing our meeting and hurting my daughter." Leah's pupils flared with anger.

"How come love hurts so badly?" Charlie looked through the fringe of her lashes. "All I want is to spend the rest of my life loving and being loved by someone, and that's not an unrealistic dream. I want what you two have and refuse to settle for anything less!" Charlie stated, as tears breached her lids.

"Charlie, please be patient, and things always have a way of working out," Beth remarked, her tone leaving no room for argument.

"I can't and won't wait around forever," Charlie declared, her voice raised. "Leah, can you please take me to visit Diana's grave?" Charlie hoisted herself to her feet.

"Why?" Leah asked, puzzled.

"I need to figure out what's going on in Noble's head, and the best way for me to do that is to visit a key piece to the puzzle," Charlie replied.

"I'll stay here with Elizabeth, and once she wakes and has breakfast, we'll go to our house. You two do what you need to do to get our Noble back and nail this son of a bitch for the last time." Beth traded a glance with them.

"That's not an acceptable word, Grandma," Elizabeth voiced while yawning in the doorway.

"Sorry, sweetie. Grandma will try to do better," Beth said, a softness touching her lips.

"Sweetie, Mommy and Mimi have to leave for a little while. Be good for Grandma. I love you." Charlie ruffled Elizabeth's hair.

"Where's Noole?" Elizabeth asked.

"She's at home. Noble has a lot on her plate right now. We'll see her in a couple of days." Charlie nervously bit the inside of her cheek.

"Okay."

"Are you ready, Leah?"

"Yes, let's go."

As they drove into the cemetery, the sun was high in the sky and a beautiful shade of orange. Leah parked the car and led Charlie to Diana's graveside.

"I'll wait in the car, sweetie." Leah embraced Charlie, kissed her on the cheek, before heading back to the car.

"Starting the conversation is tricky for me, but here it goes. People say you were not only a great cop but an even better person." Charlie took in a shaky breath. "Noble stole my daughter's heart, and I've fallen in love with her," she continued. "Diana, I know you and Noble wanted your own family, and I'm so sorry it was taken away from you," Charlie finished, holding her tears at bay.

A rustling of the tree branches above Charlie's head caused her to look up. There on the branch sat the most beautiful red-tailed hawk. It looked down at her, turning its head like it was listening to Charlie's one-sided conversation.

"I see you. This might be a good sign." Charlie nervously laughed out loud.

"As I was saying, we might know who killed you and took you away from Noble. I can't know what she's going through, but I can promise that I will patiently wait for her to get her head out of her ass and realize that it's okay to love again." The edge of her lips turned upward in a grin. "Even if you believe she might never have what you two had before, I'm here to let you know I will love her the way she loved and worshipped you till the day I die," Charlie vowed, standing strong with her head held high.

The hawk landed on Diana's headstone and looked at Charlie intensely.

"Okay, buddy, are you trying to send me a sign, or are you ready to attack? You have some big talons there. Here's to hoping you're here for a reason." Charlie belly laughed.

The hawk made a rasping scream that sounded like a high-pitched *kree-eee-ar*. It jumped to the grassy area at the base of Diana's headstone and started pecking at something in the grass.

"What've you got there, Ms. Hawk?" Charlie inquired while she bent down to the grass. Her fingers hit something metal. She crouched, watched the hawk stare at her, and picked up a coin. It wasn't a regular currency coin but a challenge coin.

"It appears you're a smart hawk. Let's see what's on it." Charlie began wiping off the coin as it was covered with dirt and grass.

The hawk flew to the tree branch it had initially been on and watched her with intensity.

"Wow. It seems like this has been here for quite some time," Charlie mumbled while using her shirt to wipe off the dirt.

At hearing another high-pitched *kree-eee-ar* from the hawk, Charlie looked down at the coin and saw some words and a Templar Knight.

Do Not Pray For An Easy Life. Pray For The Strength To Endure A Difficult One, Charlie read on one side of the coin. Upon flipping it over, it had the words Honor, Courage, Integrity, and Compassion with a sword and shield.

Charlie looked up when the tree branches started rustling and making noise. The hawk appeared to shake its head toward her.

"I think the message is loud and clear, Diana. Thank you, and I will love her forever," Charlie replied, putting the coin in her pocket and walking toward the car.

"Are you okay?" Leah asked as soon as Charlie sat and closed the passenger door.

"Yes, better than okay. Diana gave me a sign, and it's time to get this fucker out of our lives so I can help Noble realize we belong together. She should understand on her own that life without Elizabeth or me is not an option." Charlie spoke in a calm, steady voice.

"That's my girl. You looked animated over there." Leah chuckled while looking at Charlie.

"Yes, it was a spirited conversation between me and a red-tailed hawk. I'm sure Diana sent her to get me through this. The hawk even gave me something. It found a Templar Knight challenge coin." Charlie reached into her pocket, removed the coin, and handed it to Leah.

"Wow. It's been here all this time. Unbelievable," Leah stated in shock.

"What's the backstory, Mom L?" Charlie shifted her gaze to the coin.

"Your mom and I gave it to Noble at Diana's funeral." Leah drew in a deep breath. "She always carried it, whether working or on a day off. Per Noble, it helped and guided her at work and in her personal life." Her breath stalled. "She lost it about a year ago, and let's say she took it hard." A shadow came over her face.

"I can't wait to give it to her when the time is right." Charlie brushed her palms together.

"Are you ready to head to my office to review some things? Not sure if she'll be there, but we need to get Russell into custody before he kills anyone else." Leah put the car in drive.

"Let's go," Charlie replied, closing her fist around the coin and saying a brief prayer.

Chapter Thirty

"Excuse me, are you okay?" a man's voice asked, followed by a knock on the glass.

"What the hell? Where am I? Oh shit!" Russell yelled as he looked at the man beside the driver's side window.

"Oh, thank goodness you're alright. I'll go over and tell that officer who arrived that everything is okay," the older man declared.

Russell couldn't believe his eyes when he glanced at the rearview mirror and spotted the patrol vehicle. "You've got to be kidding me?" he exclaimed.

The older man talked with the officer as Russell stepped out of the car in case he had to run.

"See, I told you he was okay," the man confidently stated as Russell's eyes locked with the officer's.

"Well, fuck me. I think that cop knows who I am." Russell saw the patrol officer's eyes get as big as saucers as he was trying to open his car door.

"Excuse me, sir. Stay where you are. Onserf Police, show me your hands," the officer yelled as he exited his patrol vehicle.

Russell took off running down the alley, jumped the fence into the second backyard, and kept jumping fences until he needed to catch his breath. He was smart enough to grab his scanner and turn it low to hear what they were saying.

"Officer requesting multiple units for a perimeter, K-9s, and a helicopter if possible."

"Copy. What crime do you have?" dispatch asked.

"We're searching for a white male adult named Billy Russell. He's wanted for absconding parole and possibly murder," the officer announced, panting. The officer yelled that he was in a foot pursuit, southbound in the alley south of Blade's Brewery.

"Copy. Multiple units are currently headed to your location. I've sent them where to respond to for a perimeter via their car computer. There is a call into Sergeant Harper and the shift sergeant," dispatch stated.

"I've lost visual. The suspect hopped into someone's backyard. I'm still walking southbound in the alley, heading toward a barking dog coming from the area. He went over the fence," the officer advised dispatch.

"We will post up on each corner of the house," another officer advised.

"Copy. Backup should come northbound and southbound in the alley. Advise when you see the officers," the dispatch operator stated.

"Two units are in the alley with me. We're entering the backyard of the address to check for the suspect."

"Copy. This channel is on emergency traffic," the dispatcher barked.

Beep…beep…beep…beep…

"Your status?" dispatch asked.

"Status check?" dispatch barked again.

"It appears there's a window broken in the back of the house, and the suspect has possibly gained entry," the officer relayed over the air.

"Copy. Sergeant Harper, should be arriving shortly," dispatch advised.

"FYI, homeowners have run out the front door and notified us that an unknown subject is in the house and armed with a handgun."

"Copy, updating Sergeant Harper."

"FYI, the suspect is yelling commands, and there was a shot fired inside the house," the officer advised dispatch over the radio.

"Copy. Do you know what the suspect is saying?" dispatch asked.

"He wants Detective Gentry here."

"Copy, relaying the information," dispatch advised.

CHAPTER THIRTY-ONE

"Sex Crimes, Sergeant Harper. How may I help you?" Leah rattled into the phone receiver.

"This is dispatch supervisor Lujan. We have a situation on channel five. They've got a barricaded suspect, possibly Billy Russell, and he's asking for Detective Gentry," Lujan conveyed.

"Fuck. I've got my team here and one at the courthouse. Have the officers lock down the perimeter. I'll send my officer to the courthouse to meet with a judge and get the no knock warrant signed. It'll take only five minutes, and they can fax it to them. Once it's signed, we'll head out to make entry," Leah rattled off before she hung up. "I want all our bases covered, and that includes the no knock or silent entry warrant. Remember, Russell is an absconding parolee and a felon in possession of a firearm. A firearm that he has discharged," Leah uttered to the empty office while writing down notes on her notepad.

"What's going on, Sergeant?" Vistole propped his shoulder against the doorframe. "It's not good to be having a one-sided conversation with yourself."

"I need you to get the unit together, gear up for a search warrant, and be ready to go in under thirty minutes. They have Russell contained in a house. I'll update the SPAT agents and have them meet us at the scene. And Vistole, do me a favor and tell Gentry to get her ass in here like yesterday," Leah barked.

"Yes, ma'am," Tony answered as he ran out of Leah's office.

†

"Hey Leah, Tony mentioned that you wanted to talk to me. And regarding Charlie…" Noble cautiously inquired as she stepped into the office, uncertain if Charlie had let them know.

"Stop. This is not the time, Noble. After this call, we'll discuss your head-up-the-ass philosophy on life, and how you made my daughter cry and question coming back home to Onserf," Leah barked. "Anyway, it appears they have Billy Russell locked down inside a house he broke into when he ran from his vehicle earlier."

"What? When can we arrest that fucker? I can't wait to interview him. He needs to be locked up for good with no chance to ever see the outside of a prison again. I want my life back." Noble peppered Leah with questions.

"You know he wants you there, and I'm half inclined to send you home. I shouldn't let you near this, but we're shorthanded, and I'll beg for forgiveness afterward." Leah's jaw slammed shut and hardened. "Noble, are you comfortable with being part of the entry team with District Crime

Suppression Teams? I don't have to let you know how serious this is. I need your head in the game, not anything else."

"I know the DCST teams are shorthanded city-wide, so yes, I'm ready." Noble's chin cocked a degree. "There are many unanswered questions, and only Russell can provide the missing pieces."

"Salinas has been instructed to respond to the command post when he leaves the courthouse. Once he arrives, we'll be ready to brief with SPAT in about five minutes. Go grab your gear, we'll meet in the briefing room, and head out to the scene," Leah directed.

"Last question I have is why do we need to do a search warrant? Weren't officers in hot pursuit?" Noble shrugged.

"They lost sight of him for almost five minutes. I don't want to take any chances and want to do this by the book," Leah stated. "All occupants are out of the house, and the house is locked down. Time is on our side to end this standoff peacefully, with Russell in custody." Leah gave a clipped nod.

"Makes sense. I'll go grab my gear." Noble exited Leah's office.

†

Noble walked into the briefing room and saw only one empty chair beside Charlie. She looked directly at Charlie and raised her eyebrows as if asking permission to sit there. Charlie turned her head and launched into a conversation with another coworker. *Why should I expect a warm reception when all I did was rip her heart out and stomp on it? She deserves better. I can't believe I fucked this up when all I want is to be with her and Elizabeth. I need to make this right.* She sat in the chair and tapped Charlie on the shoulder.

"What?" Charlie barked.

"After the search warrant, can I meet you for coffee and a talk?" Noble asked, her voice a shred of a whisper.

"I'm really hurt, Noble. I just need some time. I know we need to talk, but not today."

"Okay. That's fair," Noble answered, knowing that she had loads of work to do to make it right.

"Everyone, I need your attention. Let's head to the command post now," Sergeant Harper said as she walked into the briefing room.

CHAPTER THIRTY-TWO

As the officers arrived, they gathered at the police mobile command center. The atmosphere was charged with anticipation. Officers exchanged glances, their expressions a mix of determination and concern.

"We will serve the search warrant at a location for suspect Billy Russell. Each of you now have a packet with suspect information and the house layout given to us by the homeowner, perimeter team, and entry team. We will work off Channel 8."

Sergeant Hawthorne's voice cut through the tension, relaying critical information. "A gunshot echoed through the area roughly twenty-five minutes prior." The urgency in his tone was palpable as he noted the failed attempts to reach the suspect, Russell, via the homeowners' house phone and over the PA system.

Lieutenant Torch, his brow furrowed in thought, turned to Sergeant Harper, giving her a subtle nod that signaled it was time for her to step in and lead the next phase of their operation. The air was thick with the sounds of radios crackling and the distant hum of sirens, underscoring the gravity of the situation.

"Perimeter team, head out to your assigned locations," Sergeant Harper commanded, her tone firm yet steady. The officers moved with purpose, the sound of boots crunching on gravel echoing in the stillness. "Once each of you confirms you're in position, the entry team will proceed to the address listed in the search warrant." The gravity of the moment was underscored by the knowledge that suspect Russell was believed to be inside the residence, armed, and dangerous. "Stay safe out there and we'll notify you when we're code four after entry is made, residence is secure, and suspect is in custody," she concluded.

The weight of their mission hanging in the air as they prepared to act.

†

"5Paul11, I'm on the perimeter with 5Adam11."

"5Paul12, I'm on the perimeter with 5Baker11."

"5Paul13, I'm on the perimeter with 5Henry11."

"5Paul14, I'm on the perimeter with 5Edward11."

"Copy, 5Paul11, Paul12, Paul13, and Paul14," channel eight dispatcher answered the perimeter units.

"5Sam10, I'll advise you shortly on our approach to making entry," Sergeant Harper notified the channel eight operator.

"Copy," dispatch advised.

"Everyone, please fall into your assigned spot in the stack. Agent Matthews and her partner, Mike Taylor, will bring up the rear," Sergeant Harper stated. "Make sure you're on channel eight and remember that the suspect's status is unknown, but he was armed with a handgun when he entered the residence over half an hour ago."

"We're ready, Sarge." Noble glanced at the back of the line and made eye contact with Charlie one last time.

"Ready in the back, Sergeant Harper," Charlie announced.

"5Sam10, we're making our approach."

"Copy."

"5Mary14, clear the air for emergency traffic," Detective Gentry declared.

"5Mary14 copy. This channel is on emergency traffic," dispatch replied, advising officers on channel eight.

Beep…Beep…Beep…

†

As the officers slowly approached the front door in a single file, Noble uttered a silent prayer. *Please let all officers be safe and return home to their families today.*

With their guns out at the low ready position, ballistic helmets on, multiple eyes watched for any movement at any of the windows they could see.

Officer Den tried the front door, and it was locked. He motioned to Officer Leal who approached and struck the front door with the ram, knocking the door in on the first hit. Officers methodically entered the residence, working in multiple teams to clear the house.

Special Agent Matthews and Noble eventually became a team of two as they approached the hallway on the same side of the wall. Special Agent Taylor and Detective Vistole were up to take the closed door on the left. Officer Pat and Noble looked down the long hallway with multiple doors. The last door on the left was open.

Using only her hand to gesture, Officer Pat pointed to the first door on the right. She pointed toward Special Agent Matthews and Noble to take the room to the right, gesturing that she would stand by and watch the hallway until they cleared the room.

You've got to be kidding. Of all the people to go through a door with, Charlie must be the one. Having to go with Charlie is karma for breaking her heart. I deserve it. You better not fuck it up, Gentry.

Noble and Charlie nodded in synch and turned toward the closed door on the right. With a gentle squeeze on Charlie's shoulder, Noble conveyed her readiness to proceed and enter the initial room. Officer Pat and Special Agent Taylor stood by, their eyes fixed on the closed doors and the open one at the far end of the hallway.

As Charlie took a few steps forward and opened the door to her right, Noble caught movement from the room at the end of the hall with the door open. Noble looked up and saw Billy Russell pointing a gun in their direction.

"Gun!" Noble yelled as Billy started firing his weapon. Instinct took over, and Noble pushed Charlie forcefully into the door, causing the door to swing violently into the bedroom. Charlie practically stuck to it and fell to the floor in a heap.

"Shots fired; shots fired!" Tony's voice thundered through the radio as he watched in horror as Noble's body jerked as each bullet struck.

The sound hit her like a slap across the face at high velocity. Noble's ears rang from the proximity of where the gun discharged. The burning smell of gunpowder mixed with blood floated through the air. At that moment, she knew.

Eerily silent, she lay there frozen until her brain told her to breathe, and she gasped for air.

Chapter Thirty-three

The pain was immediate in her left leg, stomach, and upper shoulder. *Fucker got me right below and right above my vest. What are the fucking odds of that happening in one incident?* It felt like someone was sticking her body with a hot poker they'd pulled out of a fire in a fireplace. As she continued firing at Billy, it seemed as though time had slowed down around her. Noble kept shooting until Billy had fallen to the ground and was no longer a threat. She wasn't aware that she'd reloaded a fresh magazine into her gun until she heard the old one hit the wooden floor and crash into the wall. As Noble collapsed, one side of her body lay in the hallway while the other rested in the bedroom they were getting ready to enter. *Oh fuck, this damn well hurts. I can't believe I let that douchebag get the drop on me. Fuck.* Noble gasped for air.

Noble could hear, "Shots fired. Officer down, officer down!" as Officer Salinas and Tony yelled into their lapel mics. *Why do they sound so far away?*

She looked up and mumbled, "How is Charlie? Why should I wear a vest when it can't even protect me? How's Charlie?" She wasn't sure if anyone could hear her. Noble's body hurt, and she felt numbness taking over with the darkness. Noble heard officers yelling to get her into a patrol car, that it would be quicker to transport her to the hospital than wait for the ambulance. *When is this ringing going to stop? Shit, some of these guys have dirty patrol vehicles. I don't want to ride in the backseat of one of them.*

Noble wanted to keep her eyes closed; the pain was unbearable, and her clothes felt wet! The wetness was likely from all the blood she was losing.

Clomp! Clomp! She could hear boots as they approached her, she assumed, trying to clear the last bedroom while confirming that Billy was no longer a threat. *I could have told you the suspect was down! There was no way he was getting more of a drop on me than he already had. There was no way he survived.*

"Dammit, Noble, stay with me. Hang in there and keep your eyes open. You did good today," Leah kept telling Noble.

Noble felt herself being lifted off the ground and carried outside. *Where the hell is the gurney? It must be serious if they're carrying me out.*

"You got him, Noble, you got him." She heard Tony say.

I hope I didn't push Charlie too hard. I should've never broken it off with her, but I didn't want Russell to kill her, too. When is the pain going to stop? So damn bad. Noble could only stare out the patrol car window, hoping this was all a figment of her imagination.

Noble heard Officer Hightower advise dispatch that he was driving a code three to the hospital with an injured officer and to have the ER personnel standing by for their arrival. The wailing of sirens echoed sharply as Noble lay there, realizing that her breath had turned heavy, fighting for air. Her entire left side was in excruciating pain, and she wanted to cry but knew that she had to be strong and not go into shock.

"Is Charlie…is she okay?" Noble mumbled in an inaudible whisper.

"Don't talk, Noble. Keep your eyes open and stay awake. Look at me if you must, but don't you dare close your eyes," Leah barked, swallowing tears.

"I need to know she's alright. I fucked up, and if something happens to me, she needs to know that I love her. And I want to make it right," Noble hissed as a sharp pain caused her to grimace.

"You're going to be alright. We're only a few blocks from the state's best trauma hospital. You can tell her anything you want after they tend to your wounds. Once again, quit talking. You'll need that energy if they need to operate." Leah squeezed Noble's hand.

"Leah, I'm sorry. I promised you I'd never hurt Charlie, and I did. I…"

"Would you shut up, Noble? We'll work on your fucked up love life and decision-making after you get better. And don't think for one second that you're off the hook with me because you got shot. You can make amends later."

"Okay…" Noble gasped and then lost consciousness.

†

"Step the fuck on it, officer." Leah closed her eyes, looked up, and whispered a prayer.

"Yes ma'am," he replied in a whisper.

"There's no way in hell you're dying on my watch, Noble. I don't want to face Beth and Charlie alone." A host of emotions overlapped on her face.

†

It felt like hours had passed when abruptly, Noble felt like she was sliding off the seat and onto the floorboard of the patrol vehicle as it jerked to a stop in front of the emergency room doors. *I guess we're at the hospital. They almost killed me trying to get here to keep me from dying from the gunshot wounds. Fucking rookie drivers.*

People were yelling orders, or at least voices Noble believed belonged to medical personnel. She felt herself being lifted and roughly handled out of the back seat and placed onto a gurney. She heard popping as her buttons flew off her shirt. People she assumed were nurses and doctors poked and prodded her body. She guessed they were evaluating her injuries in the hospital parking lot at the emergency room entrance. *Wow, seriously, right here in front of all the news cameras and fucking citizens of Onserf.* She couldn't understand what they were saying but heard Leah bark orders. *I'm not sure Leah understands that she's not their boss.*

"You need to get her inside and do the assessment. Too many cameras out here. Let's move!" Leah ordered in her supervisor's voice.

"Give us a second, and we'll be on our way," a male voice answered.

Noble could have sworn that she heard a clicking noise that sounded like a camera but was powerless to look. At one point, Noble thought she heard a woman, maybe the on-call doctor for the emergency room, trying to tell her what they were doing as they took her into a triage room.

†

Officers and staff lined the hallway at the hospital, waiting for any word regarding Noble. Word spread quickly around the department, and everyone, whether working or on days off, responded to the hospital. Noble had been in the department for many years and was a favorite among patrol officers and among staff within the department.

"How could I let this happen?" Leah clenched her fists and hit the wall in the waiting room.

"You let nothing happen, Mom L. This is the nature of the beast, the shitty part of the job." Charlie pulled Leah into a tight hug. "And I can't fucking believe she pushed me out of the way. Who the hell does that? That should be me in there." A groan accompanied the roll of her eyes. "She better make it so I can throttle her myself. Look at the knot on my forehead from slamming into that damn door."

"Oh, honey, it's going to be alright. We'll bring our Noble home," Beth reassured Leah.

"Noble does that, Charlie, as if you'd question why. She loves you, and her hard, unsecured head impedes her rational thinking." Leah lifted her shoulder in a half shrug. "You scare her because I don't think she expected to feel this way ever again after Diana died. The thought of losing you like she did Diana scared her because she loves you." The flicker of a smile passed her lips.

"Leah, I couldn't agree with you more about that. She's had four years of mourning the loss of Diana and the open case the department still has on her death. You come into the picture, and some crazed guy is insinuating that he'll do the same thing he did to Diana. It scared her," Beth replied in an even tone.

"Ending a relationship is ridiculous because you're afraid of losing that person." Charlie pinned her crossed arms over her chest.

"It's different from ending a marriage or walking away. I know you don't understand, Charlie, but Noble would readily die herself than have anyone lose their life because of her. She doesn't think she's worthy of love. Noble has taken a long time to get over Diana. She's like a literal knight," Leah explained about her dear friend Noble. "Beth, remember that Templar Knight challenge coin we gave her after Diana died? It holds. And guess what, honey, Charlie found it at Diana's gravesite." Leah looked at Beth and Charlie.

"I'm seeing that, Mom and Mom L. It's painful, you know? I can't help but wish she hadn't ended things before we even had a chance to begin. I'm still upset, and I blew her off at the briefing. What if I can't ever talk to her again? And what do I say to Elizabeth?"

"She's going to be okay. You must believe, and besides, she has something worth fighting for, you and Elizabeth," Leah stated.

"Sergeant Harper?" a man in scrubs came walking down the hall, looking confused about whom he needed to speak with.

"Yes. How is Detective Gentry?" Leah glanced at his name badge, which he was holding so she could address him by name.

"She's in recovery now, but Noble is still in critical but stable condition. She's lost a considerable amount of blood and is weak. I removed all the bullets, and she should make a full recovery, barring any complications. The next forty-eight to seventy-two hours will give me a better idea," Doctor Griffin replied as he clipped his name badge on his clean surgical scrubs.

"Thank you so much, Doctor Griffin," Leah said.

Beth, and Charlie hugged the doctor simultaneously.

"She's not out of the woods. But based on what she was saying in the operating room, I'd bet that Noble will recover a little every day."

"Doctor Griffin, can you please walk with me?" Leah turned and walked toward the empty hallway.

"But…" Charlie muttered, shaking her head.

"This is work, and you'll have to wait." Leah walked away with Doctor Griffin.

"It's just you and me. Can you please tell me what Noble was talking about? I need to make sure it doesn't pertain to the search warrant she was on."

"Well, let's see how I can make it PG." Doctor Griffin laughed as his face turned bright red.

"Hah…" Leah belted out a deep, guttural laugh.

"Something to the effect that she messed up and lost her future, and it wouldn't surprise her if none of them took her back."

"Oh, did she say who any of them were?"

"Yes, Charlie, Elizabeth, Beth, and Leah. It sounds like she might have been dating multiple women, Sergeant. More power to her, if that's the case. I must be lousy, I can only handle having a puppy." Doctor Griffin laughed.

"Well, the good thing is she's not dating multiple women. Unfortunately, she made a choice she believed was right, but it turned out to be the wrong one," Leah remarked with a sad smile.

"Noble seems to be the determined woman who will right her ship and fix it. I shouldn't have jumped to conclusions."

"No worries, Doctor Griffin. Three of the individuals she mentioned are here. The main one is my daughter, who was with me earlier, our granddaughter, my wife, and myself."

"Don't give up on her. She'll need help to get through this. Before I can discharge her, someone will need to stay with her for the next couple weeks."

"What?" Leah stammered.

"Taking care of her at home and ensuring she gets to therapy will be crucial. Moreover, finding someone who won't fall for her tricks but can assert authority over her is equally important."

"Well, it'll be me or my wife. Noble has no other family that lives nearby."

"Good. If you give me your card, I will add you as a contact if we need to advise you of anything."

"Thank you for everything, Doctor Griffin. You saved a good friend and possibly a future daughter-in-law."

"I was only doing my job, but today was a good day, a win if you want to call it that."

"Yes, undeniably a win. Can the three of us see Noble? Just for a couple of minutes."

"For only a few, she needs to rest."

"Let me grab them and let the other officers know what's happening. That way, I can clear some of your hallways. Be right back."

Leah walked over to the officers, gave them a brief update, and headed toward Beth and Charlie. Out of the corner of her eye, she saw Tony and Mike sitting in the waiting room. Tony had been crying. She headed that way.

"Vistole, are you hanging in there?" Leah squatted before him and placed her hands on his.

"I'm waiting to hear how Noble is doing, Sarge." He shifted in the chair.

"According to the doctor, she's out of surgery and in critical but stable condition. We should know much more in the next seventy-two hours," Leah shared.

"Whew. Good news," Tony replied. He took a deep breath and covered his face with his hands to wipe away any tears that might have slipped through.

"The doctor told me we could go in for a couple of minutes. Come with us. Mike can wait out here for you."

"I'll be here, Tony. Check on your partner. She's going to be okay."

"Not today, Sarge. It's more significant that Charlie, you, and Beth see Noble. I'm not leaving here tonight, so they'll let me see her after they get her to a private room."

"Are you sure?"

"Yes. She needs to hear Charlie's voice. Her voice will help Noble fight and return to us all." A grin creased his face. "And before I forget to tell you, it looks like Bridget's ex-boyfriend was contacted and he hasn't been in Onserf since the day they had that argument. He has an alibi that was confirmed. He's an asshole, but not a murderer." Tony finished up with a chuckle.

"You're a good man, Tony. I know Noble thinks of you like a brother, and I see why. I'll come check on you when we leave for the night. And thank you for the ex-boyfriend info." Leah stood, turned, and walked back to Charlie and Beth.

"You ready to go see her for a couple of minutes?" Leah traded a glance with Beth and Charlie.

"Why did you pull the doctor away?" Charlie asked, throwing up her hands.

"I needed to find out if she blurted anything pertinent to the case. You should know why I had to do it." Leah shot her a narrow look.

"We do, Leah. There's no need to snap. It's been a long day. Let's see how Noble is doing, and we'll go from there." Beth embraced Leah.

"I'm sorry. It's been a long day. And I almost lost an officer who's a good friend." Her voice faded into a wisp.

"It's okay, Mom L. She's important to all of us. Sorry if I sounded accusatory." Charlie walked up and joined in on the hug.

"Charlie, why don't you go in? Remember to keep it short; she needs all her strength to get through this," Leah said.

"You and Mom can go. Unless you want to stay longer." A panicked expression flittered across Charlie's beautiful face.

"Get in there. It would be best if you saw Noble for yourself." Beth nudged Charlie toward the door.

"Okay. Okay. I'm going—"

"We'll be right out here," Beth and Leah announced.

CHAPTER THIRTY-FOUR

Upon turning the knob with caution, Charlie gently pushed the door open, only to be greeted by the rhythmic sound coming from the equipment beside Noble's bed. Charlie didn't know what to expect, but this was nowhere close to what she'd imagined. Noble had all kinds of tubes, and an IV going into her hand. Her right hand and wrist had a TLC splint, known as "Touch, Look, and Compare" to help stabilize the IV line. This splint allowed nurses more straightforward access to monitor the IV insertion site with minimal disruption to Noble.

Crazy, some of the stuff you pick up and remember doing this job.

"Oh, good lord, Noble. What were you thinking when you pushed me out of the way? I'm sorry this happened to you." Charlie walked to the side of the bed and covered Noble's good hand with her own.

Charlie looked at the heart rate monitor and noticed Noble's heart rate starting to beat faster. She slowly leaned in and kissed Noble on the forehead, seeing a spike in her heart rate again.

"Excuse me. I need to grab Detective Gentry's chart," the nurse, who'd entered the room undetected, whispered.

"Okay," Charlie replied, never taking her eyes off Noble.

"Thank you." The nurse quietly shut the door.

"What am I going to do with you, Noble? You broke my heart and saved my life," Charlie whispered as her shoulders dropped with a sigh. "When you get better, we will need to talk. Please know that whatever happens between us, I will always love you. Even if we're apart." Her forehead creased with uncertainty.

Alarm bells from the heart monitor were going off. Charlie looked up and saw that Noble's heart rate had escalated and most likely sent a notification to the nurse's station nearby.

"You could've asked me to leave instead of getting the nurses to escort me out. Rest easy, Noble, and I will see you soon." Charlie's smile fell away.

"I'm sorry, but visitation is over. Detective Gentry needs her rest," the head nurse concluded.

"Yes, I understand. I didn't mean to raise Noble's heart rate. My apologies," Charlie replied to the nurse.

"It's good because it means she was listening to you. But we should error on the side of caution and let her get her rest so she can heal and talk to you when she's better." The nurse smiled and helped settle Noble down with some medication.

"Get well, Noble." Charlie lightly squeezed her hand and felt Noble squeeze back.

Once outside the door, she saw her parents staring questioningly at her.

"What happened in there, Charlie?" Beth asked, her eyes doubled in size.

"Mom, I was telling her that whatever happens between us, I will always love her. She must've been semi-awake to hear me say it. Suddenly, her heart rate monitor went off the charts." Charlie held her arms around herself.

"So, you were hoping she was asleep, and instead, she wasn't, and you referred to possibly not being together? What did you think was going to happen?" Leah interjected, the muscles in her neck twitched.

"I sure as hell didn't think that was going to happen, Mom L. Cut me some slack," Charlie clipped back. "Just because she saved my life today doesn't negate that less than twenty-four hours before that, she broke my heart."

"Okay, you two. Make nice." Beth wagged her finger at them. "Charlie, I'm taking you back to our house. Elizabeth will be there waiting for us. Our neighbor, Mrs. Duke, is watching her." Beth steepled her long fingers together. "Leah, it would be best if you stayed with Tony for a while. Someone will check in with you later tonight."

"Sweetheart, I'm sorry. We know you've been through a lot this last week. Come here." Leah wrapped her arms around Charlie and kissed her gently on the forehead.

"Me, too! Please keep us updated if there's any change."

"Will do. Love you." Leah leaned in and softly kissed Beth.

"Bye," Beth and Charlie announced in unison.

†

Leah sat in a chair next to Noble's room. Leaning back and placing her head against the wall, she closed her eyes and took a deep breath. Slowly, the tears streamed down her face as the thoughts of today's events finally caught up to her.

"Excuse me, Leah," a female voice spoke.

"Yes." Leah sat up straight, opened her eyes, and stared at a familiar face.

"I thought you could use some coffee. You've been asleep for about an hour."

"Thank you, Quincy. Sorry to see you under these circumstances."

"Yes, but at least it's good to see you. I got the call from Dani today about what happened, and I wanted to make sure I came by to see you for a bit."

"I'm glad you did. It's been a couple of months since we last saw you two. Hope all is going well with everyone," Leah said.

"Yes, we're busy as usual," Quincy replied. "Dani is assigned to the Southwest District, working day shift patrol. She's keeping busy. And it's always busy here at the hospital. I'm off shift, but I wanted to swing by to bring you some coffee. Also, here is a sandwich, as I'm sure you had no dinner." Her grin softened into a genuine smile.

"You're a life saver," Leah replied as her stomach growled, letting her know it was time to eat.

"I'm heading home. Let's get something on the calendar in the next month so we can all get caught up. Can we meet up with you in a few weeks? I want your opinion on something from law enforcement and women's perspectives," Quincy asked.

"Of course. Call or text, and we can review our calendars to set a time. That sounds like a plan. Our daughter and granddaughter have moved back so we could have a BBQ at our house, and you could meet them. I'll check with Beth and send you a text."

"I hope your detective is doing okay. And I look forward to your text."

"Yes, she's got a long recovery, but she should do well. Thank you. You'll be hearing from me soon. Good night." Leah unwrapped the sandwich and took a huge bite. "Is everything alright?"

"I'm not sure, but it can keep till we get together," Quincy replied, walking down the hall, and disappearing around the corner.

"I wonder what that was all about." Leah inhaled the rest of her sandwich and leaned back to rest her eyes for a couple of minutes.

†

"Sarge, wake up." Leah heard a male voice say.

"I'm awake, just taking a moment to rest." Leah slowly opened her eyes.

"Sounded more like you were sawing down a forest, but okay, stick with the 'resting your eyes' bit." Tony took a step farther away from Leah.

"You know I'm your boss, right?" Leah tilted her head.

"Yes, ma'am. Sorry, a little punchy from lack of sleep," he replied as he looked down at the ground.

"I'll let it slide this one time. How is Noble doing?"

"She's awake and cranky. Pissed off at the world, or more so herself, for how she hurt Charlie. Being shot is not on her top ten list. It's all about getting Charlie back and righting her wrong."

"Well, my daughter can be stubborn. And it won't be a simple task for Noble, but everything will work out."

"This is the first time I've seen Noble look so lost. I mean, it devastated her when Diana died. But this is different. She knows she controls how it ends, and Noble picked the wrong play to secure the touchdown. It's fourth down, and she's got one chance to make it right."

"Well, aren't you the football commentator? You go home and get some rest. And I've cleared you to take the next few days off. I will check on the quarterback and see if she has any better play calls to make."

"Thanks, Sarge. I'll check in with you later. Chief Raynor wanted me to let you know that she'll be here in about fifteen minutes. Something about wanting to talk with you about an urgent matter. She wants you to hold off seeing Noble until you speak to her."

"Okay, thanks for the heads up. Speak of the devil…" Leah heard the clicking of high-heeled shoes heading her way.

†

"Sergeant Harper, how's our patient doing today?" Chief Raynor smiled from ear to ear.

"Hi, Chief. Detective Vistole stated she was grumpy, but otherwise, she was doing as well as expected. He mentioned you wanted to see me. Is there a problem?" Leah asked.

"No, not a problem, but new information regarding a cold case," Chief Raynor replied.

"Is it connected to the shooting?" Leah asked, puzzled.

"It's linked to Noble, the suspect, and a cold case."

"Okay, care to share that information?" Leah sat up in her seat and made direct eye contact with Chief Raynor.

"Here is a copy of a note removed from suspect Russell's pants pocket. Please read it."

You haven't pulled the pieces together yet, have you, Detective? Too bad that I'm tired of waiting. It's funny really, I almost wished you would've figured it out because it would have been more challenging, but deep down, I know no woman—least of all you—could ever outsmart me. I'm on a level far above you. Let me cut to the chase. Picture my utter surprise when I connected you to that pathetic female officer I ran down ages ago. You never did pin that rape on me. If it weren't for that bitch, Tracy, I'd still be free. It's a pity I didn't finish her off like I did your bitch. She had a certain good look about her before I turned her into roadkill. If time had been on my side, I'd have had my way with her after I hit her—after all, I was the last thing she saw as she lay there dying. Knowing she was near death was a thrill. Still, the real fun would've been with that little bitch, Tracy. Imagine my shock when they decided to let me out on a technicality. I thought it was the perfect time to rewrite that inconvenience and perhaps pay your new bitch and her kid a little visit. And you? Oh, rest assured, you'll be on my list too. It's time for women like you to recognize your rightful place. One by one, I will come for you. Just watch. I'll always be several steps ahead, while you'll never be smart enough to catch me. And remember, you only exist for one reason—serving whatever a man dictates.

"That son of a bitch!" Leah snarled through gritted teeth.

"I, for one, am glad that he'll no longer be a threat to women, much less the city of Onserf," Chief Raynor replied.

"How did his name not get flagged for Diana's hit and run? His DNA was in the system." Leah clenched her hands.

"Even though the hit and run involved an officer, the case took a backseat behind murder and sex crime cases with DNA." Chief Raynor claimed a chair next to Leah.

"Is this letter for me to show Noble? Or do you want me to tell her without showing it to her? It's a good thing she killed him, or you know she'd hunt him down," Leah stated, her eyebrows drawn together.

"If you think she can handle it, it might be better to show her. She needs to know that we finally got Diana's killer. We can officially close her case. And yes, I know what she'd do. It's the same thing any of us would do."

"I'll head on in and check on her. Thanks, Chief, for bringing this to me. In this moment, we have closure. Let's hope we get our Noble back."

"Go on in, and I'll check with you later."

"Wish me luck." Leah exhaled and opened Noble's hospital room door.

†

"I'm getting out of here in two days, so maybe, the next time you see me, it will be in my own home," Noble muttered when she saw Leah enter her hospital room.

"Get some rest, Noble. I'll check in with you tomorrow to see how you're doing. There's something I need to have you look at, and it would be better if your mind is clearer and not clouded by your pain medication. I heard Tony offered to stay with you until you can get around. We offered, but Tony begged to be the one. You've got a good friend in him, too. Always remember that."

"Always. I realize I have many great friends, and I'm thankful for every one of them. Get home to Beth and send her my love. I'd tell you to do the same for Charlie, but I don't think she'd want to hear it yet."

"Give it time. You need to heal from your wounds physically and mentally, heal from everything that's happened, and lastly, figure out which way you want to head on that long and winding road. I'll close your door so you can get some rest."

"Don't worry, you know me. I will never give up on something I believe so strongly in. See you soon, Leah. I love you, Char…" Noble's timed painkiller shot made its way through her IV. As the medication started taking effect, Noble's eyelids fluttered closed, her breathing became controlled, and she slipped into a deep sleep.

CHAPTER THIRTY-FIVE

Noble heard a click and saw her hospital room door open as Leah peeked inside. Pushing the button, she lifted the top of the bed so she could partially sit up.

"Hi, Leah. Come on in."

"Hey, Noble. Checking in to see how you're feeling. Do you need anything? I can ask the nurse if you do," Leah asked while she sat beside Noble's bed.

"No. I'm good. Thank you. I still can't eat solid food, but the doctor says I should fully recover."

"I heard that from the doctor last night. You scared the shit out of all of us, Noble. I'm glad you survived because it's still a tossup if I'm going to kick your ass or not." Leah laughed as tears streamed down her face.

"I was doing my job. Nothing more, nothing less. However, desk duty for a while isn't too bad. And please stop crying, or it will make me cry as well," Noble begged as water bordered her eyelids.

"Well, you'll be off until you heal enough to return to that desk." Leah wiped her tears away with a Kleenex.

"I know. Been bugging the nurse to let me walk so I can start the rehabilitation process." Noble smiled.

"Don't rush things, Noble. We want you to heal so you can eventually return to work if that's what you want." Leah looked directly at Noble.

"By we, does that include Charlie?" Noble's face divided into a nervous grin.

"You hurt her, Noble. It was heartless." Leah's chin jerked high. "She's going to need some time to rethink things. Give her that time. That's all I ask of you."

"I can do that. I don't want Charlie to see me like this, you know, weak." Noble took a deep breath. "She always calls me a Noble Knight, and I'm not feeling like a knight right now. I feel more like a terrible human being who hurt someone that I care deeply about." A desperate gasp clipped the silence.

"Give it time. You're anything but a terrible human, Noble." Leah squeezed Noble's hand.

"Thanks for being here, Leah. You and Beth have helped me through a dark time, and I will always be grateful."

"Speaking of that, I need you to look at something. It's a note found on Russell's body that he addressed to you. Are you up for it?"

Leah slowly unfolded the piece of paper that Chief Raynor had given her. She had folded it multiple times and placed it inside her jacket pocket to ensure she wouldn't lose it. The paper appeared weathered and no longer crisp or new looking.

"Give it here. I can't fathom what that asshole had to say to me," Noble spouted.

†

Leah handed over the note to Noble and watched her closely. She noticed Noble's eyebrows lower, and nostrils flare. Her trembling lips thinned because she pressed them together, and her lower jaw thrust forward. Tears rolled from her eyes down her face at a rapid rate.

"I'm so sorry, Noble. He was right under our noses. Because of homicide and sex crimes cases taking precedence, his DNA wasn't in the system yet. The system failed," Leah said in a throat-roughening whisper.

"I thought we only had prints on Diana's case. Where was his DNA located?" Noble looked a little confused.

"He exited the vehicle to check on Diana after hitting her, leaving traces of his blood on her shirt, likely from having injured himself in the accident." Leah's expression went blank. "The officer who collected the sample at the scene submitted it per department policy. Still, due to Detective Morales' injury and absence from work, the results ended up in his email inbox. Eventually, the department forced him to retire after a few years, resulting in him never having the opportunity to review the information before leaving," Leah spat out the words through gritted teeth. "Consequently, the results remained in his designated inbox until another officer took over and gained access. The sergeant failed to check his inbox for assignments that needed reassigning to another detective until there was a new one assigned to replace Morales," Leah choked out.

"Why did it eventually get checked?" Noble arched a questioning eyebrow in her direction.

"I had them put a rush on it after that car incident at Charlie's house." Her lips thinned. "It was a hunch, and Chief Raynor delivered this note earlier. And right before I came in here, I received the confirmation that the blood on Diana belonged to Billy Russell." Leah's eyes locked on Noble's.

"Diana can finally rest in peace. I'm so glad I killed that son of a bitch," Noble roared. "There was no way he'll take anything or anyone else from me. My gut kept saying he was involved; I was too close to it to see." She facepalmed into her hands.

"But you saw it when it mattered most, Noble. I'm forever thankful to you for saving Charlie's life," Leah remarked, laying a hand over her heart. "Not that Charlie is. She's pissed about what you did," she snorted. "And I'm so glad you'll be okay, Noble, because believe it or not, you're loved tremendously and valued as a friend." Leah wiped the tears from her face.

"Don't cry for me, Leah. I only know that I plan on hanging around for a long time," Noble stated in a steady, lower-pitched voice. "I've some healing to do, and after that, the rest of my life will be to win Charlie back and show her that my life is nothing without her and Elizabeth in it."

CHAPTER THIRTY-SIX

Two months later.

"We'll have to wait and see what happens after today's awards ceremony. I have faith that Noble will realize that she's irrational and loves you, and that's all that matters," Beth said. "Noble wanted to be healed up before she begged you to take her back. Or at least that's my take on it. Because you always called her Noble Knight, she wants to live up to that name." Beth hugged Charlie. "Leah will save us a couple of seats. So, let's head that way."

"Thank you for being the best moms on the planet. I can't believe it's been two months, and I can't believe you're forcing me to attend the ceremony! But I'm glad I have you two to lean on," Charlie replied to express her gratitude to her mom and Leah.

†

"I don't want to be here," Noble growled at Leah. "And in my Class A uniform at that."

"Tough. You need to relax. It will only take two hours, if that, out of your day," Leah replied. "And besides, you're not the only one getting an award, Noble."

"I never wanted to be recognized for saving anyone's life. It's part of the oath we swore to uphold when we became police officers!" Noble crossed her arms in front of her chest.

"I think you're upset because you and Charlie haven't spoken yet, and I can't say I blame her. You were wrong, and you're cranky!" she stated. "Have you ever considered she's letting you heal before having that crucial conversation? You need to get your shit in order," Leah snapped.

As the awards ceremony started, Noble thought about her life. *I had it all with Diana, and circumstances out of my control took her away. I was afraid to love again, and I never assumed that there would be anyone else. Out of the blue, Charlie waltzed right in and blew the wind out of my sails. As Leah stated, I need to step up to the plate and do something if I want her back.*

"You need to quit daydreaming because it's almost time for you to go up and get your award." Leah elbowed Noble's side.

"Let's get this over with so I can get home," Noble growled. She kept looking around, hoping to see Charlie, but to her dismay, she was nowhere to be found.

"Don't worry, she'll be here, and you can talk to her after you get your award." Leah pointed to the stage.

"Our last recipient of the day is a dedicated and cherished detective in our police department, and as such, she will receive the highest award our department has ever given, the

Medal of Valor. This award recognizes her courageous act in saving the life of a fellow officer during the execution of a search warrant. Detective Gentry has been with the department for twenty years and has been an instrumental asset in each unit she's worked in. Ladies and gentlemen, it's my pleasure to introduce Noble Gentry," Chief Raynor announced.

Noble felt Leah elbow her in the ribs and tell her to get up, but her feet and legs felt like Jell-O.

"Crap," slipped from Noble's lips, "here goes nothing." Standing, she walked toward the stage.

As Noble ascended the stairs and arrived at the top, she received a hug from Chief Raynor. Noble stepped up to the podium and looked out into the audience. *You can do this; look out into the crowd and say a few words,* Noble thought. As Noble looked for Leah, a friendly face who'd reassure her that everything would be okay, her eyes met Charlie's, who was sitting in the seat she'd vacated moments before.

"I'd like to thank everyone for coming today. What is the fuss about other than I did my job, which many of us do, and got injured in the process," Noble stated in a matter-of-fact voice.

"We love you, too, Noble!" someone in the audience yelled, causing the room to fill with laughter.

"As I was saying. Two decades ago, when I began my career, a few veteran officers told me it took a special person to be a police officer," she stated and took a deep breath. "We see and hear things that regular citizens should never have to see, some things we don't talk about away from the job." Noble looked down at the podium in front of her. *Come on, keep focus; you can do it.*

"Amen to that!" an unidentified person shouted.

"The department becomes your extended family that you come to rely on, and we forge a bond that will never break. I did what any of my family members would have done for me—take them out of harm's way!" Noble held her head high. "I don't regret my decision at all that day. Some officers are lucky to find love, marry, and have a family. I've been one of those individuals lucky enough to find love. I know how it feels to have that love stripped away by the actions of another person."

"We're always family, no matter what," Tony yelled from the back of the room, drawing a thunderous round of applause.

"I love you too, Vistole. You sometimes feel powerless, at fault, and lost. Your extended family is there to help you through the most challenging time of your life." She looked at Tony and winked. "You go forward in life and try to make that person you lost proud of you. Your friends tell you that you'll never forget those lost, but that you'll move on and possibly find someone new to share your life." *Time to step up to the plate,* Noble locked eyes with Charlie.

"I didn't believe them until it happened. Until I collided with her in the hallway and got knocked to the ground. I never thought about a second chance in a million years," Noble stammered, her throat muscles straining to contain emotion. "I've made it difficult for her and tried to push her away because of my insecurities. In a nutshell, I was afraid to love again, fearing it would get stripped away." She swallowed, causing the lines of her neck to move.

"Glad you've realized, Gentry," Leah spoke out in her commanding voice loud enough to draw another round of applause.

"Being injured has opened my eyes. I need to take hold of what and who I love and live for today, not worrying about tomorrow."

"Amen, Noble. We got your back," multiple people in the crowd yelled.

"Cherish what you have in front of you, and everything will follow. I hope this second chance will give me a lifetime of happiness with the woman I lost my heart to and love with every ounce of my being." Noble shifted from one foot to the other. "And a bonus to losing my heart is her daughter, or preferably our daughter, I hope." She shoved her hands in her pockets. "It's an honor to accept this award with graciousness and humility," Noble asserted. *Not only did I step up to the plate, but I hit a grand slam.* Noble felt relieved. *At least, I hope I did. This moment is the time to find out.*

Noble was unaware of how she made it down the stairs. It took forever to make her way over to Charlie, Elizabeth, Leah, and Beth. She noticed Beth hugging Charlie and whispering something in her ear.

"Gracious speech." Leah hugged her.

"Thank you, my friend, for helping me pull my head out of my ass." Noble returned a rib-crushing squeeze.

Beth hugged Noble and stated, "You hurt our daughter again, and you'll have to worry about me. Do you understand?"

"Yes, ma'am, I truly am sorry and will spend the rest of my life if she'll have me, making up for my lapse in judgment," Noble replied. "I'm glad you came today." Noble turned to Charlie, looked her in the eyes, and smiled hesitantly.

"There was no other option on my calendar." Charlie hit Noble with a nasty glare.

What an ass! I made her cry, Noble thought.

Noble gently lifted her hand up to Charlie's face and wiped away a single tear rolling down her cheek.

"I swear if I take the rest of my life to make this up to you and prove that I'm worthy of your love, it will all be worth it." Noble's smile warmed her lips. "I love you with everything I am, and I hope you can find it in your heart to forgive me and give me another chance," Noble stated as their eyes linked.

"How can I believe you won't get scared again and push me away, Noble?" Charlie asked, her expression reflecting uncertainty.

"Believe it or not, Charlie, but when I got shot, I had a personal tour of my life—past, present, and future. And I didn't like that there was the potential of not having you in my life," Noble expressed, a hint of sorrow reflected in her smile.

Charlie looked at Noble, confusion evident on her face, and asked, "Can you please explain!" Her lips formed a flat line.

"As I was lying there, being worked on by the doctors, I felt a presence in the room…." Noble responded.

"Go on." Charlie took Noble's hands.

"Diana was there and helped me see I was pushing you away and blaming myself for her death, which she insisted was ridiculous." Noble smiled and squeezed Charlie's hands. "Diana showed me that my life would either be me dying or fighting for a chance at happiness with you. She told me this was a simple decision and not to blow it!" Noble's eyebrows went skyward. "So, I fought like hell to wake up long enough to yell at the doctor that he better fix me because I sure as hell wasn't ready to go; I was in love!" Noble declared. *She'll think I'm nuts and make an exit right out of my life.*

"I don't think you're as looney as it seems. Diana made her way to me, too." A small smile touched the corner of Charlie's mouth.

"For the first time in my life, I was afraid. With Diana, I didn't have any input or control over her death. With you, I pushed you away for the mere fact of being afraid of losing you instead of telling you all my fears." Noble took a deep breath. "I fled like a coward. I will always regret the pain and heartache I caused you. And make no mistake, it will never happen again," she vowed. "You're my today, my future, and my forever, Charlie. I am in love with you," Noble whispered, looking into Charlie's eyes, waiting for a response. "I would consider it an honor if you and Elizabeth would share the rest of your life with me."

"For someone who doesn't like to make me cry, you sure are doing a splendid job today!" Charlie replied as tears chased one another down her cheeks.

"You promised you would never make my mom cry," Elizabeth shouted. Looking up at Noble with a disappointed look, she crossed her arms.

"I'm sorry, Bug. It's the one regret I've ever had in my life. I'm hoping you and your mom can forgive me, and we can become the family I've been looking for my entire life." Noble squatted down and looked directly into Elizabeth's eyes.

Noble tilted her head to make eye contact with Charlie. *Crap, I blew it! I need help to do something right.*

"Noble, you're my present day, will be my future, and will always be my forever. I love you, and nothing will ever change that." Charlie pulled Noble up and lightly kissed her.

"I love you too, Noole." Elizabeth hugged Noble's leg.

"I love you so much. Let's get Grandma and Mimi and go home. To our home." Noble scooped up Elizabeth and put her arm around Charlie.

EPILOGUE

"Are you ready to get out of the car?" Charlie asked Noble at the cemetery.

"Indeed, I am," Noble replied, her slight nod conveying agreement.

As they approached Diana's grave, hand in hand, Charlie took out a bag and handed it to her.

"What's this?" Parallel lines formed over the bridge of Noble's nose.

"Isn't it obvious? Or do I truly need to spell it out to you?" Charlie laughed.

"I know it's a coin, but what should I do with it?"

"Well, this is the coin Beth and Leah gave you. You know who they are, right? Mom and Mom L. Well, I thought it would be a sign of respect to give it to Diana." Charlie locked eyes with Noble.

"There's no need to get snarky, sweetie. I'm a little confused. Why don't you wrap it up for me and tell me why here and why this moment?" Noble tilted her head to the side.

"Remember, I told you I had a visit from Diana? Well, it was here, and she directed me to this coin in the grass by her headstone. It only fits that the original coin is here with her in the flower canister. I have it in a baggie, so it won't get wet or tarnished." She placed it into the vase holder and added flowers to mask it from the public eye. "I figured maybe you and I would carry new coins and realize that even though Diana is gone, she'll always be an important person in our life." Charlie leaned in and kissed Noble on the cheek.

"You mean the world to me. I never thought I'd be this happy again. Thank you for giving me a second chance. I will never disappoint you again." Noble pulled Charlie into her arms. "I am truly grateful to Diana for giving me a reality check when I was out of it in the emergency room after being shot."

"She guided us together for a reason—for us to find happiness finally. Noble Knight, I love you for your honor, courage, integrity, and the compassion you exalt as a person. I can't wait to continue showing you the love I have, which will only keep growing." Charlie tightened her arms around Noble.

As they turned to walk back to the car, they saw a red-tailed hawk land in the tree near Diana's headstone. Once again, the hawk made a rasping scream. It sounded like high-pitched *kree-eee-ar*, like the last time Charlie was there. Another hawk landed on the same branch and interacted with the first.

"I think everyone is getting another chance at love." Charlie embraced Noble, and the hawks flew away together.

About the Author

LJ is a retired police officer from the State of California. In her spare time, LJ is an avid reader and loves to be with family and friends, enjoying a good glass of wine or taking trips in the RV. Born and raised in central California, LJ currently lives in the State of Arizona with her wife B. They have two children, a son and a daughter, and two grandchildren.

Other Affinity Books

The Princess Needs a Wife by JM Dragon

Since birth, Princess Sophia Osric has led a charmed life. When a family tragedy forces her to shift from casual obligations to specific royal duties, it results in a decree from her father to find a wife or risk losing her special privileges. But there's always a catch—it must be a commoner. How on earth can she do that? Where will she find a commoner other than someone to wave or smile at?

Perhaps fairytale romances happen for princesses, too.

Without Borders by Stacy Reynolds

When the opportunity to become a war correspondent opens at her news agency, journalist Nicole Sheppard jumps at the chance to go to Ukraine. Her lifelong goal to gather news firsthand in the heat of battle and to test her mettle against the turbulence of war will finally be realized.

What she doesn't anticipate is having her heart and emotions tested as well when she meets the beautiful French doctor, Marie Dubois. As Nicole dodges bullets and Marie extracts them from the wounded, the two women struggle against a growing attraction to one another.

But when Nicole and Marie are kidnapped by a ruthless Russian mercenary, they must work together to find a way to escape.

The only thing they can't escape is falling in love.

The Invisible woman by Annette Mori

In a world where logic meets the extraordinary, Tamara, a brilliant forensic scientist, discovers a mysterious purple plant that blesses her with superhuman abilities, including invisibility. Teaming up with her best friend, Annalise, a passionate FBI agent haunted by scars from her past, the two friends embark on a quest to bring down a brutal serial killer known only as The Hunter. As the danger intensifies, their bond deepens, and secrets are revealed. Will Tamara and Annalise finally admit to their feelings despite being polar opposites? Join these extraordinary women in this gripping tale of love, friendship, and the fight for justice, where heroes are born from pain.

<u>Never Too Late by Glenda Poulter</u>

After the death of her long-time partner, and a scandal at the school where she taught music and art, Janice Halston emerged as a shadow of herself. Feeling shaken, cautious and artistically blocked.

Tam Murphy lost her wife and son within a short time of each other. She tries to fill her emptiness with her daughter Mae, and granddaughter, Ocee.

Janice and Tam are brought together by the precocious Ocee. As their friendship deepens, so do their feelings for each other. Their deepening feelings send both women spiraling…in different directions. One toward what could be, the other away from fear of another loss. Will their spirals lead them back to each other, or further apart?

Nothing But Net by Ali Spooner

Hunter James, a rising star in college basketball, has her career and life sidelined after experiencing a family tragedy.

An opportunity for a fresh start opens the door to return to what she loves most: playing basketball. Hunter rushes through that door to make the most of her second chance.

Back in the basketball arena, doing what she loves, will she open herself and her heart to another chance to forgive herself and fall in love?

The Kitten Trap by Annette Mori

Inspired by the classic movie, *The Parent Trap*, two adorable black kittens, Midnight and Onyx, play matchmakers for their human mothers, Mac and Carmen. Struggling with the complexities of farm life, Mac can barely believe her beautiful girlfriend, Carmen, has agreed to move to the drafty old farmhouse to live with her and her beloved Pops. When Carmen is forced to leave the farm to care for her ailing mother, Midnight and Onyx as well as Mac and Carmen must struggle with the difficult separation. Just when it appears Carmen and Onyx may come back home to the farm, cruel fate raises a further challenge, one that will need the help of two mischievous kittens to overcome.

To Autumn by Katie M Hall

Sixteen-year-old Robyn Gale, along with her younger sister Anne, is sent away for the summer holidays of 1997 to stay with her grandmother at a caravan park in Devon.

Robyn's had a tough few months: trying to cope with the fallout of their mother's attempted suicide, messing up her GCSEs, and finding herself attracted to girls. Perhaps getting away from her real life is just what she needs…she can focus on finding a boyfriend, watching *Neighbours,* and swimming. A solid plan, until she meets charismatic Australian lifeguard, Autumn, and her life is turned even more down under.

Fairytail Farm by Ali Spooner

Dr. Hill McCall and her wife Alice dreamed of developing a sanctuary for unwanted cats and dogs to live out their lives as a retirement project. Hill has secretly worked on the project for months when a wealthy benefactor surprises her with a large donation, allowing Hill to be more aggressive with the project's opening. A group home operator approaches Hill about summer volunteer positions for four girls as Fairytail Farm becomes more than just a sanctuary for the animals. It creates an environment of love and kindness for the animals and all that support the project. Several love stories develop from first love to mature couples who have found their forever person. Fairytail Farm is more than a dream come true. It is a home for happily ever afters.

The Love Demand by Annette Mori

In the dazzling realm of reality television, where love and drama entwine in a complicated dance as old as time, a groundbreaking series emerges that transcends the ordinary. *The Love Demand* is not your typical reality show. Lacey Fellows isn't sure she wants to subject herself to further humiliation, however, on the off chance her girlfriend may agree to accept a second marriage proposal, Lacey reluctantly consents to participating in the new reality show. What she doesn't count on is meeting a kindred spirit—one she can't seem to shake from her thoughts. Jaimie would do almost anything for her girlfriend, including following her to the ends of the earth and participating in a conniving television show that puts her in front of a camera, which happens to be her least favorite place. Her girlfriend, Sabina, hasn't met a camera she doesn't like. They couldn't be more opposite, but Jaimie still hopes Sabina will want marriage, kids, and the whole shebang. The last thing she expects is to fall in love with someone else. Let the games begin.

<u>Sullivan's Trace by Ali Spooner</u>

Micah "Sully" Sullivan has settled into a solitary life at the family horse ranch after her father's death. When her long-term vet, Doc Barton, plans to retire, his granddaughter, Bryn, arrives to take over his practice. An attack on one of Sully's prized horses throws Sully and Bryn into a whirlwind as they fight to save the young animal. Just as Sully is becoming comfortable with her growing attraction to Bryn, tragedy occurs, and her brother and his wife are killed in an accident. Sully's solitary life drastically changes when a family of three is born.

<u>Love Sins by Annette Mori</u>

Jessica Green's life is predictable and boring. As the chief engineer for Solar Flair, her career is right on track. Her love life, not so much. The last thing she expects is a call from her estranged father's attorney. Too curious to ignore the message, she can't resist meeting with him and discovering more about specific instructions related to his estate, as well as the letter her father left for her. Rattled by what she finds at her father's home, she promptly dials 911.

Special Agent Amanda Forrester is perplexed by a call to join a homicide investigation until she arrives at the scene and learns the victim is not only a serial killer but an elite assassin the authorities have been after for years. To Amanda's increasing irritation, the daughter recognizes a picture of the last target and insinuates herself into the investigation. As the case takes a surprising turn, Amanda finds she has landed smack dab in the middle of a complicated and dangerous situation. The facts lead her to a puzzle weaving together the recent suicide of a wealthy businessman with the activities of several prominent politicians. Amanda must join forces with a mysterious organization and the persistent woman she finds increasingly hard to resist. Her instinct to protect the alluring and vulnerable Jessica Green kicks into high gear, taking the reader on a roller-coaster journey for the last book in *The Next Generation* series.

Affinity
Rainbow Publications

eBooks, Print, Free eBooks

Visit our website for more publications available online.

https://affinityebooks.com/

Published by Affinity Rainbow Publications
A Division of Affinity eBook Press NZ LTD
Canterbury, New Zealand

Registered Company 2517228

www.ingramcontent.com/pod-product-compliance
Lightning Source LLC
LaVergne TN
LVHW020656110826
845149LV00012B/2017

* 9 7 8 1 9 9 1 3 5 7 3 2 8 *